RETURN TO THE WILD

SEEKERS

THE MELTING SEA

SEEKERS

Also by Erin Hunter

WARRIORS

THE NEW PROPHECY

POWER OF THREE

OMEN OF THE STARS

EXPLORE THE
WARRIORS
WORLD

RETURN TO THE WILD

SEEKERS

THE MELTING SEA

ERIN
HUNTER

HARPER

AN IMPRINT OF HARPERCOLLINS*PUBLISHERS*

2/18

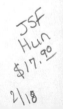

The Melting Sea

Copyright © 2012 by Working Partners Limited

Series created by Working Partners Limited

All rights reserved. Printed in the United States of America. No part of
this book may be used or reproduced in any manner whatsoever without
written permission except in the case of brief quotations embodied in
critical articles and reviews. For information address HarperCollins
Children's Books, a division of HarperCollins Publishers,
10 East 53rd Street, New York, NY 10022.
www.harpercollinschildrens.com

Library of Congress Cataloging-in-Publication Data

Hunter, Erin.

The Melting Sea / by Erin Hunter. — 1st ed.

p.   cm. — (Seekers: Return to the wild)

Summary: Toklo, Kallik, Lusa, and Yakone trek onward toward the
Melting Sea, the site of Kallik's traumatic cubhood—and prepare to be
separated for the first time since their journey began.

ISBN 978-0-06-199637-5 (trade bdg.)

ISBN 978-0-06-199638-2 (lib. bdg.)

[1. Bears—Fiction.   2. Fate and fatalism—Fiction.   3. Fantasy.]   I.
Title.

PZ7.H916625Mel   2012   2011044629

[Fic]—dc23   CIP

                                                                          AC

Typography by Hilary Zarycky

12 13 14 15 16   LP/RRDH   10 9 8 7 6 5 4 3 2 1

❖

First Edition

Special thanks to Cherith Baldry

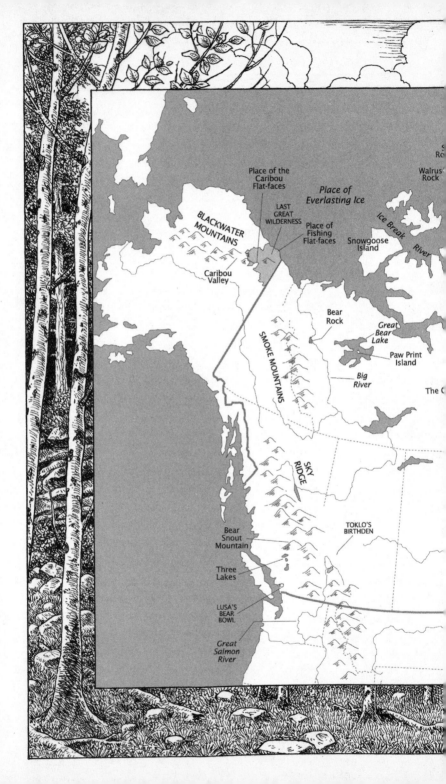

The Bears' Journey: Bear View

Lusa — — — — —
Kallik and Yakone -----------
Toklo ------------------

The Melting Sea

BURN-SKY
GATHERING
PLACE

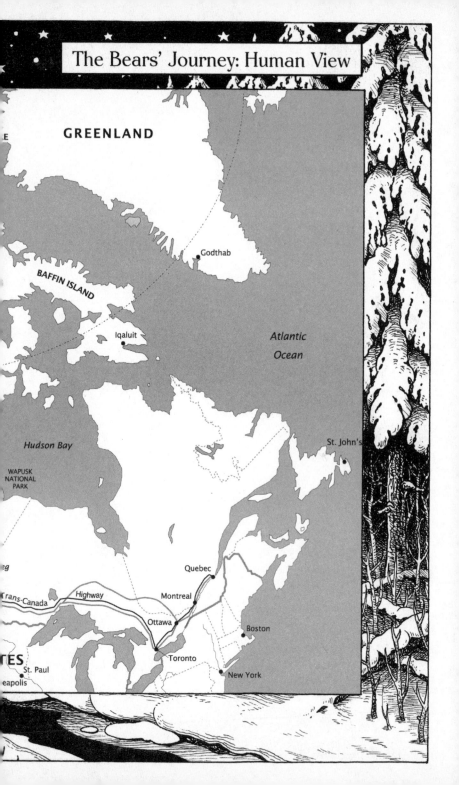

The Bears' Journey: Human View

GREENLAND

Godthab

BAFFIN ISLAND

Iqaluit

Atlantic Ocean

Hudson Bay

St. John's

WAPUSK NATIONAL PARK

Trans-Canada Highway

Quebec

Montreal

Ottawa

Boston

Toronto

New York

UNITES

St. Paul

eapolis

CHAPTER ONE

Toklo

Toklo's paws churned up snow as he hurtled across the ground, ice clogging his belly hair. He could feel his heart pounding. His breath came in hot gasps.

Glancing over his shoulder, Toklo saw Kallik on his tail. A wild light shone in her eyes as she pounded along. Yakone was racing after her shoulder, less than a snout-length behind. Forcing his aching legs to move even faster, Toklo faced forward again. A steep, rocky outcrop loomed up in front of him.

If I can only reach that . . . he thought.

Somewhere behind him he heard Lusa stumble and let out a yelp that was quickly muffled by snow. Toklo was sure the small black bear had fallen into a drift, but he didn't stop or even look back.

Lusa will have to look after herself. I need to keep going.

One set of the thundering pawsteps behind Toklo halted, and he realized that Yakone had dropped back to help Lusa.

The rocky outcrop was just ahead. With a mighty leap, Toklo flung himself at the lowest ledge, but his paws slipped

1

on the icy surface and he fell back, rolling over in the snow in a tangle of flailing legs.

Kallik sprinted past him and sprang onto the rock, scrambling to the summit and sending a shower of yet more snow down onto Toklo.

"I won!" she roared.

Toklo hauled himself to his paws, shaking clotted snow out of his fur. "No, you didn't," he retorted, annoyance welling up inside him. "I got to the rock first. It's not my fault my paw slipped."

"First to the top of the rock, that's what we said." Kallik slid down to join him, giving him a friendly poke with her snout. "Don't be a sore loser."

Toklo just grunted. He was angry with himself more than with Kallik. *I should* have won! *If I'd just been a bit more careful* . . .

"Well done, Kallik!" Yakone called as he came puffing up with Lusa. "You're really fast. You too, Toklo."

"Thanks for checking on me—not!" Lusa added.

Toklo stifled a snort of amusement as he looked at the little black bear. She was covered in snow; even her ears were filled with it. "I know how much you like falling into snowdrifts," he said to her. "Besides, it could have been a trick to make me slow down."

Lusa shook her head from side to side, trying to dislodge the snow from her ears. "I never had a chance of winning," she murmured sadly. "My legs are so short."

Seeing her beginning to shiver, Toklo padded over to her and started to lick the snow out of her ears. "Cheer up," he comforted her. "You'd win in a tree-climbing race."

"I'm not sure I would." Lusa looked dejected. "I'm so out of practice. I can't remember the last time we saw a real tree!"

"True," Kallik agreed. "There's not much of anything on this island, and it seems to just go on forever. Are you *sure* this is the right way to the sea?"

"This is the way Nanulak's family told us to go," Toklo replied.

"And we trust them?" Yakone muttered. "After what Nanulak did?"

Yakone's words revived the pain of betrayal, as sharp as a thorn piercing Toklo's heart. He had believed that Nanulak was his friend, that he could teach and take care of the young bear just as he had taken care of Ujurak.

But all Nanulak wanted was to use me, to get revenge on his family.

The memory of Nanulak's father flashed into Toklo's mind so vividly that he almost thought that the huge white bear was looming over him. He saw blood patching the bear's white fur, and remembered the pain of his own wounds.

I could have killed him because Nanulak lied to me. How could I have been so wrong about Nanulak?

Kallik gave Toklo a gentle nudge, drawing him away from his hurtful memories. "Why don't we hunt?" she suggested. "It won't be light for much longer." Her eyes gleamed with amusement as she added, "I won the race, so I think you should all bring food for me!"

"In your dreams!" Toklo exclaimed, relieved that she hadn't mentioned Nanulak. He gave her a harder nudge in return.

"You're so fast, you should be the one chasing prey!"

Toklo took the lead again as the bears headed onward, making for the crest of a low range of hills that lay across their path. His belly was bawling with hunger, but so far there was no sign of any prey. Snow-covered slopes rolled into the distance on every side, broken occasionally by jutting rocks or a few stunted thorn trees. For days they had been heading toward the setting sun, meeting scarcely any other bears. Even traces of flat-faces were rare in this desolate landscape: only the occasional small den, or thin tower poking into the sky.

Pushing the thought of Nanulak to the back of his mind, Toklo tried to relax and enjoy the company of his friends. The race had been fun, even though he had lost. Yakone, the reddish-pelted white bear they had met on Star Island, was settling into the group. And they had directions now that would take them to a narrow stretch of sea that divided this island from the mainland. Everything was looking good.

But the parting that was soon to come nagged at Toklo's mind like a rough pieces of ice between his toes. The whole point of this journey was to reach the Melting Sea, where Kallik and Yakone would stay with the other white bears who made their homes there. The little family they had created through so many difficulties and dangers would be broken up. Soon Lusa, too, would find bears like herself and live with them among the trees that were her true home.

If only Nanulak . . .

Toklo cut off the thought, stifling a sigh. Everything seemed to lead back to Nanulak. Once Toklo had believed that he would build a new life with the young mixed bear, living in adjoining territories so that he could teach Nanulak the ways of brown bears.

That's not going to happen now. I can't believe that treacherous bear had me fooled for so long. And suppose a bigger, stronger bear does that—one who could beat me if it came to a fight? Determinedly, Toklo shrugged off the worry. *No. I'll never make that mistake again.*

"I can't wait to get away from all this snow!" Lusa's voice came from just behind Toklo; she was trotting along between Kallik and Yakone, and sounded quite cheerful, as if she had forgotten all about Nanulak and the problems he had caused. "I'm just longing to see real trees again, and to find some other black bears!"

"I'm sure you will," Kallik responded. "Every pawstep is taking you closer."

The she-bears' confidence reminded Toklo of his own blank future. Kallik had Yakone, and might even meet her brother, Taqqiq, again once they reached the Melting Sea. And Lusa was so friendly, she would find it easy to be accepted by her own kind.

But what about me? Toklo wanted to wail like an abandoned cub, and instantly felt ashamed of himself. *You'll find a territory and live alone. That's what brown bears do.* But the prospect didn't seem as enticing as it once had.

By now the crest of the hill was only a few bearlengths away. As they approached it, Toklo heard a familiar clicking sound, though it took him a moment to remember what it was.

"Caribou!" he exclaimed.

"Oh, great!" Kallik bounded past him. Reaching the top of the hill, she glanced back and added, "A whole herd!"

Toklo quickened his pace until he stood on the ridge beside her, Lusa and Yakone hard on his paws. In front of him the ground fell away in a gentle sweep of land. The herd of caribou were wandering past about halfway down the slope, nosing into the snow to find the grass buried underneath. The clicking sound came from their feet as they moved.

Memories flashed through Toklo's mind of the first time they had seen caribou in the Last Great Wilderness, and then of the time they had driven a herd of caribou into a frantic stampede on Star Island, to trample down the flat-face oil rig that was destroying the wild and driving the spirits away.

He gave his pelt a shake in an effort to banish the recollections. *We've got more urgent things to worry about now,* he thought, gazing out across the landscape.

Beyond the caribou, the slope ended in a narrow stretch of flat, white ice. On the opposite side, mountains reared up, dark and bulky against the sky.

"That must be the crossing," Toklo said, angling his head toward the ice. "The Melting Sea should be really close now."

Kallik sniffed the air eagerly, then shook her head. "I can't pick up anything familiar," she told the others. "We're still too far away—but this must be the right way to go." With a sigh she added, "It was so much easier when we had Ujurak with us."

Toklo murmured agreement, struggling once again with a pang of loss. The small brown bear had always been certain of the path they should take, even when there was nothing to guide them. Now the bears had only their own instincts to trust, and any information they could glean from other bears. *And we just have to hope we're getting it right,* he added to himself.

"If it wasn't for all this spirit-forsaken snow, we might be able to see where we're going," he grumbled.

"At least we can see the place we have to cross," Kallik reminded him. "Now, what about the caribou? We need to work out how to separate one from the herd and bring it down."

Yakone stared at her, blinking in amazement. "You *hunt* caribou?" he asked. "That's no sort of food for a white bear."

Toklo opened his jaws for an indignant retort. *If the Star Island bears had learned how to hunt caribou, they wouldn't have been starving when the seals got sick!*

But Kallik spoke first, giving Yakone a gentle nudge with her snout. "It's great food," she told him. "You'll see."

Toklo padded along the ridge to get closer to the caribou, making sure that they were downwind of the herd. The huge beasts were meandering along slowly, grazing as they went, and obviously had no idea that there was any danger.

Peering down at the caribou through narrowed eyes, Toklo spotted a young male at the edge of the herd, limping on one forehoof. Water flooded his jaws as he anticipated the taste of caribou flesh.

"That one," he murmured, pointing with his snout. "Kallik, you circle around and get onto its other side. Make sure they don't spot you."

Kallik nodded and padded softly down the slope, her white pelt scarcely visible against the snowy ground.

"Yakone," Toklo went on, "head down the slope, but keep behind the herd, in case the one we want doubles back."

"Okay." Yakone followed Kallik, then crouched in hiding behind a rocky outcrop.

"What about me?" Lusa asked, her eyes shining.

Toklo hesitated. Lusa was much smaller than the others and much more likely to be injured by trampling hooves. "Stay here," he ordered at last. "If our prey breaks away upward, roar and drive it back."

For a moment Lusa looked disappointed, as if she suspected Toklo was trying to protect her. Then she gave a brisk nod. "You got it."

Checking that Kallik was in position, Toklo rose to his hindpaws with his forelegs splayed out and roared loudly. The echoes rolled around the hills. The caribou halted, looking up, then as one they began to race away in a thunder of hooves.

Toklo dropped to all four paws and hurtled down the slope. The limping caribou was already dropping back, unable to keep up with the rest of the herd. Seeing Toklo bearing down, it swung around and fled, its hooves skidding in the snow.

Kallik was ready. Springing up out of a shallow dip, she leaped at the caribou. It swerved wildly away, tossing its antlered head, only to meet Yakone racing toward it, his jaws wide as he roared. Trapped between three bears, the caribou let out a terrified bellow. Toklo sprang at its haunches, driving his claws through its tough hide. At the same moment Kallik barreled into it from the other side and threw it off balance.

"Grab it!" she growled at Yakone.

After a moment's hesitation, Yakone flung himself at the caribou, sank his claws into its shoulder, and pulled it to the ground.

As Toklo struggled to get a better grip among the caribou's legs, he realized that Lusa had joined them and was hanging on to the creature's neck, her paws almost lifting off the ground as it fought to rise again. Toklo reached around her and slashed his claws across the caribou's throat. Blood gushed out onto the snow, and the animal went limp.

Panting, all four bears rose to their paws and stood looking down at their prey.

"Good job," Toklo grunted.

"Try it." Kallik nudged Yakone closer to the dead caribou. "You'll really like it."

Looking a bit uncertain, Yakone crouched down beside the prey and tore at its flesh, taking a huge mouthful. A low growl of appreciation came from him as he gulped it down. "That's delicious!"

"Told you," Kallik said smugly as she crouched down beside him to eat. "Thank you, spirits, for this prey."

Lusa and Toklo joined her. Toklo sighed with satisfaction as he sank his teeth into the warm caribou meat. It had been a long time since they'd been able to feast like this, with more than enough for every bear.

"You're all really good at this," Yakone remarked when the worst of their hunger was satisfied. "You make a good team."

"We've had practice," Toklo replied briefly.

"Now you're part of the team, too," Kallik added, edging closer to the other white bear. "It's good to know lots of different ways of hunting."

Yakone nodded, looking impressed. "I can see that."

Lusa had taken only a few mouthfuls of the meat. Then she turned away from the carcass and began scrabbling at the snow. "Nanulak taught me how to scent plants growing underneath," she explained, as she began uncovering a straggly bush with a few grayish leaves clinging to its branches. She took a huge bite. "This is the right food for a black bear," she mumbled around her mouthful of twigs.

Toklo stared at her, thinking how dry and unappetizing the leaves looked. "Yeah, right," he muttered. "You're welcome to it."

While they were eating, the sun had dipped close to the horizon, staining the snow with scarlet light. His belly comfortably full, Toklo began to feel sleepy. He and the others curled up in the shelter of the rock where Yakone had hidden from the caribou. Toklo relaxed into the warmth of Kallik on one side of him and Lusa on the other, but a familiar worm of dread stirred in his belly. *There won't be many more nights like this, when we're all together.*

Kallik is going home, and that should be a happy time. I'm not going to spoil it for her. She's my family, and I will look after her until I know she's safe.

CHAPTER TWO

Lusa

Cold wind whispering around her woke Lusa. She opened her eyes to see the snow-covered landscape in front of her, glimmering in the pale dawn light. As she stretched her jaws in an enormous yawn, she spotted her three companions already gathered around the carcass of the caribou.

Good. They'll be full-fed today. . . . She blinked blearily as she hauled herself to her paws and stumbled out from the shelter of the rock.

"Hi, Lusa." Kallik looked up with meat dangling from her jaws. "Come and share."

Lusa shook her head and scrabbled in the snow until she found more of the grayish leaves she had eaten the night before. Energy started to flow back into her body as she crunched up the twigs.

"All right, let's go," Toklo said at last, heaving himself up and padding reluctantly away from the remains of the carcass. "I wish we could take the rest of the meat with us, but we can't."

"Never mind." Kallik rose and followed him. "The foxes will have a feast, and at least we've had two good meals."

Yakone took a last mouthful and joined Toklo and Kallik; Lusa bounded after them as they set off down the hill toward the stretch of ice that separated the island from the mainland.

"Once we're across there, we'll be almost at the Melting Sea!" Kallik announced excitedly, picking up the pace until she was racing down the slope. Yakone let out an eager bellow and raced after her.

Lusa followed more slowly, unable to share her friends' enthusiasm. *I hate traveling across ice. It's so cold it burns my paws, and I can't find the right black bear food.* She shivered, remembering how the wind sweeping across the ice would make her ears burn and chill her to the bone. But she knew there was no point in protesting. This was the way they had to go. Besides, Kallik looked so happy to be nearing her home, and Lusa didn't want to spoil that by complaining.

At any rate, she told herself, *it sounds like it's not so far to cross. Surely it won't be so bad this time.*

When she and Toklo caught up with the white bears at the edge of the ice, Kallik and Yakone were talking together.

". . . keep an eye open for seal holes," Yakone was saying, his eyes gleaming with enthusiasm. "There are bound to be plenty out there."

Yuck! Seal meat! Lusa thought, but said nothing aloud. She knew there would be times ahead when she might be glad of seal, even though it weighed heavily in her belly and made her feel sick. *I'm going to be tough about this,* she decided. *I'm not a cub anymore!*

Spotting a thornbush growing in the shelter of a rock at the very edge of the land, she bounded over to it and gulped down the leaves. There were even a few shriveled berries clinging among the twigs.

Kallik led the way out onto the ice. Padding along in her pawsteps, Lusa paused to glance over her shoulder at the island they were leaving. The shadowy shape, dark against the brightening sky, seemed like a huge animal, hunched up as if it were about to spring.

I knew there'd be trouble before we ever set paw there, Lusa reflected, sighing with relief that they were leaving it behind. She would never forget her fear of the underground tunnels where Toklo had been lost, or the shock and disgust she had felt when they discovered Nanulak's treachery. *I don't ever want to come back here.*

Glad to turn her back on the troubled island, Lusa fixed her gaze on the hills she could see ahead of her, at the other side of the ice. They seemed so close. But almost at once she realized that reaching them wouldn't be as easy as she had hoped. The surface was rougher than she was used to, as if sheets of ice had rubbed against each other and thrust up ridges that were hard to clamber over and dug painfully into Lusa's paws.

"Look at this!" Kallik called from up ahead.

Struggling across the uneven ice to join her, Lusa saw a much smoother stretch reaching into the distance on either side, parallel with the hills on the distant shore; on its edges the ice was even more broken, like tiny mountain ranges with jagged peaks.

"What did that?" she asked.

"I think it must have been one of those flat-face firebeasts," Toklo replied after a moment. "It pushed its way through here, smashing up the ice, and then the water froze again after it left."

Lusa shuddered, remembering the firebeast they had encountered after they left Star Island, when they had been forced to swim in the freezing water while flat-faces shot at them with firesticks. "I hope it doesn't come back."

Toklo nodded. "Those things are dangerous. We'd better get moving."

Still nervous, Lusa kept looking around as she clambered over the spiky ice at the edge of the firebeast track. There was no sign of the huge creature, with its glittering, unnatural colors and its deep-throated roar, but she couldn't relax until they had left the weird trail far behind.

Her paws hurt even more as she tried vainly to pick a path through the rutted ice. Toklo was limping badly, she noticed, and even Kallik and Yakone were having trouble.

I wish my legs were longer, Lusa grumbled to herself as she struggled up the side of a steep ridge and let herself flop down the other side. *At this rate, it will take days to cross.*

She realized that she was dropping back, sometimes losing sight of the others in the dips between the ridges. But the broken ice dug into her paws, and however hard she tried, she couldn't go any faster.

Then Kallik stopped to wait for her. "Come on," the white bear said. "Climb on my back. I'll carry you for a bit."

"I'm not a baby!" Lusa protested indignantly. "I don't need you to take care of me."

Kallik sighed. "I know. But this is a lot tougher for you than the rest of us. Let me help you."

Lusa wanted to refuse, but she felt so exhausted, and her paws hurt so much, that instead she found herself climbing onto her friend's back. "Thanks, Kallik," she murmured as she crouched down into her thick white fur.

Even with Lusa's weight on her back, Kallik loped much faster across the ice than Lusa could, climbing the ridges with hardly any hesitation until she caught up with Toklo and Yakone. For a while they made good progress, and the hills ahead seemed to be drawing nearer, but gradually Lusa became aware that their outlines were becoming blurred. At the same time the air was growing colder.

"Fog," Toklo muttered. "That's all we need."

As the mist swirled around her, growing thicker with every pawstep they took, Lusa realized that she had never seen fog like this before. The air was full of tiny ice crystals that stung her eyes and settled on her pelt, striking deep into her fur like frozen thorns.

"What's happening?" she whimpered.

"I've seen this kind of fog a few times on Star Island," Yakone remarked. "It happens when it's really cold. There's nothing any bear can do about it, except shelter until it's over."

"Like we can do that out here," Toklo grumbled.

The fog rapidly grew thicker, blotting out their view of the mountains ahead. Lusa wasn't even sure that they were moving in the right direction anymore, though Kallik and Yakone strode on confidently, less worried by the stinging ice than Lusa and Toklo.

Still perched on Kallik's shoulders, Lusa thought she had never been so cold in all her life. "I'll be an ice bear if this goes on," she whispered under her breath.

Hoping for some shelter near the ground, she slid down from Kallik's back and plodded along beside her friend. For a short while the going seemed easier, but ice crystals began clogging in Lusa's pelt, weighing her down like stones, and it became harder and harder to put one paw in front of another.

She paused for a moment to catch her breath and try to scrape some of the ice crystals off her fur. But as fast as she scraped, they settled again. *I really look like a white bear now.*

Looking up, she realized that she couldn't see Kallik or the others; their shapes had melted into the thick fog. Listening closely, she thought she could hear pawsteps; then they, too, faded. Lusa wasn't even sure which direction they had been traveling.

She opened her jaws to call out to her friends, then stopped herself. *If I do that, they'll know I'm lost. They'll know I need help. They already think I'm just a cub, and I'm not!*

Remembering all the times she had needed help from the other bears, Lusa was determined that this time she would cope by herself. *When we reach Kallik's home by the Melting Sea, we'll be splitting up. Before that happens, I have to prove that I'm their equal.*

But when Lusa set out again, the fog was so thick that she could hardly see her paws. Every breath felt like thorns in her throat. She wasn't sure whether her friends even knew that she had fallen behind. *If they think I'm still with them,* she thought, pushing down panic, *they could be way ahead by now.*

Before she had gone many pawsteps, Lusa came up to an ice ridge with a deep crack running from top to bottom. *I'm sure I've seen that before! Am I going in the completely wrong direction?* She was so scared that she hardly dared move.

While Lusa still stood there, her paws frozen to the ground with fear, she heard a clicking sound. A caribou appeared out of the fog and loomed over her. Lusa was so close to panic that she barely realized how weird it was to meet a caribou out on the ice.

Oh, no! Has it come to take revenge on me, because I was part of the hunt?

Lusa braced herself for a fight, hoping desperately that she stood a fair chance against a caribou. *It doesn't have any sharp teeth or claws. How dangerous can it be?*

Then a voice spoke inside her head. "Follow me."

Lusa could hardly believe what she was hearing. Blinking ice crystals out of her eyes, she stared up at the caribou. "Ujurak?" she whispered.

The voice spoke again. "Yes, I'm here. Follow me, and we'll find the others again. Keep close to me."

"But I can hardly see you through this fog," Lusa protested.

"Then follow the sound of my feet," Ujurak responded.

He lowered his mighty antlered head and began to shoulder

his way through the fog. Lusa followed, sometimes losing sight of Ujurak's huge shape, but always able to hear the sharp, distinctive clicking of his feet as he paced over the ice.

"I don't want to slow the others down," Lusa confessed out loud, trying not to sound self-pitying. "But I'm worried they might go on without me if they think I'm lost."

"They would never leave you." Ujurak's voice sounded reassuringly in her head. "You're a family. You belong together, and they all know that."

Gradually the fog was thinning out, and Ujurak led Lusa to a place where there was no more than an icy mist. Ahead she could hear voices, and see shapes circling anxiously.

"Lusa! Lusa, where are you?"

"Here!" Lusa ran forward to her friends. "I got lost, but Ujurak found me. He's a caribou—look!" She whirled around, to see nothing but the wall of ice fog. The caribou had vanished.

"At least you're safe," Toklo grunted.

"And it's good to know that Ujurak is still with us," Kallik added, her eyes shining.

"He shouldn't have to watch over us," Toklo snapped back at her. "We should be able to look after ourselves!"

Feeling guilty because she was the one who had needed Ujurak's help, Lusa wondered what Toklo was so angry about. She thought he would be glad to know that Ujurak still cared about them, even though he had gone back to his starry home.

"It's too tough out here," Toklo went on, glaring at Kallik. "Maybe we should have crossed somewhere else."

"But maybe somewhere else the ice is starting to break up," Kallik retorted, beginning to sound exasperated.

"Yeah, this is the way Nanulak's family told us to go," Yakone added, backing up the white she-bear.

"Then we need to move faster," Toklo responded gruffly, "and make sure we don't lose Lusa again."

Even in the midst of the freezing fog, Lusa felt hot with embarrassment that Toklo was singling her out as the one who would hold them back.

"I can keep up," she insisted.

"You'd better ride on my back again," Kallik said, padding over to her side.

For a moment Lusa felt like protesting, but all the bears were looking at her, and she thought it would be even more embarrassing to refuse. Reluctantly she scrambled onto Kallik's back, and had barely gotten settled when the white bear lurched forward beneath her. Within a few pawsteps the fog grew denser once more. As Lusa gazed ahead at what little she could see of the ice ridges, she had to admit she was relieved not to be struggling along on her own paws anymore.

Yakone took the lead, picking up the pace until Lusa could see that Toklo wasn't comfortable.

"What's the rush?" the brown bear panted.

"We need to get out of this fast," Yakone responded. "You said so yourself."

Toklo gave an irritable grunt. "The ice isn't going to break up right now, you know."

"It's not that." Yakone hesitated, looking uneasy, then

added, "Back on Star Island, some of the older bears said you could get sick by breathing in the crystals of ice fog."

"What? Really?" Kallik queried.

"Actually, I never saw a bear who got sick like that. I'm just telling you what they said."

Lusa found it easy to believe. All of them were gasping for breath, and her belly was rolling uncomfortably.

"Even if it's true, there's nothing we can do about it," Toklo pointed out. "We've got to breathe!"

Kallik and Toklo kept on, following Yakone, but Lusa realized that all three of them were growing more tired with every pawstep, finding it harder and harder to clamber across the ice ridges. Kallik's shoulders slumped beneath her, and guilt weighed Lusa down like a rock in her belly as she thought of how much more difficult she was making it for Kallik.

"This is no good," Toklo announced, halting in front of a particularly steep ice ridge. "It's already getting dark; we're never going to make it off the ice tonight."

Yakone looked as if he was about to argue, but before he could speak Kallik flopped down onto the ice and let Lusa slide off her back. "You're right, Toklo. Let's sleep here."

The fog was so dense that Lusa hadn't realized that the light of the short snow-sky day was fading. Now, looking around, she realized that true darkness was gathering. Together with her friends she huddled in the shelter of the ice ridge, wrapping her paws over her nose to block out the ice crystals. *Just in case . . .* she thought muzzily. When she glanced from side to side, she saw that the others were doing the same. She slipped into sleep.

Sometime during the night Lusa woke to find that the fog had cleared. The moon shone down on the ice, bathing it in an eerie silver light, and the stars blazed out with a frosty glitter against the black sky.

Lusa craned her neck above the hump of Kallik's sleeping body until she spotted Ujurak's constellation. *He was the youngest of all of us,* she thought, *but he turned out to be so strong and wise.* He was so strong that he had seen her from far away and rescued her from the ice fog.

"I'm strong, too, Ujurak," she whispered aloud.

The comfort of knowing that the star-bear was watching over her was like thick fur wrapped around her, and his starlight was in her eyes until she drifted back into sleep.

CHAPTER THREE

Kallik

Kallik stood facing the hills across the ice and took in deep breaths through her nose.

"I can smell the land!" she announced, excitement bubbling up inside her like a clear spring.

Daylight was seeping over the ice, and after the terrible fog of the previous day the sky was clear. Her companions were staggering to their paws, stiff after a night spent huddled against the ice ridge.

"Let's go!" Kallik urged them. "It's not far now." Without waiting to see if the others were following her, she took off at a run toward the hills.

"Hey!" Yakone shouted after her. "We should hunt first."

Kallik halted and looked back, waiting for the reddish-pelted bear to catch up with her. "There won't be any seal holes here," she told him as he approached. "All the seals will have been frightened away by the no-claw firebeasts. Besides, the ice is too thick and jagged for seal holes."

Yakone cast an uneasy glance around him. "This sure

22

is weird ice," he muttered.

"Let's just get to land," Toklo said, coming up with Lusa in time to hear the last few words. "We can hunt there."

The sun appeared above the horizon, dazzling onto the ice as the bears hurried on. Kallik's excitement grew as they labored over the last stretch of lumpy ice and at last ran onto a pebbly, snow-covered shore.

"Thank the spirits!" Lusa exclaimed. "I started to think we'd never get here."

Kallik halted at the edge of the ice, taking more deep sniffs of the air. "I'm sure the Melting Sea is nearby!" she declared.

"We'll hunt first, then head for it," Toklo decided.

Kallik's paws itched to keep going. Now that they were so close, she couldn't wait to continue her journey. *I want to show Yakone my home! And maybe Taqqiq will be there.*

Painful memories flooded over Kallik as she recalled how her brother had started to travel with them, but then left them to go back to Great Bear Lake. She had never managed to shake off the feeling that she had betrayed him by staying with her friends.

What if he didn't survive on his own? What if those horrible bears he was hanging out with got him into serious trouble? They could have been attacked by bigger bears! And maybe Taqqiq would blame me, because I abandoned him.

Kallik started at the touch of a snout on her shoulder and turned to see Yakone standing beside her. "What's wrong?" he asked.

As she looked into his kind face, Kallik's worries suddenly

seemed much less important. "I'm fine," she assured him. "Just trying to remember the route to the Melting Sea."

"I can smell sea-ice," Yakone said.

Kallik nodded; she could smell it, too, and not just the ice they had recently crossed. Farther away, she could pick up the saltwater tang where the ice had started to break up. But somehow her paws were pulling her in a different direction, away from the sea and across the hills that guarded the shore.

"We can follow the coastline," Yakone continued. "We can hunt seals and swim. It'll be great!"

For a moment Kallik was tempted to agree. She so wanted to live the life of a white bear with Yakone. But then her gaze fell on Lusa.

"She's not meant to be traveling on ice," she murmured, angling her ears toward the black bear. "We need to stay inland, and take a route over the mountains instead. It'll be quicker and more direct than following the coastline anyway."

As she spoke she spotted a flash of impatience in Yakone's eyes. "It's great that you think about your friends," he began, "but you have to put yourself first. We'll find food more easily if we follow the shore, even if it is a longer route."

With a sinking feeling, Kallik wondered if Yakone would ever realize the strength of the bond that had grown up between her, Lusa, and Toklo. "They aren't just my friends, they're my family," she insisted. "If you can't understand that, then . . . then maybe we're always going to fight."

Yakone looked startled, as if he hadn't understood how strong Kallik's feelings were. He was silent for a moment, as Kallik gazed anxiously at him. *Would he really make me pick between him and Lusa and Toklo? How could I possibly choose?*

But Yakone's eyes were warm with affection as he gazed back at her. "I want to be with you," he told her. "Even if it means going over mountains." Bending his head, he gently licked her ears. "Don't worry. We can handle everything together."

Kallik was touched by his kindness, but still unsure that Yakone really understood her attachment to the other bears. *And why would he?* she asked herself. *He's grown up with white bears. He never even knew that other kinds of bears existed until we came to Star Island.*

She knew that Yakone was a decent bear, and kind, and loyal to her. *I'm so glad to have him with us.* And she also knew that he had forged genuine friendships with Lusa and Toklo. *But he always puts me first, and even though he's important to me, I just don't feel the same way about him.*

"Hey!" A shout from Toklo interrupted Kallik's musings. "Do you want to eat or not?"

His question made Kallik realize how hungry she was; they had eaten nothing since the caribou two days before. Spinning around, she saw Toklo bounding toward her with a goose dangling from his jaws. Lusa was trotting after him.

"Wow, great catch!" Kallik exclaimed.

"Not really," Toklo mumbled around a mouthful of feathers. "I think there was something wrong with its wing. It couldn't fly, and it's really skinny."

"But it's better than nothing," Lusa declared.

When they had divided up the goose, Toklo looked up from the few mouthfuls of stringy meat. "Which way now?" he asked Kallik.

"Over the mountains," she replied, hoping that Toklo wouldn't question her decision. *He's a brown bear,* she thought hopefully. *He won't want to travel along the sea-ice, any more than Lusa.*

To her relief, Toklo just gave her a brusque nod. Once they had finished eating, he took the lead, heading inland. The mountains loomed up in the distance, jagged peaks without even a tree to break the expanse of snow-covered slopes.

Kallik noticed how quiet Lusa was, her head down as she trudged across the frozen white waste. "Cheer up," Kallik said, falling into step beside her. "It should be easier for you, instead of trekking across the sea-ice."

Lusa heaved a sigh; she didn't look as grateful as Kallik had hoped. "I'm tired out, my paws are still bleeding from crossing that rough ice, and my belly aches," she complained.

"I'm sorry," Kallik sympathized with her, touching her briefly on the shoulder with her muzzle. "We'll be at the Melting Sea soon!"

Lusa halted and faced her, fixing her with a stricken gaze. "But I don't want to get to the Melting Sea!" she whispered. "That's where we'll split up."

Kallik stared back at her. *Lusa's right!* Her longing to go home was taking them closer and closer to the place where they would separate. Suddenly her paws seemed heavier, not so eager to carry her onward. Gazing at the mountains ahead, she wondered how much longer they had left together.

"Come on!" Toklo had realized that Lusa and Kallik had dropped back, and glanced over his shoulder with an irritated look on his face. "My paws are freezing. And I've just spotted some bushes ahead. They might give us a chance at prey, and there'll be leaves for you, too, Lusa."

"I'll come with you," Yakone offered instantly.

The two male bears bounded off, leaving Kallik and Lusa to follow more slowly. Kallik realized that Yakone was trying to reassure her that now the decision had been made, he was happy to travel through the mountains. Gratitude swept over her like a warm breeze.

The bushes Toklo had found grew in a wide, shallow dip in the ground, with a frozen pool at the bottom. When Lusa and Kallik approached, Toklo was already creeping up to a twisted thornbush, its branches straggling over the water. Suddenly a white-furred lemming shot out from underneath the bush, scurrying across the open ground and right under Lusa's paws. With a squeak of surprise, the black bear swatted it, and it fell to the ground and lay still.

"Awesome!" Kallik exclaimed.

Looking more cheerful, Lusa gave a snort of amusement. "Just think what Toklo would have said if I'd missed!"

Meanwhile, Yakone appeared from the other side of the bushes with a snow-hare in his jaws. "Toklo was right," he said with satisfaction as he dropped the hare at Kallik's paws. "This is a good place for prey."

Alerted by the sound of more small creatures scuttling in the undergrowth, Kallik joined Toklo by the bushes. Soon they had flushed out two more lemmings, and settled down with Yakone to eat their catch, while Lusa stripped leaves from the bushes.

Kallik felt energy flowing back into her body as she ate. For the first time since the caribou her belly wasn't cramped with hunger, and she felt as if she could run all the way to the Melting Sea.

When they set out again, they traveled easily over the level ground. Lusa had perked up at last, seeming more like her old, cheerful self. Even when the ground began to slope up toward the foothills, they still kept up the same brisk pace.

We're all strong and fit, Kallik thought, her confidence growing with every pawstep. *We're used to this, after all the skylengths we've walked. We've traveled through places far more challenging than this.*

Then she looked ahead, to where the mountains were drawing steadily closer, and caught herself, suddenly afraid that they were moving too fast. *The journey will be over too quickly, and then we'll have to split up.*

She cast a glance at Yakone, who was padding along beside her. Once again she thought how glad she was to have him, and how much she longed to show him her home. Being left alone again once she reached the Melting Sea would have been terrifying.

But what about Toklo and Lusa? Who will they have to keep them company when they reach their homes?

Now the mountains seemed to be rushing to meet them, as fast as a no-claw firebeast. As the icy peaks loomed above their heads, Toklo halted.

"Let's stop for the night," he suggested. "We need to tackle those slopes in daylight."

Kallik agreed, relieved that for a while at least they could delay crossing the mountains. When they had curled up together under a jutting rock surrounded by thick bushes, she lay awake for a while, listening to the quiet breathing of her companions.

What will it be like, when I don't have this anymore?

Kallik was jolted awake from a confusing dream of breaking ice and the gaping jaws of orca. At first she wasn't sure what had roused her; all she could hear was a weird hissing noise, almost like wind sweeping across the ice.

"But it's not the wind," she muttered.

Then a loud shriek split the air, and Kallik recognized that sound at once. *No-claws!* Panicking, she leaped to her paws and reared up to peer over the bushes that surrounded their temporary den.

Kallik gaped as no-claws in brightly colored pelts swept toward her down the snowy slopes. They had long, flat sticks fastened to their hindpaws and carried smaller sticks in their forepaws. The hissing noise came from the long sticks as the no-claws slid over the snow.

More no-claws—without the strange pawsticks—were lining up on either side, shrieking and howling as the no-claws with sticks whisked by. Kallik's heart began to pound as she realized they were all heading straight for the den.

Dropping back beneath the bushes, she saw that her three

friends were waking, clumsy and confused by the noise outside.

"No-claw attack!" she gasped, prodding Yakone in the side to wake him properly and get him moving. "They're coming to get us!"

Toklo gave a disbelieving grunt; then his eyes widened as he peered out from behind the bushes. "Great spirits!"

Lusa and Yakone joined him to look out, and Kallik braced herself for a fight. But the no-claws with pawsticks whizzed past without even looking at them, and the rest of the crowd followed.

"They missed us," Toklo grunted. "Typical stupid flat-faces."

"Why have they got sticks fastened to their paws?" Lusa asked. "Are they trying to escape from the flat-faces howling at them?"

"Who knows?" Toklo snapped. "Why do flat-faces do anything?"

"We've got to get out of here," Yakone said.

Toklo glanced out again, then turned back to his three companions. "Okay, this is the plan," he said. "There are more flat-faces on their way down. After they pass us, we'll leap out and run. The other flat-faces will be so busy watching, they won't notice us."

Let's hope not, Kallik thought.

"When I say 'Now!' follow me—fast," Toklo added.

Kallik crouched beside Lusa and Yakone, while Toklo peered out of the bushes. A few moments later she heard the weird hissing noise again, and more howls and shrieks from the no-claws.

"Now!" Toklo growled.

He scrambled out of the den. Kallik pushed Lusa in front of her and followed, with Yakone bringing up the rear. Bewildered in the midst of the turmoil outside, Kallik swerved away from where the bright-pelted no-claws were hurtling past on their pawsticks, and bounded after Toklo as he headed slantwise up the slope, trying to avoid the crowds.

The no-claws who were watching all had their backs turned, their attention fixed on the shiny track where the snow had been packed down by the passage of the pawsticks. Briefly Kallik thought that she and her friends would escape without trouble. But then a young no-claw turned around, let out a startled yowl, and pointed toward the bears with one of his forepaws.

"They've seen us!" Kallik gasped. "Run!"

It was hard to put on speed in the loose snow. As the bears floundered upward, more no-claws turned and started shrieking and jostling one another. Kallik wasn't sure if they were trying to run away or to surround the four bears and capture them. Glancing over her shoulder, she saw that the no-claws on pawsticks had begun to make their way upward again. The long pieces of wood that had helped them skim down so swiftly were slow and clumsy when they tried to climb. For the moment they didn't seem to have noticed Kallik and the others.

But they'll spot us soon, she thought, fighting back panic.

Then they'll all be chasing us!

Still struggling upward, Kallik heard the crack of a fire-stick. Her belly lurched with fear, and she braced herself to see one of her friends drop to the ground. Instead, a bright pink cloud billowed out overhead.

What's going on?

Spooked by the noise and the crowds, Kallik didn't know where to run anymore. Just above her on the slope Yakone had turned and was baring his teeth at the approaching no-claws. Toklo was a couple of bearlengths farther up, giving Lusa a shove to help her on her way.

Some of the no-claws were fleeing, while others poured onto the empty snow, shrieking and waving their forelegs. Soon the bears were surrounded; Kallik whirled to and fro, searching for a gap where they could slip through to the wilderness beyond. More no-claws appeared on pawsticks, with firesticks in their forepaws. Kallik shuddered, certain that not all of them would shoot out harmless pink clouds. The new arrivals let out loud yowls, and the encircling no-claws parted.

"This way!" Toklo growled.

Kallik's heart swelled with admiration at the brown bear's courage as he charged forward between the lines of no-claws. Floundering after him, she halted as she saw Lusa slip and begin to fall back in the snow toward the no-claws.

But Yakone reached Lusa first and nudged the black bear onto her paws again. "Go on!" he ordered Kallik. "I'll bring Lusa."

Toklo veered away from the new no-claws, who were

raising their firesticks, pointing them at the bears. Other no-claws spilled around, shrieking. Toklo charged forward, with Kallik and the others just behind. The crowds of no-claws scattered in front of them.

Then Kallik almost crashed into Toklo as he halted unexpectedly. Small firebeasts had appeared in front of them, with no-claws clinging to their horns. From behind, the no-claws with firesticks were drawing closer, gliding on their long, flat pawsticks.

"Oh, no . . ." Kallik groaned, her heart thudding with terror. "We're trapped!"

CHAPTER FOUR

Toklo

As their pursuers closed in, Toklo glanced around. The small horned firebeasts growled threateningly in front of them. On one side was a wall of flat-faces, staring and yowling and thrashing their forelegs in the air. On the other side was a row of huge, sleeping firebeasts; Toklo could smell their stench above the snow and the fear of the flat-faces. Every instinct was telling him to avoid them, but he could see that he and his friends had no other option.

"This way," he growled, veering around and galloping toward the firebeasts.

Behind him he heard gasps of shock from the other bears.

"What are you doing?" Yakone shouted after him. "We can't go that way!"

Toklo glanced back over his shoulder. "We don't have a choice!" he snarled. "Follow me!"

His mouth was dry, and his heart pounded with fear. He knew that he was taking a huge risk, but he had to get his friends away from the flat-faces.

"They're coming!" Lusa squeaked, scrambling through the snow to follow Toklo.

Toklo led the way as they dived between the sleeping firebeasts. They were big—much bigger than any he had seen before—and square, like the dens flat-faces lived in. *I know firebeasts are hollow inside,* he thought as he dodged among the massive shapes, *because flat-faces travel around in their bellies. These are so big, there must be plenty of room in there.*

He slowed down, sniffing the air.

"Keep running!" Kallik yelped as she barreled into him, trying to shove him onward.

"No," Toklo panted. "We can't outrun those little firebeasts. We have to find somewhere to hide."

"But there are no trees here," Lusa protested. "No caves or gullies . . ."

"Then we have to make the best of what we have," Toklo told her.

Padding around the end of one of the firebeasts, he spotted a gap in the far side, with a small step up to it. Resting his forepaws on the step, he leaned in and took a good sniff. There was only a faint flat-face scent, and though he listened carefully he couldn't hear anything inside.

"Okay," he muttered, hauling himself up and squeezing through the gap. *I can't believe I'm doing this! I'm in the belly of a firebeast!*

The walls of the firebeast belly were flat and shiny; there was flat-face stuff strewn around on the floor, but otherwise it was empty.

Toklo turned back to the gap. "Come in, quick!"

Kallik's face appeared in the opening. "Have you gone crazy?" she demanded.

"Quick!" Toklo repeated, his fear making him angry. "It's the only place to hide, unless you've got a better idea?"

Kallik's head vanished; for a moment Toklo was afraid that she and the others had run away. Then Lusa appeared, her paws scrabbling on the hard floor as Kallik boosted her from behind. Yakone climbed in next, and Kallik brought up the rear. She gave Toklo a furious glare but said nothing as the noise of the flat-faces grew louder outside.

Toklo gestured to the others to draw back into the farthest corner of the firebeast, while he took a quick glance outside. The flat-face yowling was louder still, but none of them were in sight yet. A flap that was clearly meant to close the belly was folded back on the outside; Toklo couldn't reach it, and there was no time to try. He joined his friends, huddled together at the far end of the space.

"We'll just have to hope no one looks in," he murmured.

The roar of the little firebeasts grew suddenly louder, almost drowning Toklo's words. Through the gap he caught a glimpse of flat-faces gliding by on their pawsticks.

Suddenly he remembered their pawmarks in the snow, marking a clear trail up to their large firebeast, and his belly churned with fear. *Is this how our journey will end, trapped like fish in a pool?* He gazed at his friends, their eyes wide with apprehension as they stared at the gap. Then the noise of the firebeasts rumbled past and began to die away. Toklo let out a long breath and felt himself trembling.

"I think they've gone!" Kallik sounded astonished.

She rose to her paws and began to move toward the gap, but Toklo blocked her with his shoulder. "No," he murmured. "We should wait in here for a while."

For a moment Kallik looked as if she was going to argue; then she flopped down again. "What do we do if the firebeast wakes up?" she asked in a whisper.

"We'll worry about that if it happens," Toklo replied.

The floor of the firebeast was covered with flat-face pelts, and things that looked like flat-face hindpaws. Toklo and his companions settled uncomfortably on top of them. Lusa was stiff with fear, unable to speak, and Yakone looked numb with shock.

I wonder if Ujurak can see us now, Toklo thought, *cowering in the belly of a firebeast!*

Time dragged on, and Toklo slid into an uncomfortable doze, too scared to let himself sleep. He could feel his friends' tension; none of them could relax either.

He wasn't sure how much time had passed when he was roused by the clang of a flat-face hindpaw hitting the step. Before he could react, a flat-face appeared in the gap.

Toklo leaped to his paws with a fierce growl. For a moment the flat-face stared at him, his face white and his jaws gaping. Then he let out a hoarse shriek and fell backward.

"Come on!" Toklo barked.

Leading the way, he jumped out of the firebeast. The flat-face was crawling about in the snow. Toklo leaped straight over him and charged through the rows of firebeasts; he could hear his friends' pawsteps pounding after him. So far there was no sign of the flat-faces with pawsticks, nor the ones with firesticks.

The bears fled between two lines of silent firebeasts. Toklo knew that they wouldn't be unnoticed for long. Already he could hear shouts and shrieks starting to echo around him, and he spotted flat-faces appearing briefly in the gaps between the firebeasts, then vanishing again.

As they were approaching the end of the row, two flat-faces stepped out in front of them. They held sticks in their fore-paws and brandished them threateningly. Toklo veered away into another gap between two firebeasts, only to find the way blocked by more flat-faces with sticks. He halted, staring in dismay.

"Go on!" Kallik growled, shoving him from behind. "They haven't got firesticks."

Encouraged, Toklo reared up on his hindpaws and let out an enormous roar. The flat-faces scattered.

We can't stay among these firebeasts forever, Toklo thought, hurtling onward. *The flat-faces with firesticks will be here soon.*

He darted toward the empty space at the end of a row. The mountain slope stretched out ahead of him, white and empty, with nowhere to hide.

Yakone thrust his way forward and paused beside Toklo, gazing out, his eyes narrowed in concentration.

"There's nothing out there!" Toklo hissed. "They'll catch us easily!"

On his other side, Lusa was gazing up at the sky, and Toklo knew she was searching for Ujurak. *Unless he turns us into flat-faces or snowflakes,* Toklo thought, *he can't help us.*

Without warning, Yakone leaped out into the open space and began racing up the slope. "Follow me!" he ordered.

Toklo hesitated.

"Go on!" Kallik urged. "Trust him!"

Lusa nodded. "I'd rather die trying to escape than just give up." Her voice was grim, and for a moment her eyes looked old and wise.

Toklo nodded. "You're right. We can't stand here and do nothing."

Though he thought that his fear might choke him, he pelted out into the open after Yakone. Kallik and Lusa bounded alongside him, and Toklo suddenly remembered their care-free race of a few days before.

It's not so fun this time!

They were beginning to catch up with Yakone when Lusa missed her footing in the snow and rolled over, her legs flailing. Instantly Toklo veered aside to help her stand, thrusting her upright again with his shoulder.

"Thanks!" Lusa gasped. "I'm sorry, I just can't deal with this stupid snow!"

Toklo nodded, watching Lusa as she tried to scrape off the soft snow that was clogging her belly hair. Her legs were too short to keep her clear of it; the climb was far harder for her than the rest of them.

He used the moment's delay to look back. More flat-faces

had appeared around the firebeasts. He heard a shot exploding from a firestick.

"Go!" he growled at Lusa, giving her a hard shove up the slope as he began to run again.

Then, as he scanned the mountainside ahead of him, he blinked in confusion. Kallik and Yakone had disappeared.

What's happened to them? he wondered. *Have they been shot? Are they injured?*

"Kallik! Yakone!" he roared, looking around frantically. But the snow-covered slope was empty. There was no sign of his friends; the line of their pawsteps simply stopped, and the snow beyond was unmarked.

"Toklo! Over here!"

Toklo stiffened as he heard Yakone's voice, coming faintly from somewhere ahead.

"Where are you?" he asked.

"See that bump in front of you? We're behind that. We've dug down into a drift."

"Hurry up and join us," Kallik added. "Jump as far as you can so that you don't leave a trail of pawprints."

Toklo was impressed. He got behind Lusa. "I'm going to give you a boost," he added aloud. "Ready?"

Lusa nodded. Toklo worked his shoulders underneath her and thrust upward, hurling her over the bump. A deep trough of soft snow swallowed her up.

Toklo followed her, landing on the powdery surface and sinking deep, deep down, until his ears and nose and mouth filled up with the white stuff.

Kallik's head suddenly appeared beside him. "Dig down!" she hissed. "It's our only chance!"

Toklo braced himself as if he were about to jump into a river. "Okay, this is it," he whispered as he started to dig.

CHAPTER FIVE

Lusa

Lusa crouched in the snow, hardly daring to breathe. She knew that it was only a matter of time before the flat-faces discovered them.

"Yakone saw the bump in the hill," Kallik, beside her, murmured into her ear. "He felt the direction of the wind, and guessed that the best chance of a drift deep enough to hide us would be over here."

In spite of her fear, Lusa was full of admiration for Yakone. "He was right. He knows so much about snow!" she whispered. *But will it work?* she asked herself. *Is this hiding place good enough?*

There was nothing to do but wait. Lusa was so cold that she had to clench her teeth together to stop them from chattering.

"Right now I'd rather be in the belly of the firebeast," she muttered to herself. "I hated it in there, but at least it didn't freeze the blood in my veins, and I had air to breathe." She heaved a sigh. "Maybe we should have stayed there until the firebeast woke up and carried us away. We could be far, far away by now, safe from these angry flat-faces with sticks on their hindpaws."

"Hush!" Toklo hissed. "The flat-faces will hear you."

Lusa burrowed deeper into the snow. *I wonder how snow-hares manage to live down here without freezing to death.*

She could feel the thud of flat-faces approaching, their paw-steps vibrating through the snow, and hear the hiss of their pawsticks on the surface. They weren't yowling anymore, but walking quietly, murmuring to one another. Lusa could smell their fear, and guessed that they had been scared by Toklo's show of strength earlier.

But not scared enough to stop chasing us. Please just leave us alone! she thought desperately.

As Lusa tried to breathe, snow got up her nose, and she had to sneeze. The itching got worse with every moment that passed, until she couldn't bear it any longer.

I have to breathe! she thought.

To her relief, she could hear the flat-faces scrambling away, and the sound of their voices grew fainter.

Lusa exploded out of the snow, sneezing and spitting out the lump of cold stuff that had almost choked her.

The others loomed up around her, rising out of the drift like snow that had come to life. Lusa's legs felt numb with cold, and stiff from keeping still for so long. She could barely move, and she saw that her friends were having the same trouble.

We should be running while we have the chance, she thought. *The flat-faces could come back at any moment.*

But she felt so tired and cold, she didn't think she could ever run again.

"This is no good," Yakone muttered at last, flexing his legs. "We'll be caught for sure if we stay here."

"Do you think we don't know that?" Toklo snapped back at him.

"Then let's go," Yakone urged. "We're strong, we can do this. You know we can."

"I'm not sure anymore." Kallik sounded exhausted. "Just give us a bit more time."

"That's time we might not have," Yakone responded, looking down the slope to where the flat-faces were gathering.

Lusa followed his gaze. So far none of the flat-faces seemed to have spotted them, but she was uncomfortable about how her pelt and Toklo's would stand out against the snow.

"We have to move," Yakone repeated, his voice rougher now. "Kallik, come on. Toklo, you're not telling me that a brown bear is giving up?"

Toklo let out a low growl from deep in his throat. "I never give up, fish-breath!"

"Then *move*, now!" Yakone snarled. "All of you, *move!*"

First Kallik, then Toklo, began stumbling up the slope away from the drift where they had taken refuge. Lusa struggled after them, aware that Yakone was padding by her side, his fur brushing hers.

At first their progress was slow on frozen paws, but gradually they managed to pick up speed. As they climbed higher the ground grew steeper; sometimes the coating of snow was thin, just enough to hide the sharp rocks below. Almost with every pawstep Lusa would stub her paws on hidden boulders, or topple into drifts left in hidden hollows. Every time, Yakone was there, tirelessly hauling her out and shoving her upward. Lusa flashed him a look of gratitude, but she had no breath to speak, or do anything except force her paws to keep moving.

At last Lusa heaved herself up to a narrow ledge where Toklo and Kallik were waiting for her to catch up. Her throat seemed to burn as she gulped in air. Dizzy with hunger and fear, she didn't think she could take another pawstep.

"Please," she gasped. "I've got to rest for a bit."

Kallik gave her shoulder a comforting nuzzle. "I know. I'm just as scared and exhausted as you are, but we have to keep going."

Lusa nodded, glad that she wasn't alone. Somehow she managed to find the strength to keep going, farther and farther up the mountain, until the sun sank below the horizon and twilight gathered on the slopes.

Halting briefly, they looked back down the mountain to see lights appearing, illuminating the rows of firebeasts. Shouts drifted up from the flat-faces as they climbed into the firebeasts' bellies. The firebeasts woke up, their glaring eyes angling across the snow, and grumbled away, out of sight.

Lusa breathed a sigh of relief that she was up here in the open air instead of trapped in the shiny belly of the firebeast, no matter what she had thought earlier. "Are we safe?" she whispered.

"I think so," Kallik responded.

"But we can't rest yet," Yakone warned them. "The no-claws might be back tomorrow. We need to get right away from here."

For once Toklo didn't argue, just turned his face to the upward slope and began scrambling up to the next ledge.

Full darkness fell and the moon appeared. The bears kept climbing, hauling themselves from one rocky outcrop to the next. As the stars began to appear, Lusa looked for Ujurak's constellation, but she was too dizzy and tired to make out his shape.

If he's watching, I hope he's proud of us for escaping, she thought.

Lusa thought that her paws were about to drop off by the time Toklo halted. "We have to stop and rest," he announced. "It's too dark to see properly, and the mountain is getting steeper. We could fall off at any moment."

None of them, even Yakone, tried to argue.

"We'll hunt when dawn comes," Toklo added, limping toward a sheltered spot behind a huge boulder.

The others huddled down beside him. Lusa was shivering with cold, and her belly rumbled with hunger, but she was comforted by the thought that at least they were safe.

But what will happen after the Melting Sea? she wondered. *Will Toklo and I be able to survive together, without the others? Are two bears easier to catch than four?*

CHAPTER SIX

Kallik

A paw jabbing into her side woke Kallik. It was still night, but in the moonlight she could make out Yakone lying beside her. He was striking out with his paws and muttering disjointedly; Kallik leaned closer to make out what he was saying.

"Spirit-cursed no-claws! They're chasing us . . . they'll catch us! Nowhere to hide . . ."

Kallik rested her paw on Yakone's shoulder and gave him a gentle shake. "Wake up, Yakone! It's okay. The no-claws are gone."

Yakone's eyes blinked open. "Wha'?" he gulped.

"We're safe now," Kallik told him. "You saved us, with that great idea of hiding in the snowdrift."

Yakone grunted and rose to his paws, shaking the loose snow from his pelt. Padding around the side of the boulder where they had been sleeping, he gazed down into the valley. A few no-claw lights still showed there, glittering in the darkness like stars that had fallen to the ground.

"I won't feel safe until we're well away from here," he

growled, anger in his voice. "This place is full of no-claws who want to hurt us. What have we ever done to them? They should show us more respect."

"It was scary," Kallik agreed, "but it's over now. We'll soon leave those no-claws way behind."

"I can't wait to get to the Melting Sea," Yakone responded. "Then maybe we can get on with our lives in peace."

Kallik realized with dismay that he was assuming there would be no no-claws near the Melting Sea. Yakone had lived all his life until now on Star Island, where there weren't many no-claws, and those who were there left the white bears alone. He had probably never imagined there could be so many no-claws in the world.

"There are still some no-claws near the Melting Sea," she began, not quite sure how much to tell Yakone. She didn't want to tell him about the huge denning areas, swarming with no-claws and their firebeasts. She remembered how the no-claws had captured her and taken her to a huge den made of white stone, and how she had been carried in a metal bird that fell out of the sky in a storm of flame. Her belly churned as she pictured Nanuk, the she-bear who had taken care of her, dying among the wreckage of twisted metal.

What if we're captured again?

Guilt washed over Kallik like a cold wave as she wondered whether she had done the right thing by bringing Yakone with her. On Star Island he had food, family, and safety. *I can't promise him any of those things.*

"Hi." Toklo's voice came from behind Kallik; she turned to

see the brown bear lumbering out from behind the boulder. "I couldn't sleep either." Standing beside Yakone and gazing down the mountainside, he added, "I'd forgotten what it was like to travel through places with so many flat-faces. Maybe we should travel by night instead."

"That's a great idea!" Kallik told him. "Should we go now?"

"Let's," Yakone agreed. "Then we'll get to the Melting Sea even faster."

But reaching the Melting Sea wasn't the first thing on Kallik's mind. Her paws just itched to be moving, to give them all something to do. *There's no point in just standing here worrying.*

"I'll wake Lusa," she said.

Padding back behind the boulder, she found the black bear curled up in the snow with her paws over her nose. It took a long time to prod her awake.

"What's the matter?" Lusa asked, puzzled. "Are the flat-faces coming after us again?"

"No," Kallik replied. "We just think it's best to get away from here as quickly as we can."

"Okay." Lusa's jaws stretched in a huge yawn, and she scooped up a pawful of snow to rub over her face.

Kallik realized Lusa must still be tired from the frantic chase the day before, but the black bear said nothing more and looked cheerful enough as she padded behind Toklo when they set out up the mountain.

A chilly wind was blowing as Kallik and her friends climbed higher, flattening their fur to their sides and whirling loose snow from the surface into their faces. The moon shone out fitfully as the wind drove the clouds across the sky. The changing light and shadow made it hard for Kallik to know where it was safe to put her paws, and she could see the others were having the same trouble.

Lusa slipped sideways into a drift and floundered about helplessly until Yakone leaned over, gripped her scruff in his teeth as if she was a cub, and hauled her out.

"Thanks!" Lusa gasped.

"You can ride on my shoulders if you like," Yakone offered.

"No!" Lusa sounded indignant. "I'll be fine."

"Okay, okay." There was an edge to Yakone's tone, and Kallik wondered if Lusa had offended him. "Tell me if you change your mind."

"I'm starving," Toklo complained when they had trudged on a few more bearlengths. "Kallik, do you know if there's anything to eat up here?"

"How would I know?" Kallik retorted. "I've never been this way before. I—"

She broke off with a squeal of alarm as the ground gave way beneath her paws. She had lost concentration for a couple of heartbeats, and now she was sliding downward in a flurry of snow. A moment later she hit the ground with a thump that jarred every bone in her body.

Kallik gasped to catch her breath and shook the snow out of her ears. Glancing around, she realized she had fallen into a narrow crevice. On both sides and in front of her, sheer stone walls stretched up above her head. Looking up, she could just make out Yakone's pale head as he peered down at her; Lusa and Toklo were dark shapes by his side.

"Help me! Get me out!" Kallik shouted.

Icy fear was creeping through her as she realized that she would never be able to climb the rock face. There was nowhere on the surface for her claws to grip, and the crevice was so narrow that she was almost wedged between the walls.

"Kallik, are you hurt?" Lusa called down to her.

"No," Kallik replied. "But I'm stuck down here. I can't get out!"

"Kallik, don't panic." Yakone's voice sounded strong and calm. "Behind you there's a slope leading up to the top. If you can't turn around, you'll have to back up."

Relief made Kallik's legs shake for a moment, but she forced herself to take careful pawsteps backward, feeling loose grit and snowmelt beneath her pads. Soon she realized that the path was sloping upward, just as Yakone had said. Now and again she slipped on icy patches, but at last she felt the wind again, ruffling her fur. Toklo and Yakone were beside her, steadying her as she emerged from the crevasse.

"Thank the spirits!" she exclaimed. "I thought I was stuck there for good."

Another fit of shivering seized her as she wondered what it would have been like if she hadn't been able to climb out. Her friends would have had to leave her there. She would have heard their pawsteps and their voices dying away. . . .

No. I won't think of that.

"Are you okay?" Yakone asked her anxiously.

"I'm fine," she told him, blinking at him. "Let's keep going.

But we need to be really careful."

Hauling herself to the top of the next ridge, Kallik saw a flatter stretch of ground in front of her, covered with unbroken snow that gleamed silver in the moonlight.

"That looks easier," Toklo grunted.

"But that doesn't mean we can be careless," Kallik reminded him, still shaken from the ground giving way under her paws.

Toklo gave her a brusque nod and strode out across the open ground. Kallik and the others followed. The snow was soft and deep; within moments Lusa was struggling, sliding into drifts every few paces, and Yakone stayed close to her to drag her out.

Kallik's belly was rumbling; she paused briefly to see if she could spot any sign of prey, but there was no scent on the wind, and no tracks disturbed the untouched covering of snow. Glancing back over her shoulder, she could see only snow and rock and darkness; the no-claw lights had disappeared, left a long way behind.

At least we don't need to worry about them anymore.

A sudden roar from Toklo made her whip her head around to face forward again. The brown bear was wallowing deep in snow, only his head and shoulders visible. Kallik dashed toward him, her heart pounding, remembering her own fall. Yakone followed her, with Lusa left floundering along in their pawsteps.

But before Kallik and Yakone could reach Toklo, the brown bear barked, "Stop!" He heaved himself out of the snow again and stood to shake glittering drops of water and ice crystals from his pelt.

"There's a spirit-cursed stream under there," he snarled across at them. "I had no idea it was there until I felt the ice breaking under my paws."

Kallik and Yakone approached cautiously. Looking down, Kallik could see the hole Toklo had made, with splintered ice at the edges and dark water running past.

"My fur is soaking," Toklo grumbled.

"We'll all have to get across," Yakone said, standing at Kallik's side. "Is it narrow enough to leap?"

Toklo prodded at the snow with one paw, until he felt the place where the ground beneath gave way to the ice that covered the stream. "You can try," he said. "The edge is just here where I'm standing."

Yakone backed up to take a run and leaped, aiming to land next to Toklo. But he fell short; his hind paws broke through the ice and he slid backward, water washing over his haunches.

"Seal rot!" he muttered, scrambling out and shaking himself.

Kallik chose to wade across; the ice gave way under her weight and the stream surged up as far as her belly fur. She shuddered at the freezing touch of the water as it soaked through to her skin. Her pawsteps felt unsteady as she slipped on the muddy streambed, but she stayed on her paws and climbed out on the other side with most of her fur still dry.

"I think your way is best," Yakone commented.

Lusa had come up to the water's edge while Kallik was crossing, and launched herself through the snow a little way upstream. She was so light that the ice held her with only an ominous creak or two.

"Thank the spirits!" she exclaimed as she joined the others on the other side. "At least it's not always bad being small."

All four bears took a drink from the stream before they continued. The icy water cramped Kallik's belly, but refreshed her and gave her strength to go on.

As Toklo led the way onward and the bears began to climb again, Kallik realized that she could see the peak ahead outlined against the sky. Soon she spotted a pink and golden glow beginning to bloom on the horizon. The sky grew pale, and as the bears took the last weary pawsteps that carried them to the top of the mountain, the sun came up, flooding the snow with dazzling brightness.

Ahead of them Kallik could see a long, smooth slope that ended in a narrow valley. Another mountain reared up on the far side, and beyond that lay peak after peak, a range of mountains as far as the eye could see, snow-covered and shining in the morning sun.

"It's so beautiful!" Lusa exclaimed.

Together the bears lifted their faces to the light. A breeze blew across the summit, and Kallik was sure that she could hear Ujurak's voice whispering within it, bringing her words of encouragement.

Thank you, Ujurak, she responded silently.

The whispering grew louder, turning to a harsh clatter in

the sky. Kallik tensed as she looked up and spotted a metal bird only a few bearlengths above their heads, its whirling wings blotting out the sunlight.

"It's heading straight for us!" she squealed.

Pure panic seized her paws; she spun around and fled back the way they had come, down the mountainside. But she had taken only a few pawsteps when Toklo skidded past her and turned so he was blocking her path.

"What's the matter?" he growled. "Are you bee-brained? It's just a flying flat-face thing, like we saw in the Great Wilderness."

Kallik halted, struggling to stifle her deep, inward shuddering. She couldn't explain why she feared the metal birds that flew near the Melting Sea. She doubted that her friends would believe what had happened to her and Nanuk.

Toklo shoved her into the shelter of a heap of boulders, where they crouched, looking up at the metal bird. Kallik couldn't see Lusa and Yakone at all; she hoped they were in a safe hiding place beyond the peak. The metal bird swooped low over the mountainside, blasting snow from the surface. Kallik's eyes stretched wide with astonishment as two no-claws leaped out of its belly; they had long pawsticks fastened to their paws.

"It's them again!" Toklo exclaimed, anger in his voice. "They're still chasing us!"

The metal bird rose higher into the air, while the two no-claws began sliding toward the opposite side of the peak.

"They're heading for Yakone and Lusa," Toklo growled.

Kallik's belly lurched with fear for her friends. "What are we going to do?" she asked.

"I don't know," Toklo grumbled. "Maybe we should try to distract the flat-faces."

"Let's go and see what's happening," Kallik said.

Cautiously she and Toklo crept across the top of the peak, using jutting boulders for cover as much as they could. The two no-claws were gliding along on their pawsticks, and as Kallik watched, they vanished down the slope on the opposite side.

"They've gone!" she exclaimed, relieved.

Toklo grunted.

Kallik looked around, and her feelings of relief died as she saw no sign of Yakone and Lusa on the windswept peak. "Where did they go?" she asked. "Did they run away? The no-claws didn't hurt them, did they?"

"I didn't hear any firesticks," Toklo responded. "They must be here somewhere."

Together Kallik and Toklo began to search the peak, but Lusa and Yakone weren't hiding behind any of the boulders, and there were no hollows in the ground big enough to conceal two bears. Here and there the snow was trampled, but the pawsteps didn't lead anywhere. The farther slope swept downward, unbroken by anything except the two no-claws, by now tiny bright dots in their colorful pelts.

"Where are they?" Toklo growled.

Kallik tried to force down her rising panic. "Tell me what any bear could do, to vanish like this!" she snapped.

She spun around to march away from Toklo, but before she could move, her paw struck something solid beneath the snow. She started back in amazement as Yakone and Lusa floundered up out of the snow in front of her.

"Fooled you!" Lusa exclaimed, her berry-bright eyes sparkling with amusement.

"And we fooled the no-claws," Yakone added. He glanced back to where he and Lusa had been hiding, in a snow-filled dip behind a heap of rocks. "We're lucky there was a good, deep drift."

"I should have guessed you were using the same trick again," Kallik confessed, hugely relieved to see Yakone again and to realize that he and Lusa were safe.

Toklo strode across to Lusa's side and shouldered her out of the drift until all four of her paws were on solid ground again. "Are you okay?" he asked, checking her over as he brushed snow from her pelt.

"I'm fine," Lusa asserted, wriggling away from Toklo and scattering snow as she shook herself. "Yakone knew exactly where to hide. He knows how deep snow is just by looking at it. When those flat-faces appeared, he shoved me into the drift without even having to think!"

Toklo just grunted, and Kallik noticed a shadow of jealousy in his face as he looked at Yakone.

"I think we should get going right away," she said before Toklo had a chance to speak. "Those no-claws might come back, or there could be others. I'm not sure if they were looking for us, but there's no point in waiting around to find out."

Toklo hesitated for a moment, then gave her a brusque nod.

"This way," Kallik said, and took the lead as they headed down the mountainside.

I need to guide them now, she thought. *We're so close to my home!*

Pausing briefly, she raised her muzzle and gave the air a good sniff, straining to pick up a trace of the Melting Sea on the wind. Delight thrilled through her as she caught a tantalizing whiff of salt water.

But it smells just like the sea around Star Island and the Island of Shadows, she admitted to herself after a moment. However hard she concentrated, she couldn't distinguish anything special that made her think of her mother or her home. A claw of anxiety stabbed at her. *What if I don't recognize the place where I was born? I promised to show Yakone my home, but what if I can't?*

Fear gave strength to her paws, and she forged ahead, striding out determinedly to the bottom of the slope and across the valley to where the next mountain peak reared up ahead of them.

"Hey, Kallik! Kallik!"

At the sound of Lusa's breathless voice, Kallik halted and turned. The small black bear stumbled up to her, puffing so hard that for a moment she couldn't speak. Toklo and Yakone were still farther back, weaving a course through the boulders that littered the valley floor.

"What's the matter?" Kallik asked.

"Slow down!" Lusa gasped. "Even Toklo and Yakone can't keep up with you."

"Sorry," Kallik replied, realizing she had been so deep in

thought she hadn't checked where her friends were. "I'm so worried," she confessed to Lusa, panic welling up inside her again. "I'm afraid that I won't remember my home clearly enough."

Lusa padded to her side and gave her a reassuring nudge. "Of course you'll remember when we get there. There's still a long way to go."

Kallik's voice rose to a wail. "But what if I can't even find the way? What if I'm leading you wrong?"

"Cloud-brain!" Lusa said affectionately. "We know we're going the right way because of the sun and the stars. We just have to keep walking until we get to somewhere you recognize. Besides," she added, "Ujurak would tell us if we were going in the wrong direction, wouldn't he?"

Far from reassuring Kallik, Lusa's words only increased the white bear's worries. "But how does Ujurak know where I was born?"

"I'm not sure. But I know that he does." Lusa's voice was full of confidence. "He's not like us. He can see everything now that he's in the sky."

Gratitude for Lusa's faith in her and in Ujurak flooded over Kallik and revived her spirits a little. While she waited for Yakone and Toklo to catch up, she studied the mountain that lay ahead of them. Almost at once she spotted a path that wound upward among the rocks, zigzagging across the slope.

"That looks promising," she said as the male bears padded up. "Let's go."

"Just remember you're not in a race this time," Toklo

grumbled as he followed her.

At first the path Kallik had chosen seemed easy, but it was steeper than it looked, and loose grit beneath the snow made their paws slip. After they had plodded upward for many bearlengths, Kallik came to a halt in front of a pile of boulders that completely blocked their way.

"Now what do we do?" she asked.

"Can we get around?" Yakone wondered out loud. He began to climb the steepest part of the slope, which would have taken him above the blockage, but almost at once he started to lose ground, scrabbling with his paws and slipping back down in a shower of snow. Lusa let out a startled squeal and jumped out of his way.

"Sorry," Yakone said. "There are loose rocks under there. We'll never get up that way."

"Don't say we have to go all the way down again!" Lusa exclaimed.

Toklo didn't speak, but leaped up onto a rocky outcrop and began to survey the land around them. Kallik leaped up beside him; Yakone gave Lusa a boost and then joined the others on the top of the rocks.

"Look over there," Toklo said as Kallik reached his side. He jerked his head toward a narrow gully that led up the mountain at an angle. "We might get up that way."

"It looks very steep," Kallik responded doubtfully.

"It reminds me of the gully that we followed when we first reached the Island of Shadows," Lusa contributed. "That was a struggle, but we made it okay."

Yakone nodded. "It looks like there might be a stream at the bottom of it. We might get a drink there, and there could even be prey."

"But how are we going to get up to it?" Kallik asked. The gully opened up several bearlengths above their heads, across the slope where Yakone had discovered the loose rocks under the snow.

"Look there," Yakone replied, pointing with one paw. "Where the snow is lumpy? There must be boulders or maybe bushes under there, and that would give our paws something to grip."

"Then let's go!" Lusa said, giving a little bounce.

Kallik admired her cheerfulness, even though she must be almost exhausted by the difficult journey with little sleep. Her own resolve strengthened. "Okay. Follow me."

She set out into the snow, following the line Yakone had indicated. The snow-covered lumps turned out to be tough little thornbushes growing close to the ground. The thorns dug into their paws and the branches rasped against their sides, but at least it was possible to haul themselves upward from one bush to the next until they reached the mouth of the gully.

Yakone had been right about the stream. Its course was marked by a line where the snow was smoother. Toklo scraped away some of the snow to reveal an icy covering, which he broke with one blow of his paw. He plunged his snout into the hole he had made and took a long drink.

"That was good," he said as he raised his head again, shaking water drops from his muzzle. "All we need now is a fat hare or two, and we can walk for days!"

But as Kallik led the way up the gully, there was no sign of prey. Her belly grumbled, but she ignored it and concentrated on the climb. Though the gully was steep, the ground under-paw was fairly smooth, and they made good progress.

Looking back over her shoulder, Kallik saw her friends fol-lowing her in single file. *I hope Ujurak is watching us,* she thought. The fears she had felt about traveling without Ujurak were slowly fading, as pride in how they were managing the journey took over. "I trust you," she whispered to Ujurak, hoping he could hear her. "If we get into trouble, I know you'll be with us."

The sun had climbed high in the sky by the time the gully came to an end in a low wall of rock. Sharp, jutting stones made a path for the bears to climb to the top. Ahead of her, Kallik saw a stretch of level ground, many bearlengths wide, with yet another mountain slope at the far side.

"This would be a good place to stop," Toklo panted, clam-bering up beside her. "We need to hunt and rest for a bit."

Kallik and the others agreed. While Lusa began digging through the snow in search of roots and grass, the three bigger bears separated to look for prey.

Following the line of the stream, which meandered across the level ground from a frozen waterfall on the mountain-side ahead, Kallik spotted bird prints in the snow. Raising her muzzle, she sniffed the air, and the scent she picked up flooded her jaws with water.

Goose!

Glancing around, she saw nothing at first, so she padded forward on silent paws, trying to pinpoint where the scent was coming from. A heap of boulders blocked her view ahead, and as she crept around them, she spotted several geese poking about in the snow at the edge of the stream.

Kallik paused. The thrill of the hunt was rushing through her, but she knew she mustn't let herself get careless. She shifted slightly to make sure she was downwind of her prey and picked out a goose at the edge of the group: It was the closest to her, and had its back turned.

Pawstep by stealthy pawstep, Kallik crept up on the goose. When she was within a bearlength of her quarry, one of the other geese spotted her; it let out a raucous cry of alarm and took to the air in a flurry of wings. The rest of the geese followed. But Kallik was already leaping, batting her goose out of the air with a slap of one forepaw. The goose fell to the ground, wings flapping helplessly. Kallik severed its neck with another swift blow.

Triumph filled her as she picked the goose up in her jaws and turned to carry it back to her friends. Then she halted in surprise as she saw Yakone pacing toward her.

"I was watching you," the male bear said as he reached her side. "That was a terrific catch. You looked just like Toklo!"

Kallik gaped, dropping her prey. "What? Didn't I look like a white bear?"

Yakone looked taken aback. "Well, of course. I just think it's great that you can hunt like other bears."

Kallik took a deep breath. "Sorry," she murmured. "I only want everything to be perfect going home. I don't want the bears there to think I'm not like them."

Briefly Yakone buried his muzzle in her shoulder fur. "Everything will be perfect, because we're both here," he told her. "So quit worrying!"

I wish I could believe him, Kallik thought. *There's still so much that could go wrong.*

CHAPTER SEVEN

Toklo

Toklo nosed his way into the open and stood blinking in the pale dawn light. Behind him, in the den they had scraped out beneath an overhanging rock, he could hear his friends still snuffling in their sleep. From somewhere nearby came the sound of slow dripping, a sign that the snow and ice were starting to melt at last. A faint scent of pine wafted toward Toklo on the breeze, and from high above his head came the cry of a bird.

Excitement prickled at Toklo like ants creeping through his pelt. *The warmer weather is coming.* But his excitement couldn't banish his anxiety as he thought of the time when his little family of bears would split up.

Kallik and Yakone will stay at the Melting Sea. Lusa and I will have to go on alone.

Determinedly pushing away the thought, Toklo gazed at the landscape ahead of him and began planning the day's route. He and his friends had traveled through the mountains for several days, and already they were nearing the end of the range. They had descended a long way from the high peaks; from the ledge where he stood, Toklo could see a flat expanse of land stretching into the distance. The horizon was so misty and blurred that Toklo couldn't make out any details, but he wondered if he was already gazing out over the Melting Sea.

On their journey they had stayed at the center of the ridge to avoid flat-faces. To Toklo's relief they hadn't seen any more metal birds, or the weird flat-faces with sticks on their paws.

That's because we've been extra careful. For all we know, the flat-faces are still looking for us.

But even though it was so important to stay away from flat-faces, the bears hadn't been able to travel by night. The terrain was too difficult. Toklo winced in sympathy as he remembered how Yakone had stepped off the edge of a rock in the dark and wrenched his shoulder. That had meant a day of no traveling at all, so he could rest.

After that, they traveled in daylight, always alert for the appearance of more flat-faces. Toklo stifled a sigh of regret for the vast open spaces of the Endless Ice, where flat-faces never bothered them.

But we couldn't stay there forever, he reminded himself. *We're all going home, back where we belong—wherever that is.*

"Hey, the air smells different!" Lusa popped out of the den beside Toklo, her eyes gleaming as she surveyed the land in front of them. "I can smell green things growing—buds under the snow! I—" She broke off with a squeak as a drop of water fell from the overhanging rock above and splashed onto her head. "The mountain's melting!" she exclaimed.

"No, just the snow," Yakone told her, emerging from the den behind her and stretching his limbs with a mighty yawn.

Kallik pushed her way into the open behind him and paced forward to the end of the ledge, where she stood staring into the distance. After a moment she spun around. "I can smell home!" she gasped. "Look, the Melting Sea is there!"

Toklo and the others padded forward to stand at her side and looked down at the flat stretch in front of them. Peering through the mist, Toklo could just make out a difference between the farthest expanse and the land closer to the foot of the mountains.

"That's the Melting Sea," Kallik insisted, turning to Yakone. "We're home!"

Yakone's eyes lit up with joy, and he leaned closer to Kallik, who pressed her muzzle into his shoulder.

Toklo turned aside with a grunt, trying to pretend he didn't feel a hollow place opening up inside him.

"It's going to be weird, leaving them behind, isn't it?" Lusa said, coming to join Toklo and brushing her pelt against his.

"No, it'll be fine," Toklo responded, trying to sound confident. "We're all going home, right? That's the whole point of this journey."

Before Lusa could reply, Kallik leaped from the ledge and hurtled down the snowy slope. "We did it!" she called out, and Yakone let out a triumphant roar as he followed her.

Toklo launched himself forward and slid down the slope with outstretched legs and belly, exhilarated by the feeling of the wind whipping through his fur. Lusa rolled past him, waving her paws and squealing with excitement, coming to a halt half-buried in a snowdrift.

"This is fun!" she exclaimed as Toklo hauled her out. "Race you to the bottom!"

"Hey, be careful!" Toklo called out, as Lusa took off again, tucking in her head and paws and rolling down, collecting snow on her fur until she looked more like a white bear than a black one.

Toklo scrambled after her, slipping and sliding through the snow until he caught up with Yakone.

"Can you do this?" Yakone asked, flipping himself over to turn a complete somersault and landing back on all four paws. He grimaced slightly as the shoulder he had injured a few days before took his weight, but stood firmly.

"That's great!" said Kallik. She tried a somersault of her own, only to land flat on her back in the snow.

Yakone worked his uninjured shoulder underneath her to help her up. "All it takes is practice."

"Yes, but can you do *this*?" Toklo asked, scooping up a pawful of snow and flicking it into Yakone's face as he turned around.

Yakone let out a roar of mock rage, and Toklo fled, throwing up fountains of snow with his hindpaws to shower over the pursuing white bear. Joy and excitement were bubbling up inside him.

We're coming home! We survived the Endless Ice and we didn't get lost!

Toklo let out a muffled grunt as Yakone caught him up and rolled him over into the snow. "Fish-breath!" Toklo gasped out, half-choked on a mouthful of freezing crystals. "You'll be sorry!"

He scrambled to his paws and shook snow out of his pelt. Kallik and Yakone were standing side by side in front of him, while Lusa sat half-buried in the snow underneath a tall outcrop of rocks, her eyes sparkling with laughter.

Toklo glanced around. Sliding and tumbling, they had descended most of the slope, and the flat land lay in front of them. Suddenly Toklo was unwilling to head out toward the Melting Sea, wanting this time of fun and excitement to go on a little longer.

"See those rocks?" he said to Yakone, nodding toward the outcrop where Lusa was sitting. "Dare you to climb up and jump off!"

"Sure." Yakone loped across to the outcrop and clambered up until he stood on a jutting ledge. "Watch this!"

"Be careful!" Kallik called.

Yakone launched himself into the air and landed on his belly, scattering snow all around him. "See?" he said to Toklo. "Is that high enough for you?"

"High?" Toklo snorted. "You call that high? Watch *me*!"

Without hesitation he lumbered over to the outcrop and hauled himself upward until he stood on the topmost rock of all. On the opposite side from where Yakone had jumped, there was a flat stretch of snow that seemed to be inviting Toklo to land on it. "Here I go!" he shouted.

From below he heard Yakone's voice. "Toklo, wait! That's—"

But Toklo took no notice, pushing off from the edge of

the rock and hurtling downward with his paws splayed out. A moment later he landed on snow so hard-packed and densely frozen that it felt like stone. All the breath was driven out of his body, and his head was filled with glittering light and darkness.

From close by he heard Lusa shrieking. "Toklo! Move!"

Toklo's senses swam back. He could hear a deafening rumble and see a dark shape looming over him. Blinking, he made out a firebeast bearing down on him, its yellow eyes glaring and its round black paws churning the snow.

With a yelp of terror Toklo scrabbled at the hard surface, thrusting himself to one side as the firebeast roared past. He felt a blast of hot air wash over his fur and collapsed in a heap as the firebeast vanished into the distance.

Kallik, Yakone, and Lusa came slithering down to join him. Their eyes were wide with shock, their playful mood of a few moments before vanished completely.

"Oh, Toklo!" Lusa gasped. "I was so scared . . ."

"Are you completely bee-brained?" Kallik snarled, standing over Toklo. "You could have hurt yourself badly, jumping from way up there, even if there hadn't been a firebeast."

Toklo was too stunned to retort, vaguely aware that Kallik was only angry because she had been terrified for him.

"You can tell that there's a BlackPath under the snow here," Yakone began. "It's too flat, for a start. And the surface is really hard-packed ice if you look closely . . . it reflects the light differently."

"Yeah, well, we're not all snow experts, okay?" Toklo

growled, trying to conceal his fear and embarrassment. "And I'm fine, so what's the problem?"

"You nearly weren't fine," Lusa reminded him, and added, "It could have been any of us, straying onto the BlackPath without noticing. We've been away from firebeast trails for so long, we aren't used to looking for them."

Kallik nodded, scraping at the layer of frozen snow on the BlackPath with one paw. "This one's well hidden," she murmured. "Maybe the firebeasts don't want anyone to know it's there?"

Toklo scrambled to his paws and looked around, alert for any more firebeasts or flat-faces. His friends did the same; he could sense the tension behind their wary glances.

Lusa crouched down and put her ear to the ground. "There's another firebeast coming!" she announced.

All four bears dashed for the cover of the huge outcrop of rocks. Moments later a huge firebeast loomed up out of the distance and roared past on vast round paws, scattering snowmelt onto the side of the BlackPath.

Yakone's eyes were bulging as his gaze followed it. "They're so big!" he exclaimed. "Back on Star Island, the firebeasts were really tiny."

"You're not on Star Island now," Toklo reminded him.

Yakone ignored him. "You're so brave!" he said to Kallik. "I had no idea what you had to go through on your journey."

Somehow the white bear's words annoyed Toklo. "The firebeasts are no threat if you know how to handle them," he pointed out. "They mostly keep to their trails."

"It's the flat-faces in their bellies that you have to worry about," Lusa added.

Yakone gaped. "They have flat-faces in their bellies? Have the firebeasts eaten them?"

Kallik shook her head. "Not exactly. They seem fine when they get out. They're not chewed up or anything. Just like when we hid inside the firebeast when the flat-faces on paw-sticks were chasing us."

"It's time we were moving," Toklo said, his paws itching with impatience to get as far away as possible from the Black-Path. "Line up beside me, and don't try to cross until I tell you." To his relief, the others did as he told them without arguing. Toklo stood with ears pricked, making sure that all was silent. There was no sign of firebeasts in either direction.

"Now!"

All four bears launched themselves across the BlackPath, slipping and sliding on the hard-packed snow. Memories flashed into Toklo's mind of how he and his mother and Tobi used to cross BlackPaths all the time. They often walked along them through the woods, ducking into cover at the edge when firebeasts came by. Back then, the BlackPaths hadn't seemed so terrifying, but Toklo couldn't remember why they'd stayed near them.

Surely Oka should have realized that BlackPaths and flat-faces are nothing but trouble?

Once across the BlackPath, Kallik took the lead, heading away from the mountains and into the plain. "Come on!" she urged, looking back. "I want to get to the edge of the Melting Sea. It's my home!"

Toklo felt a stab of jealousy. He had no idea how to find the sunlit woods where he had wandered with Oka and Tobi. He just knew that they were a long, long way away. The hollow place inside him opened up again as he wondered whether he would even recognize the valleys and forests where he grew up.

Will I be as certain as Kallik when I get there?

For the rest of the day the bears trekked across the plain, pausing just after midday to hunt. Determined to show what he could do, Toklo stalked cautiously toward a clump of thornbushes and reeds around a frozen pool. Before he reached them, he spotted two black spots against the snow and realized that he was looking at the ear tips of a hare. His belly cramping with hunger, Toklo crept up on the telltale black specks. The scent of the hare reached his nose and he imagined sinking his teeth into the warm flesh.

Just a bit closer . . .

With a roar, Toklo leaped. His claws sank into the hare before it was even aware of him. He crushed its neck with one paw.

As he gazed down at his prey, breathing hard with satisfaction, a flicker of movement caught his eye. A second hare sprang out from behind the thornbushes, clearly alarmed.

Toklo raced after it, enjoying the sensation of his muscles bunching and stretching as he chased it across the snow. The frightened hare changed direction, dodging from side to side, but Toklo was determined it wouldn't escape. Guessing which way it would run next, he intercepted it and killed it with a blow to the head.

Pride filled Toklo as he headed back to his companions with the two dead hares gripped in his jaws. When he reached them, Lusa had uncovered a bushy plant and was chewing the leaves, while Kallik and Yakone stood close together a little way away. They didn't seem to have caught anything.

Toklo was pleased that he was able to provide for them. Padding over to them, he dropped the hares at their paws. "Here," he said. "You can have one of these."

Kallik and Yakone exchanged a glance.

"Thanks, Toklo," Kallik responded awkwardly. "But Yakone and I decided that we'll wait and hunt on the ice when we reach the Melting Sea. We want to start fresh there."

Toklo thought that was bee-brained, but he tried to conceal his rising annoyance. "The ice is too hard on Lusa," he pointed out. "We agreed to stay on land."

"I know," Kallik replied. "We won't go far, just out enough to catch a seal, and then we'll come back, I promise."

"But we've always hunted together before!" Toklo protested.

"Well, maybe we don't have to now," Kallik told him.

Lusa looked up from where she was munching leaves. "It's fine, Toklo," she said. "I think it's a great idea if they hunt on the ice. I can find food here, and we can wait for them."

Toklo glared at the white bears. *Will they really come back?* he wondered.

Yakone dipped his head. "We'll be back before you know it," he said, as if he had guessed what was bothering Toklo. "Our journey isn't over yet."

"That's settled then," Lusa said comfortably. "Come on, Toklo, eat up. I want to see the Melting Sea!"

"I'm not hungry anymore," Toklo grunted, turning his back on his catch and stalking away.

He heard pawsteps behind him and realized that Kallik had followed him. "You must eat, Toklo," she said gently. "You need your strength. *We* need your strength. There's still a ways to the shore."

Feeling slightly ashamed, Toklo returned and devoured his catch, feeling full-fed for the first time in days. When he had finished, Kallik took the lead again and they headed once more toward the Melting Sea.

From here the plain was crossed by more small BlackPaths. Yakone was good at spotting them under the snow, and Toklo tried not to feel jealous of his skill. They crossed cautiously, listening for firebeasts, and hiding behind rocks and bushes when they roared past.

They hadn't gone much farther when Lusa halted, gazing into the distance. "Look!" she exclaimed. "Flat-face dens!"

Toklo followed her gaze and saw a few dens clustered beside one of the BlackPaths. A couple of firebeasts were crouched outside, and he picked up the harsh tang of oil on the air.

It feels weird, seeing their denning places again, he thought. *It's been so long since we've been near that many flat-faces.*

"Best to stay away from them," he grunted, and took the

lead to pass the flat-face dens at a safe distance.

As the sun went down, Toklo began to realize how weary he was. Kallik's and Yakone's paws were dragging, and Lusa kept stumbling as she tried to keep up. The run down the mountain had sapped their energy, and now every pawstep took a massive effort.

"We won't be able to reach the Melting Sea today," Kallik admitted at last, her voice regretful. "We'd better find somewhere to spend the night."

Toklo couldn't help wondering if she and Yakone wished they had shared the hares when they had the chance, but he didn't say anything.

Gazing around, Toklo couldn't see anywhere that would be a good place for a den: no deep hollows or rocks big enough to give them proper shelter. They padded on into the gathering twilight and eventually found a clump of scrubby bushes.

"I suppose this is better than nothing," Kallik said, beginning to scrape the snow away from underneath the outer branches.

Lusa sniffed a spray of shriveled leaves and backed off with a disgusted look on her face. "Yuck! I wouldn't eat those even if I were starving."

While Toklo and Yakone were helping Kallik to clear the snow away, Toklo noticed that Yakone kept glancing around nervously.

"We ought to keep a watch," the white male said when the makeshift den was ready. "With all these no-claws around, and those huge firebeasts . . ."

All *these no-claws?* Toklo thought. *Wait until he sees a really big flat-face denning area!* But he knew that Yakone had a point. Now that they were drawing closer to flat-face places, they would meet all kinds of unexpected dangers. "Good idea," he said aloud. "I'll take the first watch."

When his friends had huddled down into the scanty shelter of the bushes and were snoring softly, Toklo sat gazing back at the mountains they had just crossed.

Our journey has been hard, he thought. *But would it have been better to keep traveling, instead of returning to a place where we'll have to leave our friends behind?*

CHAPTER EIGHT

Lusa

Lusa lay with her muzzle squashed against the thin trunk of a prickly bush, but in her dreams she was walking through a forest. For so long she had yearned to be back there, to watch sunlight dazzling through the branches and making patterns on the ground, to climb and feel herself rocked in the branches of a tall tree, to stuff herself with luscious berries.

But this forest was dark and forbidding. The trees loomed over her; the faces in their bark were harsh and hostile, and branches reached out to claw at her fur. She tried to push through, but the trees seemed to shift and block her path. The faces drew back their lips and showed snarling teeth.

Eerie voices filled the air, seeming to come from all directions at once, so that Lusa didn't know which way to flee.

"What are you doing here, little bear?" a voice said.

"You don't belong here!" chimed in another.

"This is not your home!"

Lusa woke with a squeak of terror and lay trembling in the den, thankful for the bulk of Toklo and Kallik sleeping beside her. Yakone, outside on watch, poked his head under the branches. "Lusa, are you okay?"

"I had an awful dream," Lusa confessed, shuddering.

"Why don't you come outside and tell me about it?" Yakone suggested, his gaze friendly. "Let the others sleep for a bit longer."

Carefully, so as not to disturb Toklo and Kallik, Lusa wriggled underneath the spiky branches and plopped down in the snow beside Yakone. Stars still shone in the darkness, though Lusa thought that the sky was paling on the horizon where the sun would rise. "I thought I was walking through a forest," she began.

"But aren't forests your home?" Yakone said, puzzled. "Why wasn't it a good dream?"

"This forest was dark and scary," Lusa explained. "And there were voices wailing at me. I felt like the trees were trapping me."

"That does sound scary," Yakone agreed. "But then, I think forests sound scary anyway. I've never even seen a tall tree!"

"Oh, but real forests are wonderful!" Lusa told him. "They're full of interesting scents, and you can find delicious berries to eat and grubs under fallen trees, and the wind rustles in the branches. . . ."

Yakone shook his head. "I'd still feel trapped, just like you did in your dream. I like looking at the sky!"

"You can still see the sky," Lusa assured him. "In little gaps between the trees. And if you climb high enough, you can see all of it. You can see everything there is!"

"Well, we're obviously very different," Yakone said, amusement in his tone. "I guess you can't wait to get home to your forests."

"I guess so," Lusa replied in a small voice, suddenly remembering what it would mean when she reached the forest, and how she would have already lost Kallik and Yakone. Pushing the thought away, she added, "The forest isn't my real home, though."

Yakone looked confused. "But I thought . . ."

"No, I was born in the Bear Bowl," Lusa told him.

Yakone's bewilderment deepened. "What's a Bear Bowl?"

"It's a place flat-faces made," Lusa explained. "There are a whole bunch of bears there. My mother, Ashia, and my father, King, and my friend Yogi. And one time I met Toklo's mother, Oka, there."

"Sounds weird," Yakone commented. "Why would the no-claws make a place like that?"

"They liked looking at us, I guess," Lusa said. "We had fun there, Yogi and I. We used to hide like this," she added, springing to her paws and crouching down behind a snow-covered rock. "And then we'd leap out and pounce!"

Imagining she could see Yogi, his bright mischievous gaze flickering to and fro as he looked for her, she leaped out of cover. The memory had been so clear it was almost a shock when her paws landed in soft, powdery snow.

"Stella was an old bear who told us all about bear spirits," Lusa went on to the bemused Yakone. "She said that when bears die their spirits go into trees, and if you look closely you can see their faces in the bark." She peered at the twisted bushes where they had made their den. "I guess bear spirits wouldn't want to make their home here."

"White bear spirits become stars," Yakone said. "I'd rather be shining up in the sky than stuck in a tree!"

Lusa gave him a friendly shove. "I guess you would. But trees are best for black bears. King taught me to climb," she added. "It's just great, racing up the trunk, going higher and higher. Can you climb trees?" she asked Yakone.

The white bear shook his head. "I've never tried. Where would I find trees to practice on?"

"Oh, yeah," Lusa said, remembering the barren slopes of Star Island. "I can teach you if you want." She peered up at the bush, then slid between the branches to rest her forepaws against the trunk. "This one's kind of small, but it'll do to start with. Look, put your paws here like this."

Caught up in her enthusiasm, Yakone pushed his way in until he stood beside her and reached up the trunk, his paws stretching way above Lusa's head. The trunk bowed under his weight and the branches waved around, dumping snow on Toklo's head.

"Uh-oh," Lusa muttered, realizing this might not have been the best idea she'd ever had.

Toklo sat up, shaking snow off his head and glaring around. "What's going on?"

His movement woke Kallik, who blinked her eyes open and scrambled out into the open. "Yakone, what are you doing?" she snapped.

Looking guilty, Yakone backed out of the bush and padded to Kallik's side. "Sorry," he said, touching his muzzle to her shoulder.

"It's my fault," Lusa confessed. "I was telling Yakone about the Bear Bowl and showing him how we used to climb trees."

"The Bear Bowl?" Toklo growled. "Not that again!"

Kallik let out a sigh. "Since we're all awake, we might as well get going."

Toklo grunted and crawled out from underneath the bush. With another glare at Lusa, he set off toward the Melting Sea, not even looking back to see if the others were following.

Lusa was aware of the tension in the air as she padded off beside Kallik and Yakone. She wished she hadn't woken Toklo, but it had been fun telling Yakone about the Bear Bowl.

"I wonder if there'll still be ice all the way up to the shore," Kallik said after a while, trying to put the morning's annoyance behind her.

"I don't mind swimming a little way to reach the ice," Yakone responded.

"But the ice melts all over, even in the middle of the sea." Kallik's voice was quiet.

Lusa guessed that she was thinking about her mother, Nisa, who had been killed by orca when she was swimming across a gap between two ice floes. She gave her friend a comforting nudge with her muzzle, and Kallik returned a grateful glance.

Gradually the light grew stronger and the stars winked out. The sun rose into a cloudy sky, revealing the landscape that lay in front of the bears. But now the ground was so flat that they couldn't see very far ahead.

Lusa could feel vibrations through her paws, and with every pawstep the reek of oil in the air grew stronger. "We must be getting close to another BlackPath," she said.

Yakone halted. "Do we have to go this way?" he asked.

"I don't know," Kallik responded. "This is the shortest way to the Melting Sea, but we might be able to avoid the Black-Path if we change direction."

"And spend all day wandering about and getting nowhere?" Toklo swung around to face the white bears. "I'm not scared. Let's keep going."

"No one's scared," Kallik said defensively. "BlackPaths just aren't places where bears belong."

"But we've crossed BlackPaths before," Toklo argued.

"And we've nearly been killed by firebeasts!" Kallik retorted.

Yakone stepped between the two bears, who were glaring at each other. "There's no need to argue. Why don't we just split up and meet again by the shore of the Melting Sea?"

Lusa winced as Toklo let out a roar. "No! We stay together."

"I agree with Toklo," Lusa said hastily. "I know BlackPaths are scary, but we'll probably have to cross them somewhere before we can get to the Melting Sea, so it might as well be now."

Kallik hesitated a moment, then nodded. "That sounds sensible."

Yakone still didn't look comfortable, but he didn't protest again, and the bears set out once more.

Soon they spotted firebeasts rushing past in front of them,

their roars growing louder as the bears approached the Black-Path. Yakone kept passing his tongue over his jaws, as if he could taste something foul.

"How can any bear breathe this air?" he asked. "I feel like I'm choking."

"It'll get better once we cross," Lusa replied.

Drawing near to the edge of the BlackPath, Lusa saw with dismay that streams of firebeasts of all shapes and sizes were passing in both directions, without any gaps that would give them the chance to cross. There was nowhere to hide while they waited; Lusa's heart pounded as she thought of standing in full view beside the BlackPath, where the firebeasts could easily spot them and attack.

"Over here!" Toklo called. "There's a ditch."

Relieved, Lusa bounded over to him, to see a narrow cleft in the ground, running along a bearlength from the Black-Path.

"We can hide here until it's safe to cross," Toklo continued, sliding down into the ditch. His head and shoulders still poked out, and he had to crouch down so that only his muzzle and ears showed above ground level.

Lusa jumped down beside him; the ditch was cramped even for her, but it was better than nothing.

"That's too small to hide a newborn cub," Yakone commented, peering down at Toklo and Lusa.

"Find a better place, then," Toklo snapped at him.

"Come on, Yakone. Get in!" Padding up, Kallik gave Yakone a shove so that he half fell into the ditch, and then followed him. "With any luck, we won't have to stay here long."

But luck wasn't with them. The stream of firebeasts seemed unending. Lusa's legs started to ache from her uncomfortable crouching position, and she knew it must be even worse for the others, because of their size. Lusa kept worrying that some firebeast would spot them sooner or later.

"I can't stand this," Yakone said after a while. "The firebeasts will come for us, and we'll be too stiff to put up a fight. I'm leaving."

He started to stand, but Kallik fastened her jaws in his shoulder and tugged at him. "No," she mumbled around her mouthful of fur. "We can't split up! That's even more dangerous."

"I don't think so," Yakone retorted, though to Lusa's relief he stopped trying to climb out of the ditch.

"We just need to wait quietly," Kallik told him, letting go of his shoulder. "Please, Yakone."

"Yeah, both of you be quiet," Toklo snapped. "You're asking for trouble."

While the argument was going on, Lusa noticed that the noise from the firebeasts had faded. Cautiously raising her snout above the edge of the ditch, she saw that the BlackPath was empty.

"Look!" she gasped, prodding Toklo hard in the side. "We can cross!"

Toklo heaved himself out of the ditch, and the others followed. After the continual noise of the firebeasts, the land seemed eerily quiet without them. When Lusa scanned the

BlackPath, no firebeasts were moving in either direction.

"It could be a trick," Yakone muttered.

As he spoke, Lusa spotted a tiny glittering speck in the far distance and heard the faint whine that warned of an approaching firebeast.

Toklo noticed it at the same moment. "Now!" he growled.

Together the bears sprang forward and rushed across the BlackPath. The distant firebeast grew closer, and others joined it, until a whole herd of them was bearing down on the bears.

"Keep going!" Toklo ordered. "It's too late to turn back!"

Lusa's whole world seemed filled with the roars of firebeasts. Some of them were letting out a weird hooting noise, like the call of an angry bird, but far louder than any bird she knew.

She let out a gasp of relief as her flying paws left the hard surface of the BlackPath and landed on the rough grass at the opposite side. Kallik, Toklo, and Yakone had reached safety, too, the firebeasts sweeping past behind them.

But Lusa's relief was short-lived. She heard an even louder hooting noise and looked back to see a firebeast veering off the BlackPath and bouncing over the rough ground as it headed straight for her.

"It's chasing us!" she wailed.

Desperately she tried to put on a spurt of speed to escape from the firebeast. Her friends ran beside her, but when she looked back, the firebeast was still pursuing. It had a squat shape with huge paws that carried it easily over the bumps in the ground, and its pelt was battered, so Lusa knew it must have been in lots of fights.

Glancing back, Lusa didn't see where she was going, and felt her paws skid out from under her as she fell into a dip in the ground. She rolled over, terrified that the black paws of the firebeast would catch her and crush her. But Kallik hauled her to her paws, scarcely breaking stride, and they ran on.

"It's no good!" Toklo panted at last. "We can't outrun it—we have to stop and fight!"

Bears fighting a firebeast? Lusa thought, admiration for Toklo's courage warring with her terror.

Toklo halted, spun around, and took a pace back toward the firebeast. Rising onto his hindpaws, he splayed out his forepaws and let out an enormous bellow. "Come here and fight if you dare!"

Lusa's heart was pounding so hard she thought it would burst out of her chest. She expected to see the firebeast batter Toklo to the ground and snap his limbs with its giant paws. Then, to her amazement, the firebeast swept around in a huge circle, let out one last hooting call, and fled back toward the BlackPath.

Toklo dropped to all four paws. "I scared it away!" he barked.

"Thank the spirits!" Kallik heaved a huge sigh of relief. "And thank you, Toklo. That was so brave!"

Yakone nodded, looking too stunned to speak. Even now that the danger was past, the white male still looked scared, continually casting glances around as the bears headed away from the BlackPath.

"It's okay now," Kallik tried to reassure him.

Yakone grunted, seeming unconvinced. Lusa felt sorry for Kallik, knowing how much Yakone meant to her. *What will Kallik do if Yakone decides to go back to Star Island?* She felt sorry for Yakone, too. *It must be so strange and frightening for him, to find himself among so many flat-faces.*

As they headed toward the Melting Sea, Toklo, Kallik, and Yakone started to look for traces of prey, but they didn't find anything.

"Not even a pawprint!" Kallik said disgustedly.

"I guess the flat-faces have scared all the prey away," Toklo responded. "My belly thinks my throat's been clawed out."

Lusa tried digging down under the snow, to find some leaves she could share with her friends, but there was hardly anything fit to eat. She found a few green shoots and chewed them up, wrinkling her nose at the lingering taste of firebeasts. Her paws hurt from running, and her mouth felt weird after breathing in so many firebeast fumes.

They still hadn't found any food when the sun began to go down, leaving them in darkness. There wasn't even a good place to make a den. Finally Kallik spotted a pile of grass and broken sticks, and although they were wary of the flat-face scent that hung around it, they were all too tired to look any longer.

Lusa curled up beside her friends, but she was too hungry to sleep. She knew that the others must be even hungrier; at least she had eaten the few shoots to keep her belly quiet.

I hate this place, she thought. *I hate feeling so scared and helpless the whole time. We're acting more like prey than bears!*

Then she remembered that flat-faces weren't all bad. She pictured the silver cans outside their dens, where more than once she had found food.

Checking that her three companions were all asleep, Lusa crept into the open and looked around. In the distance she spotted some tiny lights, too close to the ground to be stars.

Those could be flat-face dens!

Casting a glance back at the sleeping mounds of fur that were her friends, Lusa set out, padding through the darkness toward the lights. The sky was covered with cloud, so she had no way of knowing if Ujurak was watching her.

I hope you are, she thought. *Help me find some food to take back to the others.*

On her way to the dens she had to cross some small Black-Paths, but this time it wasn't so difficult. There weren't as many firebeasts as there had been earlier, and their eyes glowed so brightly that she could see them coming from a long way away.

It's really weird traveling alone—so quiet!

More than once she found herself turning her head to say something to Toklo or Kallik, and realized with a shock that they weren't with her.

This is how it will be when we've all separated to find our own homes, she thought. *I'm not sure that I like it.*

As she drew closer to the lights, Lusa made herself concentrate, imagining how surprised and delighted her friends would be when she returned to them with food. She had been right that the lights came from flat-face dens: There were several of them, clustered together on either side of a BlackPath. As she crept closer, she thought the yellow squares of light were like eyes watching her, but she reminded herself that they were just gaps in the walls of the dens.

A chill ran through her, colder than the snow, when she remembered their last attempt to get food from flat-faces, when Toklo had gotten stuck inside one of the shiny metal cans. Later they had almost been killed for trying to steal food.

But it won't be like that this time, she reassured herself. *I'll be so quiet the flat-faces won't even know I'm here. And I'm small enough that I won't get stuck inside a can.*

A long time had passed since Lusa had ventured this close to flat-face dens. Her confidence grew as she sniffed around, recognizing the scents of flat-faces and their food.

Outside one of the dens a firebeast was crouching, but it was cold and quiet, so Lusa knew it must be asleep. Skirting around it, she kept her eyes open for the silver cans, heading behind the den where she knew flat-faces usually kept them. A burst of flat-face noise and laughter came from inside the den; Lusa froze with fear, then headed on even more quietly that before.

They must not hear me!

There were no lights around the back of the den. Lusa peered through the darkness, creeping forward pawstep by pawstep as she searched for the cans. Then her next step brought her up against something solid. She felt the smooth surface of a can and grabbed at it in a near panic as it started to tilt, managing to stop it from crashing over.

As her eyes grew used to the darkness, she saw that there was a whole group of cans clustered together near the entrance to the den. Balancing on her hindpaws, Lusa tried to pry the lid off the first can, wishing her friends were with her; it was so much easier to open up the cans when two or three of them were working together.

The lid was so tight that Lusa couldn't even smell what was inside. Her paws felt too big and clumsy, and they were still sore from walking so far.

She froze for a moment as she heard louder voices from the den, and a light went on in a gap above her head. But she was so close to food now that she kept on levering at the can lid, thinking of how hungry the other bears were.

The lid flew off unexpectedly, clattering to the ground. A shout came from the den. *They've spotted me!* Not caring about the noise anymore, Lusa tipped the can over and raked through the contents that spilled out over her paws. Her jaws watered as she scented all kinds of tasty things. Grabbing some in her mouth, she turned to flee.

At the same moment, the door of the den swung open, and Lusa found herself facing two snarling dogs. From inside the den the flat-faces shouted encouragement, and a thin beam of yellow light shone out, making Lusa screw up her eyes. She started to back away, still gripping the food in her jaws.

The dogs crept closer, and one of them leaped for Lusa. She had to drop her mouthful and snarl, rearing up and thrashing her forepaws in the air. But the dog kept coming, and Lusa knew she would have to fight. Panicked, she lashed out one paw, striking the dog across its head. It let out a howl of pain but turned faster than she thought possible and snapped at her leg with sharp teeth. Lusa sprang backward, pulling her leg free, but now the second dog was upon her, leaping up and trying to close its jaws on her throat.

Lusa tried to remember how Toklo would fight. *Duck away . . . now twist . . . strike that dog on its shoulder . . . snap at the other . . . whirl and strike again.* But she didn't have Toklo's strength and skill, and she couldn't fight both dogs at once. She felt teeth meet her ear and let out a squeal of pain as she swung her head around with the dog still holding on. It didn't let go until she slammed it against the wall of the den. Blood began to run into her eyes so she couldn't see clearly.

Then Lusa heard another snarl and a deep-throated barking. *Another dog!* She closed her eyes and tried to picture her mother and father and her friends in the Bear Bowl. But all she could see was Toklo and Kallik and Yakone, searching endlessly for her, blaming themselves for letting her sneak off alone.

"I'm so sorry," she whispered.

The deep-throated bark sounded beside her ear, and Lusa braced herself for pain. She could hear vicious snarling and snapping—but felt nothing.

Am I dead already?

Opening her eyes, Lusa gaped in astonishment. There was a battle going on! A third dog was fighting the others, snapping at first one and then the other, darting out of range before they could retaliate.

New energy flowed into Lusa, and she sprang to fight alongside her new ally, not asking herself where he had come from. Together they beat the other two dogs back toward the door of the den. The flat-faces took them in and they vanished, whining, their tails drooping.

The third dog turned to face Lusa. "Come on," he said in a familiar voice.

Lusa drew in a breath of pure astonishment. "Ujurak!"

Without saying any more, the lean brown Ujurak-dog began to lead the way back through the flat-face dens. Lusa ran behind. Her wounds were still hurting badly, but she felt desperately glad to be alive.

Once they were well away from the dens, the lights receding into the distance, Ujurak halted. "Are you okay?" he asked, giving Lusa's wounded ear a lick with his long pink tongue. He nosed down her sides, checking her injuries. "There's an herb you can use," he told her. "It grows close to the ground, with narrow, grayish leaves. You'll find it beside streams, under the soil. It has a bitter taste, but it should take the pain away and help the wounds heal."

His slightly frantic tone told Lusa how worried he was. She took a pace back to stop his desperate examination of her injuries. "I'm fine, really," she assured him. "Thank you for rescuing me."

Ujurak's expression grew somber. "You shouldn't have been there," he said. "Bears don't need flat-face food! Didn't you learn that from our journey? You can find your own food now, you and all the other bears."

Lusa backed away even farther, shocked by how stern Ujurak sounded. "Okay, I'm sorry," she said. "I just wanted to help the others."

Ujurak's voice softened. "You can help by finding leaves they can eat and signs of prey. You won't help them if you go off and get attacked by dogs."

Lusa nodded. "I know."

She followed Ujurak as he led her back across the plain, halting when the pile of grass and sticks came into sight.

"Come with me," she begged Ujurak. "Kallik and Toklo will be so happy to see you!"

Ujurak shook his head, making his long, thin ears flap. "No, not like this," he said. "I am with you all, always. Remember that."

Lusa let out a long sigh. She wanted Ujurak to be with them in his old bear shape, just as he had been on their first journey, but she knew that was impossible now. "Good-bye, Ujurak," she said. "And thank you so much."

"Good-bye." Ujurak touched his wet nose to Lusa's ear. "We will meet again."

Reluctantly Lusa turned away and limped toward the pile of sticks where her friends were sleeping. When she looked back, there was no sign of the dog, and no pawprints in the snow where it had walked.

"Don't leave us, Ujurak," she whispered into the air.

CHAPTER NINE

Kallik

Kallik sprang to her paws, shaking, as a roar sounded close to her ear. Sleep still clung to her, and it took her a moment to realize the fearsome sound had come from Toklo. "What's happening?" she asked.

"Wake up, Kallik. It's Lusa." Toklo was standing by the pile of sticks with Lusa beside him. "Look at her—she's covered in blood!"

Morning had come while Kallik slept, though the sun was hidden behind clouds. The ground was covered with wisps of white mist. Through them Kallik stared at Lusa; her fur was matted with blood, and one of her ears was torn. The tang of blood hit Kallik's throat. "Lusa, what happened?" she gasped.

"I tried to find some food by the flat-face dens," Lusa explained, her head bowed miserably. "You know, like we used to. But the flat-faces sent dogs to attack me."

"I'll mangle them!" Toklo exclaimed, tensing his muscles as if he was about to dash off across the plain. "I'll spread their guts from here to the Melting Sea!"

"No!" Lusa stood in front of Toklo, blocking him. "Ujurak came in the shape of a dog, and he helped me to fight them off."

"Ujurak!" Toklo's eyes lit up. "He's here?" Calling Ujurak's name, he ran out onto the plain.

Kallik chased after him, with Lusa by her side and Yakone, just struggling out of sleep, bringing up the rear.

"Toklo, wait!" Lusa called. "He isn't here anymore."

Toklo halted and turned back. Sympathy pierced Kallik like a thorn as she saw his downcast expression. "Why didn't he stay?" Toklo asked angrily. "He didn't even say good-bye!"

Lusa padded up to him and reached up to touch his shoulder with her muzzle. "He wants you to know that he's always with us," she said.

Toklo grunted. "It's not the same." Hesitating, he added more fiercely, "Do you promise you're telling the truth?"

Lusa drew in a shocked breath. "Of course! Ujurak is watching over us all," she insisted. "But I was the one who got into trouble and needed his help."

Yakone nudged Kallik and drew her a little ways away. "Do you believe Lusa?" he asked.

"Of course I do," Kallik replied. "Ujurak would never abandon us."

Yakone looked doubtful. "He wasn't there when the no-claws chased us on their pawsticks."

"We saved ourselves that time, didn't we?" Kallik retorted, determined not to hear a word said against Ujurak.

Yakone sighed, nodding. "I know how important Ujurak

was to you. I liked him too. I just don't want you to put your-self in danger because you think he'll save you every time."

"I won't," Kallik promised. *And I hope the others won't either,* she added silently to herself.

Toklo padded back to the white bears with Lusa limp-ing by his side. "It's time we headed for the Melting Sea," he announced.

"We can't," Kallik objected. "Lusa needs to rest."

Toklo glanced at Lusa, clearly realizing that Kallik was right, though he said nothing.

"We need food, too," Yakone pointed out, "or none of us will be strong enough to travel. Look, suppose Kallik and I—"

"I told you before, we're not splitting up," Toklo inter-rupted, a trace of aggressiveness in his tone. "Come on, Lusa, I'll carry you."

Lusa looked embarrassed, but she didn't object as Kallik gave her a boost onto Toklo's shoulders. "I'll be fine soon," she insisted, "and maybe you could find this herb that Ujurak told me about. He says it grows beside streams under the snow and will help me feel better."

"What does it look like?" Yakone asked.

"It's a low-growing plant, with narrow, grayish leaves," Lusa told him, remembering how Ujurak had described it.

"Sure, we'll find that for you," Yakone promised. "Come on, Kallik. Let's look."

"Just don't go wandering off and get lost," Toklo warned them.

"We won't," Kallik assured him as she followed Yakone,

glad that there was something she could do for Lusa.

Yakone halted when they had padded several bearlengths away from Toklo and Lusa. "We have to find a stream running through the snow. Do you know how to do that?"

"You're the expert," Kallik replied.

"But you're learning." Yakone's eyes were filled with amused affection. "Try to show me what you know."

"Okay." Kallik raised her head and tried to pick up the scent of running water, but the scent of snow, firebeasts, and the distant salt tang of the Melting Sea drowned out anything else she might have smelled.

So I need to look at the surface of the snow. There have to be signs. . . .

Glancing at Yakone, she padded forward, keeping pace with the distant Toklo, who was trudging onward with Lusa on his shoulders. At first she thought the ground all looked the same under its covering of snow, except for humps that meant there were buried rocks or bushes.

Yakone was watching her expectantly, and Kallik realized that he had already spotted what they were looking for. *He knows I can find it,* she thought with a twinge of excitement.

Beginning to enjoy the puzzle, Kallik scanned the ground more carefully. At length she noticed that some of the humps in the snow formed a curving line. *Bushes often grow on the banks of a stream. . . .* Beyond the humps was a swath of flat snow, about a bearlength wide, smoother than the surrounding ground and following the same curve.

"Over there!" she exclaimed, pointing with her muzzle.

Yakone nodded and let Kallik take the lead as the two white

bears raced toward the frozen stream. Kallik pushed through the line of bushes, dislodging snow from their branches, and began scraping away at the water's edge.

At first she only found grass, and some small plants with round, dark leaves that obviously weren't what Lusa needed. Yakone was searching on the opposite bank, but he hadn't found anything either.

Suddenly worried that they might lose Toklo and Lusa, Kallik glanced up. Her friends were still visible in the distance; the brown bear had halted and let Lusa slide to the ground, where she sat slumped in a heap. The sight of Lusa so obviously miserable made Kallik search even harder. Her paws thrust the snow aside, and eventually she found the plant she needed, straggling over stones at the very edge of the stream. It had the grayish leaves Lusa had described, and a sharp, pleasant scent.

"I think I've found it!" she told Yakone.

He came to join her and bent his head to sniff the plant. "That looks like it," he commented. "Let's take some to Lusa."

Very carefully, so as not to crush the juices from the leaves, Kallik picked several of the stems and bounded back across the snow with them gripped firmly in her jaws.

"Here!" she exclaimed, coming to a halt by Lusa's side. "Are these right?"

Lusa raised her head, her eyes weary and pain-filled. "They look right," she said, giving the leaves a cautious sniff. "And they smell good. Thanks, Kallik."

"You took your time," Toklo remarked impatiently while

Lusa chewed up the herbs.

"Well, that's how long it took!" Kallik retorted, fed up with Toklo's grumpiness.

Before Toklo could say any more, Yakone interposed, "Anyway, we can get going now. Lusa, do you want to ride on my back?"

"*I'll* carry Lusa," Toklo insisted with a glare, crouching down to let the small black bear scramble onto his shoulders.

As they plodded on across the plain, Kallik could see that the herbs were working for Lusa; she visibly relaxed as the pain ebbed, and finally sank into a doze as she lay splayed out on Toklo's back. She didn't even wake when they had to cross a couple of small BlackPaths, and only stirred uneasily as they skirted a no-claw den where a couple of dogs were barking.

"I wonder if those are the dogs Lusa had to fight," Kallik murmured to Yakone.

"I've no idea. We'd best stay well away from them to be on the safe side."

The sun was sliding toward the horizon by the time that Lusa woke up. She looked much brighter and more alert, sitting bolt upright on Toklo's back. "Look over there!" she whispered after a few moments. "Aren't those tracks in the snow?"

Kallik looked where Lusa was pointing. At once she spotted the pawprints, leading in a straight line toward a clump of bushes several bearlengths away.

Toklo bent his head to sniff. "A snow hare," he said. "And the tracks are fresh. Come on, Yakone."

Lusa slid down from Toklo's back, and the two males set out, creeping cautiously toward the bushes. Meanwhile Lusa started to dig down into the snow. Kallik could see that her legs were still stiff and her paws painful after the fight; she was too clumsy to dig effectively.

Kallik crouched down beside her and began to help, thrusting the snow aside until she uncovered some plants.

"Thanks." Lusa tore off a mouthful of leaves and chewed. "I'm sorry, Kallik," she went on. "It was stupid of me to go off on my own like that."

"It's okay," Kallik told her, giving her a friendly touch on the ear with the tip of her muzzle. "You were very brave. . . ."

Her voice trailed off, but Lusa seemed to understand what Kallik hadn't wanted to say and finished Kallik's thought. "One day, I'll be on my own all the time."

Kallik felt a stab of sadness. "I'll miss you, Lusa," she whispered.

"I'll miss you, too," Lusa responded.

A sudden shriek broke the silence between them. Kallik looked up to see a scuffle in the snow where Toklo and Yakone had gone to stalk the hare. A moment later Yakone straightened up with the white body of a hare dangling from his jaws.

"They got it!" Kallik exclaimed.

With Toklo hard on his paws, Yakone returned and dropped the hare beside Kallik. "It's a big one," he said. "And we wouldn't have caught it if you hadn't spotted the tracks, Lusa."

Lusa's eyes shone at his praise.

By the time Toklo, Kallik, and Yakone had shared out the prey, the sun had gone down. With no obvious denning place in sight, Kallik and Yakone piled up the snow to make a windbreak, and all four bears settled down in its shelter.

Kallik dreamed of wind scouring across the ice, and woke in the cold light of dawn to see Yakone standing at the top of the hollow, staring at the horizon. Careful not to disturb the sleeping Toklo and Lusa, Kallik scrambled up to join him.

Yakone turned his head to look at her, his eyes gleaming with excitement. "I can smell waves," he told her.

Kallik stood beside him, the wind blowing into her face and flattening her fur against her sides, and took a deep sniff. Yakone was right! The air was carrying the salt tang of the Melting Sea, far stronger than she had scented it before.

Quickly Kallik slid down into the hollow again and prodded Lusa and Toklo awake. "Hurry!" she urged them. "We have to go. We'll reach the shore today!"

Toklo grunted sleepily and heaved himself out of the hollow. Lusa was more difficult to rouse. When her eyes blinked open at last, she stared at Kallik, then shook her head as if she was trying to clear it.

"Sorry," she murmured. "I can't hear you very well. And my ear feels funny, like there's something stuck in it." She started to claw at it.

"Stop that." Kallik gently pushed her paw away. "You'll make it bleed again."

Lusa nodded, but she still looked uneasy and kept shaking

her head as she climbed out of the hollow.

"Get on my back." Toklo bent down and spoke loudly into her other ear.

"I can walk," Lusa retorted. "And you don't have to shout." Her eyes glimmering with sudden amusement, she added, "It's not all bad. If my ear's blocked, I can't hear you bossing me around!"

"Cloud-brain!" Toklo exclaimed, giving the smaller bear an affectionate shove. "Now, are we going or aren't we?"

Kallik's paws itched to bound across the plain toward the sea. The pace set by Lusa, who was still limping, seemed agonizingly slow. Kallik struggled with her impatience, but she didn't suggest splitting up. She knew how Toklo would take that suggestion.

Besides, it's not just Yakone who will see my home for the first time. It's the others as well. I want us all to be together when we get there.

Excitement and memories bubbled up inside her. "I remember my BirthDen," she told Yakone. "Nisa used to tell me and Taqqiq such wonderful stories—stories about Silaluk and Robin, Chickadee, and Moose Bird, who hunted her. She taught us so much, too . . . how to find a seal hole, and sit there very quietly. . . . I remember the first time I caught a seal. It tasted so delicious! And the games I used to play with Taqqiq—" Kallik broke off suddenly. "I'm sorry, Yakone. I've told you all this before, haven't I?"

"Yes, but I don't mind hearing the stories again," Yakone replied. His eyes sparkled. "The Melting Sea isn't just your home," he added. "It will be mine now, too."

The land began to slope gradually upward, and Kallik caught sight of long, dark shapes standing upright across their path. She stared at them, puzzled, for a heartbeat, until she realized that they were pine trees.

It's been so long since I've seen a tree. . . .

Lusa quickened her pace, still limping, and stumbled up to the nearest tree, pressing her face against the trunk. Kallik caught up to her in time to hear her murmur, "I've come home."

Yakone gave a start of surprise. Hardly able to wrench his gaze away from the pines, he asked Kallik, "Lusa doesn't come from here, does she?"

Kallik shook her head. "No, but she has a really strong connection with trees. Black bears believe that their spirits live inside trees after they die, and the patterns in their bark are the faces of their ancestors."

Yakone nodded slowly. "Lusa told me about that." Giving the pine trunks an intense stare, he added, "Now that I have seen trees, I can tell it would be easy to believe. I feel like I'm being watched."

Kallik saw that Yakone remained uneasy as they headed into the belt of trees, constantly looking up at the sky. "I feel trapped," he confessed to Kallik. "I know the trees aren't thick, but . . . how does any bear know where it's going?"

In contrast, Toklo was clearly at home, striding confidently through the pines. He paused to sharpen his claws on a trunk, then gave Lusa a boost to the lower branches so that she could nibble some pine needles.

Leaving them to follow, Kallik led Yakone onward.

"Are you sure this is the right way?" Yakone asked. "I can't smell the sea anymore. I can't smell *anything* except for these pines!"

"I'm sure," Kallik replied. Though the heavy, resinous scent of the pines was all around her, she could still distinguish the sharp scent of the sea, drawing her inexorably toward it.

Then, before she had expected it, Kallik broke out of the trees and found herself at the top of a slope that led down gently to a sweep of shoreline.

The Melting Sea!

"I'm home!" Kallik gasped. Suddenly she felt a warm presence near her. She felt sure that she could hear her mother whispering, *Welcome home, little one.*

Feeling as if she had wings on her paws, Kallik ran down the slope to the edge of the sea and gazed out. Close to the shore, the ice had melted.

That's okay, she told herself. *The weather is getting warmer; the bears won't be out on the ice for much longer, anyway.*

Still, a fierce longing swept over her to swim out to the ice she could see in the distance bobbing on the black waves. She could smell seals and fresh snow and the salty tang of sea ice.

"It's beautiful."

Kallik started with surprise as she realized that Yakone was standing by her side. Lusa and Toklo were at the top of the slope, just emerging from the trees.

"Come on!" Kallik called to them. "Come and see my home!"

A harsh clattering noise drowned her last few words. The distinctive *clack-clack* of a metal bird sliced through the air. Kallik flinched and looked up, seeing the familiar shape in the distance, heading straight for her.

Yakone gave Kallik a shove, back toward the trees. "We need to get under cover," he said urgently. "There might be no-claws with firesticks planning to shoot at us."

Kallik bounded beside him, up to the line of trees where Toklo and Lusa were waiting. But before they plunged into shelter, something made her turn back. As the metal bird drew closer, she spotted something dangling underneath it.

"What *is* that?" Lusa asked curiously.

Kallik's belly lurched with horror as she realized that the metal bird was carrying a net with white bears inside, just like the one that had carried her and Nanuk. A wave of bile gushed into her throat and she stood still, frozen to the spot as she watched. She was sure that the metal bird was going to crash.

"Kallik, what's wrong?" Yakone asked anxiously.

Kallik barely heard him. Instead, she was filled with memories of her own terrifying flight, crushed against Nanuk, her paws snagged in the meshes of the net, hardly able to breathe through the freezing, rushing air. Then the clacking sound had changed, becoming sharper and more irregular, until the last dreadful plummet to the ground. . . .

Kallik winced and shut her eyes, then opened them again, compelled to watch the destruction she was sure would happen. But the metal bird didn't crash. Instead, it swooped low and the net that carried the bears dropped to the ground. The metal bird hovered for a moment, then rose and flew away. The net unwrapped, leaving the white bears lying on the ground a few bearlengths away from the shore.

As the clattering noise of the metal bird died away, Kallik ran down the slope toward the white bears.

"Kallik, wait!" Toklo shouted.

"Be careful!" Yakone added.

Kallik ignored her friends. As she drew closer, she saw there were three white bears huddled on the shore: a mother and two cubs. She halted as she reached them, almost unendurable pain coursing through her. She felt like she was seeing herself with her mother and Taqqiq. She felt like she was seeing herself and Nanuk. Or it was like she was seeing Ujurak, lying dead in the snow. All the death and pain she had seen in her life washed over her in a wave of horror, choking her so that she could hardly breathe.

"Kallik?" She heard Yakone calling to her.

Kallik wrenched her head around to face him. "They're dead."

CHAPTER TEN

Toklo

Toklo halted at Kallik's side and stared at the white she-bear and the two cubs. Almost at once, he realized Kallik was wrong. The bears weren't dead; already they were beginning to stir. Something was wrong, though: They seemed muzzy and confused, struggling to lift their heads and making strange patting motions at the ground with their paws, as if they wanted to get up but were too weak to manage it.

He nudged Kallik in the side. "It's okay," he reassured her. "They're not dead. Look, they're moving."

Kallik didn't seem to hear him. She went on staring at the bears with an expression of horror on her face. Then the she-bear grunted and rolled over; Kallik blinked and seemed to come out of her daze.

"The metal bird brought them here," she whispered.

"Why?" Toklo asked. He had heard Kallik's story many times, of how she had traveled beneath the metal bird that had fallen out of the sky, but he had never truly understood what it meant.

Lusa and Yakone stood by, looking startled; Yakone in particular seemed frozen with shock.

He doesn't know how close flat-faces and bears can get sometimes, Toklo thought.

While they were talking, the mother bear was waking up, blinking and licking her lips as she tried to sit up.

Lusa stepped forward, dipping her head, obviously meaning to say hello, but before she could speak, the mother bear lurched to her paws, growling as she placed herself between Lusa and her cubs. Lusa took a pace back, flattening her ears with nervousness.

"Who are you?" the she-bear demanded. "Where am I? How did I get here?"

Toklo braced himself for a fight. The mother bear was clearly terrified, but aggressive in protecting her two cubs. "It's okay," he began. "You're—"

Another growl from the mother bear drowned his words. "Stay away from us. Touch my cubs and I'll rip your pelt off!"

"Toklo, back off." Kallik pushed past him. "Your color is scaring her. She probably hasn't seen brown or black bears before." Facing the mother bear, she spoke gently. "We won't hurt you. The metal bird brought you here. Do you remember?"

The she-bear stared at Kallik for a moment without replying. Toklo could see that the sight of a bear of her own kind was calming her. "I remember no-claw dens. . . ." she murmured at last. "A firebeast came roaring up . . . I felt a sharp pain, and then everything went black."

"Yes!" Kallik said. "And then you woke up in a huge white stone den, with other bears?"

"That's right . . . we were stuck behind gray columns. No-claws came and looked at us."

"I was there once, too, trapped behind the columns," Kallik told her. "They put sticky stuff all over my fur. It smelled terrible."

The she-bear looked confused. "I never had that." Curiously, she added, "How did you escape?"

"I didn't. The no-claws made me sleep again, and when I woke up I was flying underneath a metal bird, with another she-bear called Nanuk. It's the same way that you got here. But my metal bird crashed, and Nanuk died."

The she-bear looked startled. "Thank the stars that didn't happen to us."

She turned to nuzzle her cubs. The two tiny bears weren't entirely awake yet; Toklo thought they looked very young, much smaller than Kallik when he first met her.

The she-bear nudged her cubs to their paws and helped them disentangle themselves from the net. "My name is Akna," she said. "This is Iluq, and this is Kassuq."

"Hello," Kallik responded, dipping her head. Her gaze lingered on the cubs, and Toklo heard her whisper, "Just like Kissimi . . ." Then she continued, "I'm Kallik, and this is Yakone. The brown bear is Toklo, and the black one is Lusa."

Akna shot an uneasy glance at Toklo and Lusa; Toklo remembered how peculiar white bears had looked to him the first time he had seen them.

The two cubs were whimpering softly; Iluq, who was a she-cub, bigger than her brother, tottered up to her mother and pummeled her with her forepaws. "I'm hungry!" she wailed. "I want to feed!"

"Me too!" Kassuq added.

With a sigh, Akna sat and drew the two cubs into the curve of her belly. "I haven't enough milk for them," she confessed to Kallik. "And I'm hungry, too. I have to find food."

"Why did you leave the ice?" Kallik asked, surprise in her voice. "There's plenty of food out there."

Akna shook her head. "The ice started melting very early this year," she explained. "Almost as soon as my cubs were old enough to leave their den. I had to take them straight to land."

"That must have been so hard!" Kallik said sympathetically.

"It was. I had to swim with them on my back. And when we reached land, there were so many other white bears, forced off the ice, just like us. It was a real struggle to find food."

Kallik's eyes stretched wide with dismay. "That's terrible!" She paused for a moment, then added, "Akna, did you ever meet a bear called Taqqiq? He's my brother; I'm looking for him."

"No." Akna's response was definite, and Toklo could sense Kallik's disappointment. "I stayed away from the other bears, to keep my cubs safe. You know that male bears will sometimes eat cubs, if there's no other food." She shuddered.

"We can hunt together," Toklo said, stepping forward.

Akna swung her head around to gaze at him, her expression

terrified. *Does she think I'm one of these cub-eaters?* Toklo wondered.

"What kind of bear is he?" Akna asked Kallik, her voice nervous. "Are there any more of him?"

"Er . . . it's a long story . . ." Toklo began, before Kallik could reply.

"We've been on a journey!" Lusa announced eagerly, bouncing forward. "We've been all the way to Star Island on the Endless Ice, and now we're going home."

Akna gave her a shocked look. "The Endless Ice doesn't exist! It's just a tale for cubs."

"It does exist," Kallik assured her. "We've seen it. But it's too far for you to walk to with your cubs. You need to learn how to survive here. Let Toklo and Lusa teach you how to find food on land."

A faint growl came from Akna's throat. "What do a brown bear and a black bear know about white bear hunting? That little black bear is only the size of a seal!"

"That's not the point," Toklo began, struggling hard to keep his temper. "We—"

"You should listen to them." To Toklo's surprise, Yakone stepped forward and spoke to Akna. "Kallik and I wouldn't have survived without them."

Akna still looked unconvinced. "My cubs belong on the ice!"

Toklo didn't know what he could say to the she-bear to make her understand that he and Lusa could help. "Come here a moment," he said to his friends, jerking his head to signal them to follow him a few bearlengths away.

"I hope you're not going to tell us we have to leave Akna and her cubs to take care of themselves!" Kallik began before Toklo could speak. "I won't do it!"

"That's *not* what I was going to say," Toklo growled. *Kallik has bees in her brain because she keeps thinking about her mother and Taqqiq.* "I've got a different idea. You and Yakone should swim out to the nearest ice and see if it's worth helping Akna and the cubs to get out there. Maybe you could hunt for her while you're there. Meanwhile Lusa and I will find some food for all of us onshore."

Kallik blinked in surprise. "That's a great idea! Thank you, Toklo!"

Toklo cleared his throat in embarrassment. "Strangers have helped us often enough," he said brusquely. "I'm not going to leave Akna and her cubs to starve, and she's in no state to hunt on her own."

"Oh, Toklo, thank you!" Kallik repeated, stepping forward as if she was going to give him a grateful nudge, but Toklo backed off. He didn't want a fuss. "Come on, Yakone," Kallik continued, her eyes shining with excitement. "Let's tell Akna what we're going to do."

Toklo and Lusa followed more slowly as the two white bears hurried back to Akna. They came up in time to hear the end of Kallik's explanation.

"We'll be back in no time. You'll see!"

She and Yakone ran down to the shore and swam out into the water. Toklo watched them go, fascinated to see how their bodies changed as they launched themselves into the sea. On land they lumbered, their pelts rolling awkwardly when they ran, but in the water they were as sleek and graceful as seals, hardly leaving a ripple as they struck out toward the distant sheet of ice.

Akna, too, had turned her head to watch them, a mournful look in her eyes.

"I know you want to go with them," Lusa said sympathetically, "but you have to get your strength back first."

Akna's two cubs had given up trying to feed. Instead, they were scrabbling around near their mother's paws, nibbling at sticks and bits of debris scattered along the shore. They looked more awake now, half forgetting their hunger to tumble over each other with playful squeaks.

"Why don't I keep an eye on the cubs while you hunt?" Lusa suggested to Toklo. Turning to Akna, she added, "You can trust me to look after them. And you need to rest."

The white she-bear grunted agreement, though Toklo noticed she never took her eyes off the cubs.

"Come on, Iluq, Kassuq," Lusa said, determinedly cheerful. Seizing a stick, she added, "Which of you can pull this out of my jaws?"

"I can!" Iluq squealed, throwing herself at the stick.

Lusa has her paws full there, Toklo thought, as he headed up the slope, back into the belt of pine trees.

Plunging into the shelter of the trees, Toklo spotted tracks in the snow almost at once, and picked up the scent of muskrat. Following the trail, he leaped through the woods, feeling strong and confident now that he was in more familiar territory. Weak sunlight sliced through the branches, and for a moment he felt as though he'd come home.

This must be how Kallik feels when she gets back to the ice, he thought.

"We're all so different," he murmured to himself. "It has to be a good thing that we're all going back to our homes."

He tracked the muskrat to its den among the roots of a tree, killed it, and left it there while he searched for more prey. Soon he spotted a lemming skittering across the surface of the snow, and remembered how Tikaani, the white she-bear, had taught him to hunt lemmings on the Island of Shadows. Now he caught up to the tiny creature in a few bounds, and tossed it into the air before killing it with a hard blow of his paw.

Where there's one lemming, there might be more. . . .

Toklo settled down to wait in the shadow of a pine, and soon another lemming scuttled straight at him, trying to veer aside only when it was too late. Gripping both lemmings and the muskrat firmly in his jaws, he headed back to the shore.

Lusa was lying on the ground with both cubs on top of her, battering at her with their soft paws. "Toklo, save me!" she gasped. "Save me from these fierce white bears!" Iluq and Kassuq burst out into squeaks of amusement.

Toklo padded past her and dropped his catch in front of Akna, who was sleepily watching the antics of her cubs.

"That's amazing!" she exclaimed when she saw the prey. "When I first came off the ice, I hardly caught anything to eat."

"I can teach you what to do," Toklo promised, glad that the mother bear seemed to have lost her hostility toward him and

Lusa. "It's not hard to hunt on land—catching a seal is much more difficult!"

As Toklo spoke, he spotted Kallik and Yakone swimming strongly for shore. When they heaved themselves out of the water, he saw that they were carrying a seal between them.

"Great catch!" he called out.

Akna's eyes lit up when she saw the seal. "Then there is good hunting ice out there," she said to Kallik as Kallik and Yakone came up and deposited their prey in front of her.

"Yes, but it's melting like the rest of the sea," Kallik told her. "You and the cubs can reach the ice once you're strong enough to swim, but you wouldn't be able to stay there for long. You'll have to live on land until burn-sky is over."

Akna looked worried, glancing from Kallik to Yakone and back again as if she hoped they would be able to tell her something more hopeful.

"You'll be okay," Lusa assured her, coming up with the cubs, who were giving the prey an interested sniff. "We can show you how to hunt on land."

The sun was starting to go down, casting red light over the shore as the bears gathered around their prey. Akna chewed up some of the seal meat and gave it to Kassuq and Iluq before taking any for herself.

Toklo spotted Lusa taking a few mouthfuls of the muskrat.

"This isn't bad," she mumbled with her mouth full. "Much better than seal!"

But soon she abandoned the catch and climbed the slope;

Toklo spotted her stripping leaves from a bush near the edge of the trees.

With food in their bellies the cubs looked sleepy and contented, and huddled into the curve of their mother's belly to suck milk from her.

"At least I should have some milk now," Akna sighed, looking almost as drowsy as her cubs.

As darkness fell, Kallik coaxed the white bear family to get up and head for the shelter of the pines, in the lee of the slope to be out of the wind. Toklo and the others settled down beside them.

"It feels good to be helping other bears, for a change," Kallik murmured quietly to Toklo.

"It's what Ujurak would have done," Toklo responded.

As his friends fell asleep around him, Toklo stayed awake for a little while, sitting alone on the shore and looking up at the sky. Ujurak's stars shone brightly, even brighter than the others, it seemed to Toklo.

Are you watching us? he asked silently. *Is this what you wanted us to do?* Looking at the sleeping shapes of Kallik and Yakone, he added to himself, *At least it keeps us together for a little longer.*

CHAPTER ELEVEN

Lusa

"*Dig your claws into the bark* and peel it away like this," Lusa instructed.

Akna watched her carefully, while the two cubs attacked the base of the pine tree, scratching at the bark with soft claws.

"But what's it for?" Akna asked.

"You can eat this soft green layer just under the bark," Lusa explained. "Try it. It's really tasty."

Akna doubtfully sniffed the green layer and swiped her tongue over it. "Hmm . . . not bad, I suppose," she commented. "But I'd need an awful lot of it to fill my belly. And only squirrels feed off trees!"

"Well, let's catch a squirrel, then!" Toklo suggested, striding up through the pine needles.

"Yes!" Iluq bounced up and down with excitement, while Kassuq blinked eagerly at Toklo.

"You're too young," Lusa told them. "Don't worry, we'll find something fun to do while your mother hunts."

As Lusa turned toward the shore, Kallik and Yakone

appeared through the trees and padded up to the other bears.

"We're going onto the ice again to hunt for seals," Kallik announced.

Lusa spotted Toklo giving the two white bears a worried look. *He must be afraid that they won't come back.* She wanted to reassure him, but she knew the gruff brown bear would never admit to his feelings. A wave of affection for him washed over her.

Kallik and Yakone headed down to the beach again, with Iluq and Kassuq scampering after them.

"We want to come, too!" Iluq squealed. "It's great out on the ice."

"Yeah," Kassuq added. "We'll catch the biggest seal!"

"Hey—stop right there!" Lusa told them, dashing after them and blocking them. "You're too small to swim so far."

"We aren't," Iluq insisted, dodging around Lusa while her brother tried to wriggle past on her other side.

"*No.*" Lusa reached out with one paw to grab Iluq before she could go any farther. "You're coming with me, and . . ." She thought rapidly. "And I'll show you some stuff you can do to help you grow big and strong."

"Yes!" The two cubs bounced up and down with excitement.

Through the trees Lusa could hear Toklo teaching Akna how to follow the trail of a snow hare. "They're not like seals. It's no good sitting still and waiting for them. You have to find tracks and then follow them."

Not wanting the cubs to disturb their mother and Toklo,

Lusa steered them out of the trees and farther along the shore until she found a place where a large amount of driftwood had been washed up.

"Look here," she said, clawing a piece out from the rest and pushing it in front of the cubs. "Are you strong enough to pick this up?"

"Easy!" Iluq boasted, grabbing the wood in her jaws.

"Very good," Lusa praised her. "Now let Kassuq try."

The male cub, who was smaller than his sister, still managed to pick up the wood, while Iluq nosed about in the pile until she found a bigger piece.

"Watch! I can carry *this* one!" The little she-bear hefted the piece of wood into the air, but it was so big and awkward that she lost her balance, staggered, and flopped down on her side.

"Cloud-brain!" Kassuq teased her.

"You try it then, if you're so clever!"

Kassuq grabbed the big piece of wood, straining to lift it off the ground. It was too big for him to manage, but at last he raised it about a whisker's width into the air, and dropped it again with a huge gasp. "There! And I didn't fall over, either."

Iluq leaped onto her brother and the two cubs rolled over, lashing their paws in a play fight.

"That's enough," Lusa said, suppressing laughter as she separated them. "This is something you can do anytime. Keep practicing and lifting heavier and heavier pieces, and it will make your muscles strong. And there's another thing I want to show you."

"What's that?" Iluq asked.

"When you're on the ice, you can make dens out of snow, right? But what will you do when there's no snow?"

"There's always snow," Kassuq objected.

Lusa shook her head. "You've already seen the ice starting to melt. When burn-sky comes, the snow will melt, too. Then what will you use for shelter?"

The two cubs were staring at Lusa, big-eyed. Lusa hoped that she hadn't scared them.

"We could dig into the ground," Kassuq suggested at last.

"Yes, good idea," Lusa said.

"Or hide among trees," Iluq added, pointing with one paw toward the pines at the top of the slope.

"That's a good idea, too," Lusa told her. "Or you can build something. If we pile up this wood, then it'll make a good shelter from the wind."

Iluq's eyes sparkled. "Let's do it! Then there'll be a comfortable place for Mother when she comes back."

Lusa checked for the direction of the wind and began helping the cubs to pile up the driftwood into a windbreak. Contentment welled up inside her as she felt the different pieces of wood beneath her paws.

I've been away from forests for so long. . . .

"Hey, look!" Kassuq's voice distracted Lusa from her reflections. "This piece of wood looks just like a squirrel!"

Iluq scampered over to gaze at the driftwood her brother had found. "You're right . . . look, there are its eyes and its nose. It's staring at me!"

"Let's hunt it," Kassuq suggested.

Lusa watched, amused, as the two cubs crept up on the piece of driftwood. Their eyes sparkled, and they let out little snorts of excitement. *A real squirrel would have been way up a tree by now.*

At last Iluq pounced, her forepaws landing hard on the piece of wood. She bent her head, growling. "Got you! Now I'm going to eat you."

"Me too!" Kassuq grabbed one end of the wood in his teeth.

As the cubs tussled over the driftwood, Lusa got a better look at it. She realized that the knotholes and the grain of the wood really did look a bit like a squirrel's face.

"You know, black bears like me believe that there really are faces in trees. We think that when we die, our spirits go to live there," she told the cubs. "Sometimes you can see the spirits' faces in the bark. Like your squirrel. Or this one." She snagged an old, bleached branch with her claws. It had two scraps of bark still clinging to it that could have been eyes, and a knothole like a gaping mouth.

Iluq and Kassuq dropped their "squirrel" and came to stare at the new branch. Iluq stifled a snort of laughter and prodded it with one paw. "Hey, old bear, can you hear me in there?"

Kassuq started scrabbling among the scraps of wood and grabbed a piece in his jaws, waving it at his sister. "Here's a bear coming to get you!" he mumbled around the stick.

Iluq squealed and darted away, nearly knocking over the carefully piled-up shelter. "That's not scary! I'll find a bigger one to get *you*!"

"Hey, have a bit more respect!" Lusa said, stifling laughter.

"That old bear might leap out of the tree and eat you up!"

Both cubs froze, staring at her with huge, terrified eyes.

"Really?" Kassuq gasped.

"No, not really," Lusa reassured them. "But I think we've had enough of that game for now." She knew that if they went on play-fighting, the shelter would be completely destroyed. "Let's walk along the shore for a bit."

"Will you tell us more black bear stories?" Kassuq asked as they set out.

"Sure I will," Lusa told him. "I was born in a Bear Bowl," she began when the two cubs were padding along, one on each side of her. "That's a place built by flat-faces—sorry, no-claws—for bears to live. The flat-faces would come and look at us, and if we waved our paws and looked cute, they would throw fruit at us."

"Like this?" Iluq tottered up onto her hindpaws and waved her paws in the air.

"What's fruit?" Kassuq asked. "Did it hurt?"

Amusement bubbled up inside Lusa. "No, it's nice," she replied. "It's sweet, squashy stuff that grows on trees, and you eat it."

"These trees?" Iluq asked, giving the belt of pines an interested look.

"These aren't the right kind," Lusa told her. "But later on in burn-sky you'll find trees and bushes with fruit on them."

Kassuq's tongue swiped around his jaws. "Is it as good as seal?"

"Black bears like me think it's better," Lusa said tactfully.

"But seal is the best food for white bears. So," she went on, "I escaped from the Bear Bowl, because I had to find Toklo and give him a message," she said, skipping over the part about Oka.

"And did you find him?" Kassuq asked.

"Of course she did, cloud-brain!" Iluq darted at her brother and gave him a prod. "Toklo's that big brown bear who's teaching Mother!"

"Yes, I found him," Lusa said, gently pushing Iluq away from Kassuq before the cubs started fighting again. "And we went on a long, long journey, right up to the Endless Ice, where the spirits dance in the sky." She sighed, remembering. "It's so beautiful!"

"I want to go there!" Iluq asserted.

"Maybe you will, when you're bigger," Lusa responded.

"No, I want to go there *now*!"

"There are all kinds of other interesting places you might travel to," Lusa went on, hoping to distract the little she-bear. "There's Great Bear Lake, where lots of bears gather to celebrate the Longest Day. I met Kallik there, and—"

Lusa broke off. The *clack-clack* of a metal bird sounded overhead, growing louder with every heartbeat. Looking up, she saw the bird hovering close by, with another net of white bears dangling underneath it.

"Is that how we got here?" Iluq asked, staring up with fascination in her eyes.

"Yes." Lusa's heart was starting to pound. Glancing around, she spotted an outcrop of rock a couple of bearlengths away.

"Let's get behind there," she continued, herding the two cubs in front of her. "We don't want to be underneath it when they drop those bears, do we?"

"We'd be squashed flat!" Kassuq squealed.

Lusa and the cubs dived behind the rocks as the metal bird swooped lower. Lusa crouched down and tried to shield the cubs with her body. A fierce wind swept over them, ruffling their fur, and deafening noise blasted their ears.

"I don't like it!" Kassuq wailed. "Make it go away!"

"It will soon," Lusa tried to reassure him, but the cub was in too much of a panic to listen. Wriggling out from underneath Lusa, he darted away from the rock, fleeing toward the trees.

"No! Kassuq! Come back!" Lusa sprang after him, grabbing him by the scruff, and dragged him back, still wailing, into shelter. To her relief, Iluq hadn't moved; she was pressing herself, shaking, into the rock, her eyes huge with fear.

The metal bird sank down and placed the net of bears onto the shore a few bearlengths closer to the water's edge. As the metal bird climbed back into the sky, two white males rolled out of the net and onto the stones.

"Look!" Iluq whispered, peering out from behind the outcrop. "They're so big!"

Lusa realized that white bear cubs were brought up by their mother, so these two might not have been so close to a white male before.

"Do you think one of them is our father?" Kassuq asked. "Shall we go and ask them?"

"No," Lusa said sharply, shuddering as she imagined the

two cubs trotting up to these huge bears and giving them a friendly prod. "I don't think it's a good idea to go too close."

"Why not?" Iluq asked. "Look, that one's waking up."

The white bear nearest to the rock had just stirred and opened a beady eye. Lusa dragged both cubs back into shelter.

"Because white males sometimes eat little cubs like you," she told them sternly, remembering how scared Akna had been when they first met, and how she had been ready to fight to protect her cubs. "Especially when they're starving."

Kassuq gulped. "Really?"

"Really." Lusa was sorry she had to frighten the cubs, but she needed to make them understand what a dangerous position they were in. "You'll be fine," she added. "We're going to get away from here, as quickly and quietly as we can. Don't make a sound, and do exactly as I tell you."

Both cubs gave her a scared nod.

The white bears were slowly waking up and fighting their way out of the meshes of the net. Lusa glanced up the slope toward the pine trees. *We'd be safe there, but how to get there . . . ?*

The shore was empty of anything that might have offered cover, except for another outcrop of rocks about halfway to the trees. It was smaller than the one where they were hiding now, and Lusa didn't think that they could all hide behind it.

But that's all there is.

"Okay, this is what we'll do," Lusa told the cubs. "When I say 'now,' we'll run as fast as we can to that rock over there. Then we'll hide until we see what the white bears are doing. Okay?"

"Okay," Iluq responded tensely, and Kassuq nodded.

Lusa peered out again from behind the rock. The white males had clambered to their feet and were swinging their huge heads around, checking out their surroundings. One of them let out an experimental bellow, and Kassuq jumped with fright.

"Now!" Lusa said. "Hurry!"

The two cubs sprang out from behind the rock, heading for the smaller outcrop. Lusa followed, casting glances over her shoulder at the white males. They still didn't seem to have noticed her and the cubs.

They had almost reached the rock when Iluq suddenly let out a yelp and toppled onto her side. Lusa ran toward her. "Get behind the rock!" she told Kassuq. "Iluq, what's the matter?"

"I'm stuck!" Iluq wailed.

Reaching her side, Lusa saw that the little she-cub had gotten her paw stuck under a piece of driftwood. The wood itself was jammed between two boulders, and however hard Iluq tugged, she couldn't free herself.

"Don't worry," Lusa gasped, remembering how scared she had been when she got her paw stuck in the ice on the Island of Shadows. "I'll get you out."

A rumbling roar came from farther down the shore. Glancing up, Lusa saw with horror that the two white males were gazing in their direction. They still looked dazed, and their movements were uncoordinated, but after a moment they began to lumber toward Lusa and the two cubs.

Lusa felt her whole body grow tense as she braced herself

for trouble. *They're bound to challenge me when they see that I'm a black bear.*

She heaved at one of the boulders that were jamming the driftwood, but she couldn't shift it. Iluq noticed the white bears and let out a shriek of terror. She struggled even harder to free her paw, but it was no use.

Then Lusa heard a high-pitched squeal from close by. "Hey, you bears! Over here!"

It was Kassuq, jumping up and down and waving his paws at the two male bears.

"No, Kassuq!" Lusa cried, even while she admired the little cub's bravery. "Go and hide, like I told you."

But it was too late. One of the white males veered over to Kassuq, and Lusa had a horrible vision of him tearing at the cub's flesh with his sharp fangs. Instead, the huge bear thrust his muzzle out at Kassuq, sniffing him curiously, then pushed him back with short jabs of his snout until he was pressed up against the outcrop of rocks where Lusa had hoped to hide.

The second white male padded up to Lusa and Iluq, who was still helplessly stuck. "What have we here?" he rumbled, sniffing at Iluq. "Three cubs?" His cold, beady stare rested on Lusa. "What's wrong with you? You're not a white bear!"

Lusa shoved her way between the white male and Iluq, desperately trying to remember the fighting moves Toklo used when he confronted enemies. *Scratch their noses . . . go for their eyes and throat . . . stay out of reach of their paws . . . Oh, Arcturus, they're so big!* Pushing down her panic, she reared up on her hindpaws, her forepaws splayed out and her claws ready.

"I'm not afraid of you!" she growled.

Before any bear could move, a roar of fury erupted from the pine trees. Lusa glanced over her shoulder to see Toklo and Akna exploding into the open and racing down the shore.

"Get away from my cubs!" Akna snarled, heading for Kassuq.

Toklo thrust Lusa aside to take her place in front of the white male that was menacing Iluq. A fierce flame of battle burned in his eyes. "If you want them, you'll have to come through me first," he barked.

The male bears swayed backward. Lusa could see that they were still too unsteady for a fight, and not really in the mood to match Toklo's and Akna's aggression.

"We weren't doing anything," the first bear said, padding over to join his companion. "Keep your fur on."

"You'll have to move on," Toklo told them brusquely. "There are other white bears living here."

The two white males exchanged a glance. Lusa could still feel tension like sharp thorns in her throat, and she knew that as the bears' heads cleared and they recovered from their flight, they could still attack.

"Why do we have to do what *you* say?" one of the white males asked. "You're a brown bear!"

"Yeah," his companion added.

"*I'm* a white bear," Akna snapped, padding over with Kassuq hard on her paws. "And I'm telling you to get out of here!"

"We don't want to fight you," Toklo said. "But we will, if you stay here to make trouble."

The two white males hesitated, then turned and shambled off along the shore; one of them glanced back to give Toklo a furious glare.

"There's hunting on the ice for now!" Toklo called after them. "Maybe you should look there for food."

"I can't believe you'd help them after what they did!" Akna exclaimed.

Toklo shrugged. "Better they eat seals than your cubs, right? Lusa, are you okay?" he continued. "I can't believe how brave you were, standing up to those two fish-breathed idiots!"

Lusa had started to shake, really understanding for the first time how easily she and the two cubs could have been torn to pieces. "I'm so sorry, Akna," she said. "I put your cubs in danger."

"But you were great," Toklo insisted. "You held off two bears much bigger than you. If you hadn't, they might have hurt the cubs before Akna and I got here."

Lusa shook her head, finding it hard to accept Toklo's praise, but wondering if he might be right. *I did help save them. . . .* "I should have gotten the cubs away sooner," she said.

"It wasn't your fault, Lusa," Akna responded. "I didn't realize there would be more white bears here. I'll have to be more careful. At least I have you and Toklo to help me look after the cubs."

Toklo grunted, flashing a sidelong glance at Lusa, but didn't say anything. Lusa guessed he was wondering how long Akna expected them to stick around.

"Please," Iluq asked plaintively, "could some bear get me out from under this driftwood?"

When Akna had freed her cub, easily heaving aside the boulder that was jamming the wood, the bears headed back to their temporary den at the edge of the pine trees. Kallik and Yakone were there, calling out their names.

"We were so worried about you!" Kallik exclaimed, bounding forward to meet her friends. "We saw the metal bird bringing those other bears."

"We dealt with them," Toklo replied. "I sent them farther up the shore."

"Come and share the seal we caught!" Yakone called.

The cubs ran toward him, while Akna and the others followed more slowly. Lusa saw that Akna looked much more relaxed now.

"It was so hard to find food when we first came ashore," she said as they settled down to share the seal. "I didn't know where to look, and there were so many other bears, and no-claws everywhere. I'm lucky to have found you," she finished, tearing hungrily into the seal.

Lusa noticed that Toklo seemed unusually quiet as they ate. When every bear was full, and Akna took her cubs into the shelter of the trees to sleep, Toklo rose to his paws.

"I want to make sure that those bears haven't come back," he announced.

Kallik and Yakone withdrew to the makeshift den with Akna, but Lusa followed Toklo down the slope.

"We're not going to stay here much longer, are we?" she

asked, guessing that Toklo would want to keep going.

"This isn't where our journey ends," Toklo replied. "It's good to help other bears figure out how to find food on land, but Kallik still has to travel farther on to the Melting Sea. And our homes are still far away."

Lusa heaved a deep sigh. "I wish we didn't have to leave Kallik and Yakone behind."

"We always knew it would happen one day," Toklo pointed out.

"I know, but . . ." Lusa hesitated, then went on, "If there are trees, we could stay beside the Melting Sea, couldn't we?"

Toklo glanced down at her. "You know we don't belong here," he told her. "We still have a long way to go."

CHAPTER TWELVE

Kallik

Stars glittered above Kallik's head as she stood on the shore. Behind her, Yakone was sleeping in the makeshift den, along with Akna and her cubs. Farther down the shore, Toklo and Lusa were padding along side by side, Toklo bending his head down to Lusa as they talked.

I think I know what they're talking about.

Looking up at the stars, Kallik felt comforted by the spirits of her ancestors shining down on her. She knew that Nisa was among them, and remembered how she had seen her mother dancing in rivers of fire above the ice. *"I'm coming home,"* she whispered.

At last Lusa and Toklo turned back toward the trees. Kallik padded out a few paces to meet them. "We leave at dawn?" she asked.

Toklo nodded; there was nothing to discuss. All of them knew that they had to keep moving.

"Akna won't like it," Kallik commented after a moment, glancing back to where the mother bear was sleeping with her cubs in a heap of white fur.

"Akna will understand eventually," Toklo said.

For several heartbeats they stood looking at the horizon, where the next stage of their journey lay. Ujurak's stars twinkled icily above the snow-covered landscape.

"The four of us are still together," Lusa whispered.

Kallik woke as dawn light filtered through the pine trees, and slipped out of the den. Yakone, Toklo, and Lusa were stirring, too, though Akna and her cubs still slept.

Toklo came to stand beside her. "I think you should be the one to break the news to Akna," he said quietly.

Yakone blundered out of the den, blinking. "What news?"

"We're leaving now," Toklo told him.

"Why?" Yakone's eyes widened in surprise as he turned to Kallik. "There's food here, on the ice and on the land, and more bears are arriving every day. What if Taqqiq comes?"

A worm of uneasiness gnawed at Kallik's belly, because she knew that Yakone might be right. "I want to go back to the place where I first left the Melting Sea," she replied. "Even if the ice doesn't last long enough to go out to where Taqqiq and I were born," she added, desperately hoping that Yakone would understand. "We just have to hope that Taqqiq is still there."

Yakone bowed his head. "If that's what you want."

Kallik could see that he was still doubtful. "You have to trust me," she said.

"I do," Yakone responded, touching his muzzle gently to

her shoulder. "I want to see all the places that you remember. But I'm worried that the ice is breaking up so soon, when burn-sky has hardly begun. I don't want to walk into starvation."

"We have to risk it," Kallik replied. "I must find Taqqiq."

A rustle came from the den as Akna rose to her paws, along with drowsy squeaks from the cubs. Kallik turned to her.

"Akna, why don't we go for a walk along the shore?" she suggested, fighting uneasiness at the thought of what she was about to say. "I'll show you the nearest ice floe, where you can go hunting for seals."

Akna nodded. "Good idea."

"Can we come?" Iluq asked, bouncing with excitement. "Please?"

"No, not this time," Lusa told her, emerging from the den and rounding her up with her brother, Kassuq. "You've got to get some practice lifting bigger sticks. There are lots here under the trees. You want to grow big and strong, don't you?"

"And we'll look for black bear spirits!" Kassuq said.

"There's something I have to tell you," Kallik began when she and Akna were padding along the water's edge. She hesitated and then continued. "We're leaving today."

"What?" Akna halted, dismay in her eyes. "But how will I survive on my own? What about my cubs?"

"You'll be fine," Kallik told her, hoping that was true. "Toklo tells me you're getting really good at hunting on land, and soon Iluq and Kassuq will be big enough to help."

Akna sighed, then gave an understanding nod. "I know the

four of you are on a long journey," she murmured, "and that you haven't reached the end yet. But please—will you hunt with me on the ice just once, before you go?"

Kallik glanced back to where Toklo, Lusa, and Yakone were standing at the edge of the pine trees. She knew that they were waiting to leave, but she also felt that they owed one more hunting expedition to Akna. She had a long, hard burn-sky ahead of her, with two hungry cubs to provide for.

Hoping her friends would understand, Kallik launched herself into the sea with Akna beside her. The pale light of dawn shone on the ruffled water, growing gradually brighter as they swam.

At last Kallik reached an ice floe and scrambled onto it, waiting for Akna to join her. She relished the feeling of ice under her paws, but the floe felt incredibly fragile; the slap and gurgle of the sea was so noisy after the silence and solidity of the Endless Ice. And the ice was disappearing much earlier than when Kallik had been forced onto the shore when the last burn-sky came. This truly was the Melting Sea. The ice—along with Kallik's memories of her mother and Taqqiq—was vanishing into the black water.

"Is this the first time you've been back on land?" she asked Akna as the mother bear shook water out of her pelt.

Akna shook her head. "No, I was born three suncircles ago. I was my mother's only cub then, and I lived with her. . . . I still see her, and her younger cubs, but every burn-sky they get thinner, and more desperate for food."

Kallik murmured understandingly as she turned and

padded away from the edge of the ice floe, beginning to search for a seal hole.

"I had two cubs one suncircle ago," Akna continued, her voice tight with grief. "But they both died of hunger."

A massive wave of sympathy for the mother bear washed over Kallik. "Iluq and Kassuq won't die," she assured Akna. "You'll all be okay, I promise."

Akna turned her head and looked deep into Kallik's eyes. "That's not a promise you can make."

"I know," Kallik admitted. "But the spirits of your other cubs will be watching over you, willing you to be strong."

"Perhaps," Akna said. "I want to believe that the cubs are still in the ice, in the bubbles and shadows under my paws." Her voice shook and then strengthened again. "That way they're closer to me."

"I hope they are," Kallik told her, touching Akna's ear with the tip of her snout.

A few paces farther on Kallik spotted a seal hole, a dark blotch in the expanse of ice. She and Akna settled down beside it, a feeling of quiet companionship growing between them.

Knowing Akna was older than her, and more experienced in hunting, Kallik expected she would be the first to catch a seal. But when the water swirled and the seal stuck its nose out into the air, it was Kallik who reacted first. Lunging swiftly, she fastened her claws into the seal's hide and dragged it thrashing out onto the ice. Akna helped her to kill it with a blow to its spine.

"Great catch!" Akna said. "I wish I were as fast as you."

"You would have caught it if I hadn't been here," Kallik told her, half wishing she had hung back and let Akna take the prey. *But what if she'd missed it? I can't stick around here all day.* "Let's get this back to the others," she added.

When Kallik and Akna dragged the seal up the shore, Toklo came to meet them, with Iluq and Kassuq bounding around his paws and almost tripping him.

"What are you doing?" Toklo asked Kallik in an undertone, gesturing toward the seal. "I thought we were leaving at dawn."

"I owed this to Akna," Kallik retorted.

Toklo grunted but said no more.

Yakone and Lusa padded down from the trees to join them. "It's time we got going," Yakone said. "Akna, I hope all goes well with you."

"And with you," Akna responded. Kallik could see anxiety in her eyes. "I wish you luck," she added, sounding doubtful, as if she was imagining the dangers they might encounter.

"Thanks," Toklo said, adding to his friends, "Let's go."

"No! You can't leave us!" Iluq protested, her eyes wide as if she had just understood that this was good-bye.

"Lusa, we want you to stay and play with us," Kassuq added.

"I'm sorry, but I can't," Lusa replied. She bent her head and touched noses with each cub in turn. "Look after your mother, and remember to practice what I taught you."

"We will!" they chorused.

"Good-bye, Akna," Toklo said. "Remember everything you've learned about hunting on land."

Akna nodded. "Good-bye, Toklo. And thank you."

The time had come to leave. Kallik found it hard to walk away, and wondered if she was making a grave mistake. But her need to find Taqqiq again forced her paws onward.

By now the sun was well above the horizon, glittering on the waves and the distant ice. Kallik spotted a silver glint in the sky and made out another metal bird with a single bear in the net dangling underneath. It flew over their heads and swooped in to land farther up the coast.

I hope that bear is okay, she thought. *It'll need luck as well as new hunting skills to survive.*

"I can feel the sun soaking right through my fur!" Lusa announced. "I'd almost forgotten what it feels like to be warm."

"It's great," Toklo agreed.

Kallik exchanged a glance with Yakone. She was also enjoying the weak sunlight warming her fur, but she knew what it meant for the ice. She hoped that Yakone wouldn't start wishing that he had never left Star Island, surrounded by the Endless Ice.

Thinking of Star Island reminded her of Kissimi, the cub she had taken care of when his mother died. "I wonder how Kissimi is getting on," she said out loud to Yakone. "He's older than Iluq and Kassuq. Do you think he's learned to catch seals yet?"

"Maybe," Yakone responded. "He's still young, though."

"How soon do the mother bears on Star Island start teaching their cubs to hunt?"

Yakone hesitated. "It varies," he said at last. "I was about three moons old when I started. You have to be big enough to cope with a seal, and sensible enough to keep still while you're waiting."

"Waiting's the hardest part!" Lusa exclaimed, as she and Toklo caught up. "Kallik, do you remember how you taught me to catch a rabbit by waiting outside its burrow? I thought it would never come out!"

"That's because you're an annoying chatterbox," Toklo growled, though he nudged Lusa affectionately as he spoke. "If you could talk prey to death, we would never be hungry!"

"Speaking of being hungry," Yakone interposed, looking as if he still wasn't comfortable with Toklo and Lusa's playful quarreling, "I'm starving. Kallik, do you want to swim out and hunt?"

"Sure," Kallik replied. "If it's okay with you?" she added to Lusa and Toklo.

"That's fine," Toklo said instantly. "Bring us back a really tasty seal."

Kallik was glad that he was comfortable letting her and Yakone go out onto the ice now. *He must be sure that we're not going to leave him,* she thought. Aloud she said, "Thank you."

Toklo blinked in surprise. "I know you'll come back. We have a long way to go yet."

CHAPTER THIRTEEN

Toklo

"My paws are falling off," Toklo grumbled. Every pawstep he took felt as if thorns were driving into his pads. Lusa was limping, too. "It's time to stop for the day," he announced.

Two sunrises had passed since the bears had said good-bye to Akna and her cubs. They were walking in a shallow gully, sheltered by the wind, and separated from the shoreline by a gentle rise. The pine trees had been left behind; only a few scrubby bushes grew on the landward side of the gully.

"It's getting warmer all the time," Toklo continued as he halted, "and the days are getting longer. I guess that's why our paws feel so sore: We're walking farther every day because we're using all the daylight." He flopped on one side and rasped his tongue over his stinging pads. "We'll have to start limiting how far we travel each day," he said between licks.

"Good idea," Yakone responded.

Toklo was pleased by the white bear's agreement. He knew that Yakone found their journey easier, because his paws were suited to walking on snow.

Kallik won't like it, though, he thought. *She's more driven with every day that passes. She won't want to cut down our traveling time.*

Glancing around for the white she-bear, he saw that Kallik had drawn a little ahead and was standing at the top of the rise, looking out toward the sea. Her gaze was focused on something out of Toklo's sight; he wondered if she had spotted some prey, or another bear.

Though we've only seen one metal bird since we left Akna, and that passed straight overhead.

Scrambling to his paws again, Toklo padded toward Kallik, but before he reached her she began to walk away from him, then quickened her pace until she was running. As he reached the top of the rise, Toklo saw that her gaze was fixed on some piles of lumpy snow not far away from the water's edge.

Alarmed, Toklo ran after her. Catching up to her, he saw that Kallik was digging down frantically into the snow. "What are you doing?" Toklo asked.

Kallik ignored him. She was muttering to herself, too faintly for Toklo to make out the words, and concentrating on scraping away snow.

"What's going on?" Yakone asked, coming up with Lusa at his side.

Toklo shook his head. "I have no idea."

He watched Kallik as she uncovered a shard of metal, sharp and shiny, then hurled herself at another snowy lump and started digging again. Toklo glanced at Yakone and Lusa, but they both looked as baffled as he felt.

"Kallik, tell us what's wrong," he said, but once again the

white she-bear ignored him.

"I think I understand," Yakone said after a moment. "This must be the metal bird that was carrying Kallik when it fell out of the sky. Kallik, you can't do anything about it now."

"I've got to find Nanuk." Kallik almost spat the words out. "I left her here, all alone."

Unearthing more chunks of metal, she started heaving them aside, scraping at the snow underneath them until she reached the bare, brown earth.

"I have to find Nanuk's body," she muttered, half to herself. "I can't leave it here."

She kept digging down frantically. Toklo drew in a horrified breath as he saw that the jagged scraps of metal were scratching at her legs and paws, smudging her fur with scarlet blood.

Yakone thrust himself between Kallik and the twisted metal scrap she was trying to shift. "Kallik, stop!" he exclaimed. "There . . . there won't be anything left of Nanuk, not now."

Kallik stopped her desperate digging, raising her head to look into Yakone's eyes. She took two or three shaky breaths; at last she said, "I keep losing bears who are important to me. My mother, Taqqiq, Nanuk, Ujurak, Kissimi . . ." Toklo could hear her pain in each name as she spoke it.

"But we're still here with you," Yakone reminded her.

Kallik's gaze was still full of sorrow. "I know. But how much longer? What would I do if I lost you, or Lusa, or Toklo?"

"You won't," Toklo said instantly, then wondered if that was true. *We're bound to split up soon, to find our own homes.*

"I wish I could believe that," Kallik responded, clearly understanding what he hadn't said. "I think about those others, and I *know* sooner or later it will happen again."

"The past is the past," Yakone murmured. "We have a long way to go, and a lot more surviving still to do. . . ."

Kallik let out a long sigh. "I know. . . ." Turning to Lusa and Toklo, she added, "I don't know why, but I felt I had to see Nanuk again. I couldn't say good-bye to her properly before, and I wanted to."

"We understand," Lusa responded sympathetically.

Kallik gave Toklo a doubtful look, as if she expected him to dismiss her grief, or to make a joke.

But I know all about losing bears who mean a lot. Toklo knew he would never forget the little mound of earth and sticks that had covered Tobi.

"Yes, it's okay," he assured her. "I'll help you look for Nanuk, if that's what you want."

Kallik's eyes widened in surprise. Looking back at the piles of half-buried metal, she shook her head. "No. We should let her rest where she is," she replied. "Yakone's right. Her spirit isn't there anymore."

"So this is where you started your journey," Lusa said, glancing around. "How did you know where to go?"

"I didn't, at first," Kallik told her. "But then . . . come on, I'll show you."

Kallik led the other bears inland, up a long, gentle slope and then down the steeper descent on the other side. The land was barren, just a few stalks of long, coarse grass poking up here and there out of the snow.

"Careful," Yakone warned. "That's a BlackPath at the bottom."

Toklo spotted the hard-packed snow the white male was pointing out, and stayed well away from the edge. "Do we have to cross?" he asked Kallik.

"No, but we follow it for a while," she replied. "This way."

The BlackPath led alongside thorn thickets with a stunted tree here and there, twisted by the wind. Toklo sniffed the air and picked up the scent of water again, though he thought that they had left the Melting Sea some way behind.

Finally Kallik's trail left the BlackPath as she led the way up another long, snow-covered slope. Reaching the top, Toklo looked down. The ground fell away sharply in front of his paws; a dark stretch of water lay a few bearlengths below, lapping gently at the reeds that grew at the water's edge. The opposite side was just visible, a dark smudge of flatter land in the twilight.

"This smells salty," Yakone observed. "Is it part of the Melting Sea?"

Kallik nodded. "It's as if the sea is stretching a paw out into the land," she explained, her voice still quivering a little. "I remember standing here, looking across the water, and wondering where I should go next. Then the moon came out, and the spirits showed me a silver path along the surface, pointing inland. I knew that was the way I had to go." She stifled a snort of shaken laughter. "I think if I'd known how far away the Endless Ice would be, I would never have started the journey."

Lusa pressed her muzzle against her friend's flank. "I'm very glad you did."

Toklo thought that Yakone was looking at Kallik in a new way, as if he hadn't fully realized until then what the white she-bear had accomplished. "I know we've come a long way from Star Island," Yakone said, "but the first part of your journey was even farther, and you were all alone."

"You must have been so lonely," Lusa murmured.

"Sometimes," Kallik responded. "But there was a fox. . . . I first met him just back there, and I was so hungry I stole his prey. He kept following me, so later on I gave him part of a goose I'd caught." She scuffled the snow with one forepaw in embarrassment. "We were . . . sort of friends."

"Friends with a fox!" Toklo exclaimed. "Now I've heard everything."

"And I had Nisa and Taqqiq to keep me going," Kallik went on, her eyes deep pools of memory. "Sometimes I thought I could see them. I often heard my mother's voice, encouraging me. . . . So I wasn't really alone."

"You'll never be alone again, Kallik," Yakone told her.

"But I still have to say good-bye, don't I?" Kallik seemed to have recovered from the shock of finding the metal bird, but her voice was filled with sadness. "I'm going to lose you, Toklo and Lusa, and I wish I didn't have to."

"Well, that's the whole point of going home," Toklo pointed

out. "We're going back to our real lives, remember?"

He abruptly turned to go, then halted and looked back at Kallik. "Do you want to spend the night here?" he asked her.

Kallik gave him a surprised look. "Yes, please," she replied.

The bears scrambled down the steep slope and found a sheltered spot beneath a rock about halfway to the water's edge, and dug into the snow to make a den.

"This stuff is getting wetter," Toklo grumbled, scooping out pawfuls of half-melted crystals. "It's going to be really uncomfortable to sleep on."

"We've slept in worse places," Lusa said, curling up inside the den.

"True," Toklo admitted, crawling in after her.

Kallik and Yakone didn't follow them into the den. Instead, they walked off side by side, down the slope as far as the shore, where they sat together on a rock that jutted out over the sea.

Lusa sat up again. "Should we go with them?" she asked. "Do you think Kallik's okay?"

"Let them be," Toklo responded. Looking at the two white bears so close together, he felt a sharp pang of jealousy. Kallik needed Yakone now, more than she needed him and Lusa. *Yakone is the bear she will share the rest of her life with,* he thought, trying to thrust away the pain.

He lay for a long time with his nose on his paws, watching Kallik and Yakone on the rock. When at last they came back, treading softly so as not to disturb their friends, he pretended to be asleep.

* * *

The following morning, the bears got ready to set out along the edge of the sea, where the sparse outcrops of trees gave way to a bleak, empty landscape.

"Maybe we should swim out and hunt on the ice," Yakone suggested to Kallik as they emerged from the den.

Kallik halted. "Maybe . . . but the ice is a long way out. I think I'll just stay here and hunt with Toklo."

Surprise pricked Toklo. *I wonder if Kallik thinks the ice is breaking up too fast. She might be afraid of meeting orca.*

"Come on." Yakone tried to persuade her. "The ice isn't all that far." He gestured with one paw; in full daylight it was easier to see where this long paw of water met the main sea, with the ice shimmering on the horizon. "We won't have many more chances to hunt seal."

"You go," Kallik said, clearly uncomfortable. "I'll stay here."

Weird, Toklo thought, though he knew there was no point in looking for reasons. It would be good to hunt with Kallik again.

"Okay." Yakone briefly touched Kallik's ear with his snout before striding away toward the water. Glancing over his shoulder, he added, "I won't be long."

He splashed his way through the reeds and plunged into the sea, swimming strongly down the narrow channel until his head was just a little cream-colored dot in the water.

I'm glad I don't have to swim out all that way to hunt, Toklo thought.

Instead, he led the way inland, climbing a low hill. Before he reached the summit, he could hear a muted rumbling sound and glanced up at the sky, half expecting a storm. But the sky was a clear, pale blue from one horizon to the other.

Then Toklo reached the crest of the hill. His jaws gaped as he took in the scene in front of him. A gentle slope led down into a flat plain; moving across it was a herd of bison. They were huge, their shaggy pelts blasted by the wind, and there were so many that Toklo couldn't begin to count them.

Whirling around, he dashed back down the slope until he reached Lusa and Kallik. "We have to hunt now!" he gasped. "There are bison over there—a whole herd of them!"

"What?" Lusa exclaimed, her eyes stretching wide in shock. "Those things are huge!"

"Exactly," Toklo replied. "That's why we'll all sleep full-fed tonight."

"Why not wait until Yakone comes back?" Kallik suggested.

Toklo shook his head. "Who knows how long he'll be? The bison might move on. No, it's too bad we have to do it without him, but we can't miss this chance."

Kallik hesitated a moment, then nodded.

Toklo led the way back to the crest of the hill and peered out from behind a rock. Kallik and Lusa crowded up behind him.

The bison were making their way across the plain, leaving a broad swath of trampled snow behind them. They moved slowly, pawing at the snow with their hooves to uncover the grass, then stopping to graze.

"This is what we'll do," Toklo said, the thrill of the hunt rising up inside him as a plan formed in his mind. The rumble of the bison's hooves seemed to echo his heartbeat. The scent that wafted toward him on the wind made him want to hurl himself down the slope and into the midst of the shaggy beasts, to fasten his jaws in the throat of his prey. But he made himself stay calm and focused.

"We'll start by getting the bison running. Then, Lusa, I want you to run along the outside of the herd," he began. "Be sure to stay downwind. Pick out one bison—a calf would be best," he added, suddenly realistic about the size of animal they could tackle successfully, "and drive it away from the rest of the herd."

"But all the others will come after Lusa," Kallik objected. "She'll be squashed flat."

"That's where you come in, Kallik," Toklo told her. "You follow Lusa, and once she cuts her bison out of the herd, you attack the rest of them. Drive them back so they stay away from Lusa."

"Drive back a whole herd of bison," Kallik muttered. "Yeah, Toklo, I'll get right onto that."

"I'll be ready," Toklo continued, ignoring her comment. "Once Lusa's bison is separated from the rest of the herd, I'll dash in to chase it and kill it. Job done."

Kallik took a deep breath. "Lusa, are you okay with that?"

Lusa hesitated, then nodded firmly. "I'm ready."

"Okay." Toklo's excitement tingled right through him, from ears to paws. "Let's do it."

He leaped out from behind the rock and let out a loud bellow. The nearest bison looked up at him, and some of them started to back away, their movement rippling outward into the rest of the herd. Bellowing again, Toklo charged down the slope, his paws moving faster and faster on the steep incline. He could hear Lusa and Kallik racing down after him.

Panic began to spread through the herd. The nearest group of bison turned to flee, jostling one another as they tried to push their way into the center of the herd. More and more of them lurched around, heading away from the bears, their pace picking up as the herd began to move as one. By the time Toklo reached the bottom of the slope, they were surging like a wave across the plain, their drumming hooves louder than thunder, louder than firebeasts.

"Lusa, now!" Toklo roared.

Lusa began racing alongside the stampeding herd. Toklo and Kallik ran after her. Soon Toklo saw her fix her gaze on a half-grown bison calf that was pounding along on the edge of the panicked animals. As he watched, she darted in, nipping at the calf's hooves, forcing it to lumber off at an angle, away from the rest of the herd.

"Great job, Lusa!" Toklo shouted.

Kallik rushed past him, facing the other bison as they swerved to pursue Lusa and her quarry. Roaring fiercely, she tried to force them back, a lone white shape facing the rising tide of dark, shaggy animals.

Toklo braced himself for the final chase and kill, where he knew his greater strength would be needed. But then fear jolted in his belly as he realized that Kallik was in trouble. Too many bison were heading her way, and for all her courage, she was in danger of being engulfed in the tide.

One bison charged past her, heading straight for Lusa. Before the black bear could flee, the huge creature was upon her. Lusa was carried off her paws and the bison ran on, trampling her with its sharp hooves. Lusa rolled away and staggered to her paws; Toklo couldn't see whether she was badly hurt.

Abandoning his plan, Toklo charged in to help the two she-bears, letting out a bellow of defiance. The leading bison turned aside, but those behind pushed them on, and there were still too many. Kallik was surrounded by them, a white spot in a surging sea of dark pelts.

And what happened to Lusa? For a moment Toklo couldn't find the black bear.

"Lusa, get out of this!" he roared.

"I'm fine!" Lusa gasped just behind him. "Toklo, get the calf!"

Toklo had lost sight of their prey. Then he spotted it, still pounding along a little way from the main herd, but he was surrounded now by the stampeding bison. Toklo struggled to stay on his paws; their reek was in his throat and the drumming of their hooves filled the whole world.

A huge, shaggy male was bearing down on him. Toklo roared right into its face and it veered aside. A gap opened up: Toklo slipped through it, shoving Lusa in front of him. Breaking out of the herd, he bore down on the calf, which fled in front of him, only to stumble over a rock half-hidden by the snow.

Toklo took the chance and hurled himself on the calf. But

his paws slipped on the snow and although the calf staggered, it didn't fall to the ground. Scrambling after it, Toklo leaped again. This time, his rush carried the calf off its hooves, and he bore it to the ground, his claws fastened in its side. While its legs thrashed in an attempt to get up, he slashed one forepaw across its throat. A gush of blood poured out, and the calf went limp.

Breathing hard, Toklo looked up. At first he couldn't see Lusa or Kallik, only more bison surging around him, as if they wouldn't abandon their herd-mate even though it was dead. They shoved him aside, butting at him with lowered heads, trampling the dead calf.

"Kallik, help!" Toklo roared.

At first there was no response; Toklo reared onto his hindpaws, his forepaws splayed menacingly, but the bison still came at him.

"Kallik!" Toklo roared again.

To his relief he spotted the white she-bear forcing her way through the mass of animals to his side. Standing together over their prey, they bellowed defiance at the bison. Lusa had climbed to the top of a nearby rock, where she added her roars to the surrounding clamor.

At last, like a slowly turning tide, the bison veered away, the whole herd thundering across the plain into the distance. Toklo and Kallik were left standing beside the dead calf, while Lusa slid down from her rock and joined them.

"Well, we did it," Toklo panted.

He felt no sense of triumph. All three of them were battered and exhausted, and the calf they had risked so much to kill was battered, too, driven half into the ground by the hooves of its herd-mates. Toklo didn't even feel like eating it anymore.

"We'd better get back," Kallik said.

Together Toklo and his friends dragged the dead bison back up the slope and down the other side to the makeshift den they had occupied the night before.

"Was it worth it?" Toklo asked as he dumped it in front of the rock, not really expecting an answer.

"No, it wasn't!" Kallik snapped. "Lusa could have been killed. You can't expect her to hunt bison; it's not fair."

Lusa was moving slowly; clearly the bison who had attacked her had bruised her badly. But her voice was steady as she replied, "It's okay."

"No, it's not," Kallik retorted. "You don't even like eating meat."

"What's going on?"

Toklo turned to see Yakone trudging up from the shore. He wasn't dragging a seal; his face and the set of his shoulders showed his disappointment that he hadn't made a catch.

"Toklo almost got Lusa killed," Kallik told him hotly.

Puzzled, Yakone looked from Toklo to Lusa and back again. "What?"

"Of course I didn't mean to put Lusa in danger," Toklo insisted, baffled at why Kallik was blaming him, and pushing away the awful thought that she might be right. "We've hunted like that before; it was just bad luck that it went a bit wrong this time."

"A bit wrong!" Kallik snorted.

"Honestly, it's fine," Lusa said. "I was scared, but Toklo's right. It was just bad luck, and everything was okay in the end."

Kallik just let out a low growl and wouldn't meet Toklo's eyes. "It was so cloud-brained I don't even have words for it," she muttered. "Now are we going to eat or not?"

But even though the quarrel was over, Toklo still felt the tension among them as they settled down to eat, and the calf's meat was dry and tasteless in his mouth. *We risked our lives for this, and now I can't even enjoy it,* he thought miserably.

CHAPTER FOURTEEN

Lusa

Lusa's legs ached as she slogged through the slushy snow, her head lowered against the squalls of rain that blew into her face. A few days had passed since the bison hunt, but her muscles still ached and her ears had only just stopped ringing from when she was trampled. But she was determined not to let the others know she was struggling.

There was no need for Kallik to make such a fuss, she thought crossly. *I may be small, but I've traveled just as far as the rest of them!*

The rain was driving down, and Lusa almost wished for snow again. It might be cold, but it didn't soak through to her skin so uncomfortably, or sting her eyes.

"Stop a moment." Toklo, in the lead, was peering through the driving rain. "There's something up ahead. Stay there while I check it out."

Lusa could just make out a dark shape, barely visible in the poor light. When Toklo returned and beckoned them forward, she realized that it was a small flat-face den. There was no scent of flat-faces around it; the sides were scarred and dented, and Lusa guessed that it hadn't been used for a long time.

"Great, let's shelter," Kallik suggested, glancing at Lusa.

Lusa struggled with indignation, certain that Kallik had made the suggestion because she thought Lusa was too small to carry on. "Don't shelter on my account," she snapped.

"Well, I'd be glad to be out of the rain for a bit," Yakone said.

The door of the den was hanging open. Toklo poked his head inside, then lumbered through the gap; Lusa and the two white bears followed.

Lusa wrinkled her nose at the stale smell inside. It was dark and cramped, and the roof had fallen down at the far end, making it tight when all four bears were inside. Rain rattled on the roof with a weird, echoing sound.

"So, Kallik," Toklo began, "where exactly are we heading?"

Kallik shook her head, looking uncertain. "I know the ice is breaking up, so I might not be able to get to the place where Taqqiq and I were born." Brightening a little, she added, "But I want to find the place where I first came ashore. There might be other bears there—including Taqqiq."

"That doesn't sound too hard," Yakone commented.

Kallik blinked. "The problem is, we'll have to go past the no-claw denning place where I was captured—the place where the metal birds come from that carry bears up the coast."

"I don't want to be caught!" Lusa exclaimed, shuddering at the thought of being bundled into a net and carried through the air.

Kallik pressed herself against Lusa's side. "Don't worry. I won't let the no-claws hurt you."

Indignant again, Lusa wriggled away from the white she-bear. "*I* won't let them hurt me, either!" she retorted.

She saw Yakone giving her a warning glance, as if he was telling her not to be offended by Kallik's protectiveness. *That's all very well for him. No bear keeps reminding* him *how small he is!*

"Then we'll try to go around the denning place," Toklo said. "We'll avoid the bear-capture place altogether and keep to the wilderness."

To Lusa's surprise, Kallik didn't look completely happy with this decision. Lusa guessed she was concerned about the bears who had been caught.

"We can't help the captured bears," Toklo asserted, as if he was thinking the same thing. "And maybe it's better for them that the metal birds take them up the coast, where there are no flat-faces."

Kallik shook her head, clearly not convinced, but didn't argue.

By the time the rain eased off, night was beginning to fall. Lusa emerged from the den, splashing through puddles of mud and snowmelt, shivering in the stiff breeze that still brought with it a spatter of rain.

"My belly's telling me it's time to hunt," Toklo stated as the other bears padded into the open after her.

The bears' route that day had taken them inland, so they could avoid BlackPaths that ran along the shore, and there had been no chance of hunting on the ice.

"There are some likely-looking shrubs over there," Toklo added. "I'm going to check them out."

"I'll come with you," Lusa said quickly.

Kallik looked surprised. "Don't you want to hunt with me and Yakone?"

"We'll have a better chance of prey if we're in pairs," Lusa responded, not wanting to offend her friend.

Kallik nodded; she and Yakone set off in a different direction, while Lusa followed Toklo toward the clump of shrubs.

"Are you okay?" Toklo asked her.

Lusa sighed. "Kallik's being a bit . . . weird," she replied. "She keeps acting as if I can't look after myself."

Toklo halted and faced Lusa; she was surprised at the deep seriousness in his eyes. "Remember, Kallik has lost so much," he said. "It's only natural that she wants to keep the bears who are important to her safe."

"But she keeps treating me like I'm a cub!" Lusa protested.

"She doesn't mean it personally." Toklo hesitated, then added, "I know what it's like to lose bears who mean a lot."

"Well, I've lost bears, too!" Lusa felt annoyance welling up inside her that Toklo didn't seem able to see her point of view. "I had to say good-bye to Ashia and King and my friends."

"That's not the same," Toklo said gently. "You left them well and happy in the Bear Bowl, with plenty of food and shelter. You didn't have to watch them die, or leave them to an uncertain fate. . . ."

Lusa bowed her head, feeling that maybe she deserved the scolding. She missed her family, but she knew they were happy where they were. Still, she couldn't quite stifle her indignation. *It's so frustrating! The others still don't think of me as wild like them, even though I've lived longer in the wild than in the Bear Bowl. Sometimes I can hardly remember what the Bear Bowl looked like, or how the food tasted.*

Toklo headed on toward the bushes, and Lusa followed him. As they crept closer, she picked up the scent of a snow hare, signaling to Toklo with a jerk of her head to the bush where she thought it was hiding.

"Can you get under there?" Toklo whispered.

Lusa nodded. Stalking forward, she located the hare's exact position and crouched down onto her belly to wriggle underneath the prickly branches. The hare had flattened itself into a shallow hole; Lusa scooped it out with one paw. Blind with panic, the hare shot past her and dodged under the branches and out into the open, where Toklo killed it with a single blow of his paw.

"Great job!" Toklo exclaimed as Lusa scrambled out of the bushes again. "We make a good team."

Lusa's belly was rumbling. *I've had so many shriveled roots and frostbitten leaves lately, I could enjoy some meat.*

She was feeling better by the time she returned to the den with Toklo, her annoyance driven out by the success of their hunt. "Maybe you're right about Kallik," she confessed to Toklo. "I'll try not to mind when she fusses over me."

Back at the flat-face den, Kallik and Yakone had just

returned with a plump goose. All four bears retreated into the den to eat and then, contented and full, to sleep.

Lusa woke early and slipped out of the den while her friends were still sleeping. The rain had stopped, and a breeze was driving ragged clouds across the sky. A weak sun shone down, and under its warmth the snow was beginning to thaw.

Energy pulsed through Lusa, and she began trotting up a slope opposite the den. *I feel strong enough to run to the Endless Ice and back!* In a fit of high spirits, she let herself slide down the other side of the slope, only to have her paws skid out from under her in the slush. Landing with a bump, she saw that the marks her paws had left behind had exposed the bare ground.

Wow, the snow is so thin!

Even though the ground was made up of stones and mud, with only a few sparse tufts of grass, Lusa reveled in the feeling of it beneath her paws, along with the scent of the earth. She tried to dig down, hoping to find a juicy worm or two, but the ground was still frozen, too hard for her claws to do more than scratch the surface.

"There you are, Lusa!" Kallik was standing at the top of the slope, looking down at her with an anxious expression. "I've been looking everywhere for you."

Lusa felt her irritation rise, but remembering what Toklo had said, she forced it down. "Hi, Kallik," she said, trotting back up the slope to join her friend on the crest. "Isn't it exciting, that the snow is going at last?"

Kallik didn't look excited, and Lusa realized that it was different for her. "I want the ice to last longer," she responded, her voice desperate. "I *have* to get out onto the Melting Sea once more, so I can find Taqqiq."

Sympathy swallowed up the last of Lusa's annoyance. "I'm sure you'll find him," she reassured her friend. "If the ice melts, Taqqiq will have to come to shore, right?"

Kallik sighed, looking gratefully at Lusa, and the two bears sat close together staring out at the horizon. As the sun emerged from behind a cloud, Lusa spotted a dark smudge stretching across the route they would need to take.

"What's that?" she asked Kallik, pointing with one paw.

Kallik let out a gasp of excitement. "That's it! The no-claw denning place I told you about—the place where they take the captured bears. I'm sure of it!" She sprang to her paws. "Let's go!"

Lusa stared at her, feeling puzzled. "But it sounds like a terrible place. Why do you want to go there?"

"It is terrible," Kallik admitted, her eyes still sparkling with excitement. "But don't you see? It means I'm nearly home!"

She ran down the slope, calling to Yakone and Toklo, who emerged sleepily from the den. "Hurry!" she told them. "We have to go. We're almost there!"

Kallik's excitement was still bubbling over like a spring of fresh water as the bears set out. "If we can get out onto the ice, I'm sure I can find my BirthDen," she told Yakone. "I'd love to show it to you—all of you!"

Lusa was pleased for Kallik and tried to share her

excitement, but she was aware that Toklo was more concerned about how they would get past the flat-face denning place.

Reaching the top of the rise again, he paused to scan the landscape, then raised one paw to point. "That way," he said. "We should be able to skirt the flat-face dens and get back to the shore on the other side."

Lusa could feel her optimism rising and knew that her friends shared it as they padded along with new energy. Kallik took the lead, striding out confidently.

"Watch out for potholes," she warned the others. "Sometimes the snow just gives way under your paws. We don't want any bear to get hurt, especially now that we're so close." She paused, then added, "There are prickly plants, too, very close to the ground. Be careful not to get thorns in your pads."

The route Toklo had chosen led them around the denning place in a wide circle, but as the sun climbed in the sky, Lusa began to hear a distant rumbling sound, and feel an ominous vibration under her paws.

"Is that a BlackPath?" she asked nervously.

Skirting around a stand of stunted trees, Lusa saw that she had been right. The BlackPath stretched in front of them, blocking the route they wanted to take. It was wider than most of the BlackPaths Lusa had seen before; gigantic fire-beasts pounded up and down in both directions, roaring and wailing as their crushing black paws carried them along.

"We'll never get across that," Yakone stated.

"We'll have to try," Toklo retorted. "It's that or travel through the denning place." He gestured to the others to line up with him along the edge of the BlackPath. "When I say 'Now!'—run!"

But there was no end to the thundering firebeasts. The bears stood beside the BlackPath, their fur buffeted by the wind of the huge creatures' passing, waiting in vain for the chance to cross.

Once, in a short lull, Toklo stepped forward, his jaws parted to give the word of command, but another firebeast appeared, racing down on him, and he leaped back with a growl.

"It's no good," he admitted after another long and fruitless wait. "We'll have to head for the denning place instead." He gave a snort of annoyance.

"We'll be okay," Kallik said, still with her air of confidence. "We'll just have to hide from the no-claws."

Lusa wasn't sure that she shared her friend's certainty. They continued on, but walking so close to the BlackPath scared her, and her heart began to pound as another BlackPath joined it. It was a long time since they had been this close to so many firebeasts. On the Endless Ice she had become used to silence, and the continuous roaring and snarling froze her limbs with fear. She had to force herself to keep padding on.

"We'll have to cross this one," Toklo said, glancing up and down the new BlackPath. "It's that or go back."

At least this BlackPath wasn't as busy as the first, but Lusa was panting with terror by the time Toklo gave the order to cross. On the opposite side they found themselves on a stretch of rough ground with flat-face dens looming up in front of them. Toklo was still looking for a way to skirt around them, but in every direction the bears turned, they were blocked by more BlackPaths. Lusa thought it was as if some huge, unseen predator was herding them toward the dens, the last place they wanted to go.

As the bears crept between the dens, Lusa felt as though she was slinking along at the bottom of a deep crevasse. Strange, unexplained noises startled her, and she jumped with fright as a door opened in front of her. A flat-face popped out, looking back over his shoulder and growling something in a loud voice to someone inside. Toklo shoved her hastily around a corner, until the sound of the flat-face's pawsteps died away.

A narrow path lay in front of them, stretching into the distance. Kallik and Yakone took the lead, slipping along beside the walls and clinging to the shadows. Toklo and Lusa kept a lookout behind.

The silver cans that held flat-face rubbish stood here and there against the walls, giving the bears a little cover. Lusa's belly rumbled, but there was nowhere here to hunt, and the scents that came from the cans were harsh and unfamiliar. There was no food there.

Besides, Lusa thought, *Ujurak told me not to take flat-face food anymore. I can find my own food now.*

The ground underpaw was wet and gritty, with not much snow left except in the crevices behind the cans. Lusa winced as the slush stung her pads, and raised her paw to lick it.

"Hey, that tastes good!" she exclaimed. "It's not just melted snow."

Toklo grunted in surprise and slurped at the wet stuff on

the ground. "You're right," he said. "I wonder what it is."

"And why have the no-claws put it here?" Yakone sounded suspicious. "It's not just to give bears something tasty."

While they were still lapping at the ground, Lusa heard the loud sound of flat-face voices, coming from the end of the narrow path. "Hide! Quick!" she gasped.

All four bears ducked into the shelter of a group of silver cans, crammed uncomfortably together in the little space. Lusa was sure that some bear's paw, or some bear's ear, must be poking out somewhere.

The flat-faces are bound to see us!

But the flat-faces walked past, still talking together in loud voices, passing the cans without glancing aside.

Flat-faces never notice anything, Lusa thought, shaking with relief.

Toklo waited for the noise of the flat-faces to die away before venturing out into the open again. "Okay," he grunted, beckoning to the others. "Let's go."

As they padded onward, Lusa realized she was feeling terribly thirsty. She bent her head to lap from a puddle on the ground, but it had the same sharp tang as the stuff on the ground earlier. Somehow it wasn't as tasty as it had seemed before; she started to feel slightly sick.

"I think this stuff is making me thirsty," she said.

"Me too," Kallik agreed. "I wish we could find some water, or even snow."

Yakone grunted. "I knew there was something wrong. I just hope it's not bear poison, like whatever the no-claws were putting into the sea on Star Island."

Lusa hoped not, too. Her thirst grew until she started to feel desperate for water, yet she could see nothing except for the narrow path leading onward, crossed here and there by other paths. Weird noises echoed around her from the dens.

Are we going to be trapped here forever?

At last the narrow path came to an end. Beyond it lay a wide-open space, tufted with twiggy grass and dotted with puddles. More dens loomed up on the far side. Lusa wanted to dash out into the open and drink, but she made herself stay still while Toklo carefully scanned the space in all directions.

By now the daylight was dying, the setting sun casting dark shadows across the ground. Here and there glaring yellow lights appeared in gaps in the walls of the dens. Lusa's ears strained to listen; she couldn't hear any sound of flat-faces moving around.

"Okay," Toklo grunted at last. "Let's drink."

Still wary, the bears ventured out into the open. Lusa plunged her snout into a puddle and winced at the foul taste of the water. It reeked of firebeasts and dirt, and a trace of the sharp tang that had made her so thirsty. But Lusa needed to drink so badly that she didn't care.

Glancing up with her muzzle dripping, she realized how filthy her friends were: Kallik and Yakone had turned almost black from the dirt. Lusa sighed, realizing how used she had become to seeing their fur almost as pure white as the snow.

I can't even see the red tinge on Yakone's fur anymore.

Her own fur was just as filthy, but when she dipped her

paw into the puddle it came out with grit on it, and the many-colored sheen of oil. Her skin itched, and her nose was sore, and her eyes stung so badly that she could hardly see out of them. Her friends were suffering just as much, blundering about like cubs just out of the BirthDen.

"We'd better find somewhere to sleep," Toklo said.

He took the lead, and the others followed, stumbling over the rough ground. After a few pawsteps, Lusa sensed the surface beneath her paws grow suddenly smooth.

Hey, we must be on a BlackPath!

She was about to call out and warn her friends to get off it when she heard the sudden deep-throated roar of a firebeast. Looking up, she saw it erupt out of a gap between the dens opposite and head straight for them.

Lusa stared into its glaring eyes. Her mind was screaming at her to jump out of the way, but her body wouldn't obey her. It was as stiff and still as a tree.

Bracing herself for the impact, Lusa closed her eyes. *Oh, Ujurak, help me!*

CHAPTER FIFTEEN

Kallik

As Kallik sprang toward Lusa, the firebeast swerved madly and hurtled around the corner of the nearest den on two round black paws. There was a huge bang, and a yellow flame flashed out of the mouth of the narrow path where the firebeast had disappeared.

Kallik raced around the corner to see what had happened. The firebeast had smashed into a large den built of pale stone and lay on its side, its black paws spinning helplessly while flames leaped from its head. Two no-claws were scrambling out, backing away from the wave of heat that rolled out of the firebeast.

Kallik's belly lurched in alarm as she spotted a den made of mesh lying beside the firebeast; it looked as if it had fallen off the firebeast's flat back. It reminded Kallik a little of the cages where she had been kept after the no-claws captured her. Inside the cage a white bear was lying very still.

The fire started licking at the sides of the building. Kallik stared at it in horror. *This is the place where the captured bears are taken!* Bellows of fear and fury were coming from inside; Kallik could picture the bears and imagined their terror as they caught the scent of smoke and flame.

Three or four no-claws were running back and forth around the firebeast, shouting incoherently at one another. One of them suddenly let out a bellow of pain and fear as flames leaped across from the burning firebeast and caught on his outer pelt. Two of the other no-claws jumped on him and pushed him to the ground, rolling him over to crush out the flames.

The other bears surrounded Kallik, staring at the cage.

"Look—it's broken," Toklo said, pointing his muzzle at a spot where the metal sides were gaping open.

Kallik and Yakone raced to Toklo's side and thrust their paws between the sides of the cage, prying it farther open. A white she-bear lolled out of it, so deeply unconscious that she had no idea what was happening. She lay on the ground in an unmoving heap.

Toklo and Yakone grabbed the she-bear's fur in their teeth and heaved, dragging her away from the burning firebeast. They made it just in time, for in the next heartbeat it exploded in a ball of flame. The bears and the no-claws were driven back as the flames seemed to reach out for them. Kallik gagged on the scent of scorched fur.

The frightened bellowing still came from inside the den, louder and more desperate than ever.

"There are bears inside!" Kallik told her friends. "This is where I was held. I know my way around. Follow me!"

Gathering all her courage, Kallik plunged through the flames. A vast wave of gratitude surged over her as she realized that her friends were following. *I can always trust them!*

A gap loomed up in the side of the den, and Kallik raced through it. Inside, the heat was less intense, but thick smoke wreathed around her, stinging her eyes and catching in her throat until she choked. She led the way along a narrow passage and through another gap. Through the smoke she could just make out the white walls and straight gray columns that formed the cages where once she had been imprisoned. It was all just as she remembered it.

Inside the nearest cage were two young male white bears. They were pressed up against the gray columns, staring out with wide, terrified eyes.

"Help us!" they pleaded when they spotted Kallik. "Get us out of here!"

Kallik examined the door of the cage. She could see that it was fastened by a bar of metal, but she couldn't see how to open it. She clawed at the bar, but it wouldn't move.

"Hurry!" one of the young males gasped.

Toklo pushed Kallik aside and tried to work the bar loose with his teeth. While he struggled with it, the two captive males threw themselves at the columns again and again, while Kallik, Yakone, and Lusa yanked at the barrier with their paws and teeth.

But it was no use. The door remained firmly closed. Kallik reared up on her hindpaws and tried to batter it down by sheer strength, but all she did was bruise her paws.

The heat was growing more intense. Kallik could see the dusky glow of the flames through the thickening smoke. She knew that she and her friends had only heartbeats to get out, but she couldn't bring herself to abandon the two young males.

Suddenly she heard a high-pitched shout. A no-claw came battling his way through the smoke, flailing his arms. To her amazement, Ujurak's voice sounded in Kallik's head. *Get back!*

"It's Ujurak!" she choked out, shoving Lusa in front of her toward the outer door. "Come on!"

Glancing back as she and her friends bundled out of the den, Kallik saw the no-claw unfasten the door of the cage, then turn away and vanish into the flames.

No! Ujurak! Come back!

She raced back into the den, the flames singeing her fur, until Yakone seized her shoulder in his jaws and dragged her away. The no-claw was gone.

The two male bears in the cage staggered out, breathless with smoke and fear. Toklo and the others got behind them and urged them out into the open.

The no-claws who were standing around the fire backed away as the bears emerged, staring at them in horror, wide-eyed and silent. Kallik gazed at each one; none of them was the no-claw who had opened the cage. *It* was *Ujurak, then.*

Kallik and Yakone shoved the two bears they had rescued into the shadows. "Run!" Toklo growled. "Get out of here!"

"Thanks!" one of them gasped as they disappeared at a stumbling run.

"I don't think there are any more bears left inside," Kallik choked out through the smoke in her throat. "Where's that she-bear?"

The bear who had been in the wrecked firebeast was still lying on the ground where they had left her. Kallik bounded over to her with the other bears hard on her paws. She was beginning to stir.

Lusa nuzzled the sleepy bear. "Come on, wake up," she pleaded. "We don't want to leave you behind!"

"Uh-oh!" Yakone exclaimed. "Time to go."

Following his gaze, Kallik spotted two new no-claws rounding the nearest corner, with firesticks in their forepaws. *Oh, no—not now!*

The bear raised her head a little, blinked, then flopped back onto the ground.

Kallik's desperation spilled over. "Get up!" she roared.

Looking terrified, the she-bear scrambled to her paws, dazed and wobbly. Kallik and the others surrounded her, supporting her as they fled. Behind her Kallik heard the crack of a firestick, but none of the bears stumbled and fell.

Another explosion sounded behind them. Glancing back, Kallik saw more flames billowing up; the no-claws who were chasing them turned back. The air was full of noise; wailing firebeasts were converging on the fire from all directions as the flames crackled and roared.

Blinded by the glaring eyes of the passing firebeasts, the bears stumbled along narrow paths, their paws slipping on the hard stone. Kallik's ears felt as though they were on fire; she paused to scoop up a pawful of snow and rubbed them, making them sting.

Yakone turned back toward her. "Are you okay?" he asked.

Kallik nodded. "I'm fine, thanks." Her throat was sore from coughing in the smoke, and her voice sounded hoarse.

Yakone took the lead as they staggered on a little farther. Then he halted. "Look over here!" he called, jerking his head toward a dark den with a wide gap in the wall. "We could shelter there for the night."

"Let's check it out," Toklo growled, brushing past him.

The two male bears paused for a few heartbeats in the gap, then vanished inside the den. Kallik and Lusa waited, supporting the white female, who was still barely able to stand.

A moment or two later Yakone reappeared. "It's okay!" he called. "Come on!"

Inside the den was a vast empty space, dark and silent. A ragged hole gaped in the roof, and underneath it was a puddle of water. As Kallik and Lusa entered, almost carrying the white bear, Toklo raised his dripping muzzle from the pool.

"Come and drink," he said. "It's clean for once."

Kallik felt some of her tension leave her as she gulped down the cool water. Exhaustion overwhelmed her, and she tottered over to the white female, who had already sunk to the den floor and was sound asleep again. Kallik collapsed beside her, with her friends huddling around her. Darkness was rushing into her head, and with a sigh of relief she gave in to it.

* * *

Light slanting through the gap in the den wall woke Kallik. For a moment she couldn't remember where she was or how she had come there. Her ears were stinging, and her head felt strange and heavy. Her fur was black with ash, and all she could smell was fire.

This overwhelming scent, and the sight of the strange white female asleep beside her, brought Kallik's memory back with a rush. She shuddered as she remembered the smoke and flames, and the panicked bears trapped in the den.

Around her, the others were beginning to wake. Lusa raised her head and looked around, blinking; then her eyes widened in sudden understanding, and she gasped, "The fire!"

"I thought we were dead for sure," Yakone said, hauling himself to his paws.

"And those poor bears . . ." Lusa whispered. "What if we hadn't come?"

"Don't think about it," Toklo grunted.

But Kallik, shaken as she was, couldn't stop thinking about it. "I was so scared when the firebeast exploded."

"And being inside the den, when we couldn't free the trapped bears . . ." Yakone pressed his muzzle into Kallik's shoulder.

"I think it was Ujurak who freed them," Kallik announced. "He came as a no-claw. I heard him speaking to me inside my head, telling me to get out."

Toklo and Lusa exchanged a wondering glance.

"It must have been," Lusa agreed. "Ujurak would never let bears die if he could save them."

A scrabbling sound distracted Kallik, and she turned her head to see the white she-bear trying to get up, her claws scraping on the hard floor of the den. Her eyes were wide with fear.

"It's okay," Kallik told her. "Just rest."

But the white bear's gaze was horrified as she scanned the group of bears, and she flinched away from them. "Your pelts are weird colors!" she exclaimed. "What sort of bears are you? Bears should be white!"

"Your own pelt is pretty weird right now," Kallik pointed out, glancing down ruefully at her filthy fur. "Lusa here is a black bear, and Toklo is brown, but they're both okay. No bear here will hurt you."

The she-bear looked slightly reassured, though her gaze flickered into the dark recesses of the den. "How did I get here?" she whimpered.

"Just relax; we'll explain everything," Kallik told her. "My name's Kallik," she went on, "and this is Yakone. Do you remember anything?"

"I'm Shila," the white bear responded. "I swam ashore when the ice started to break up, and almost at once a fire-beast came, filled with no-claws who shot me with a firestick. And then I woke up here."

"The no-claws put you in a cage on the back of a firebeast," Yakone told her. "Then the firebeast crashed, and the cage broke, so we were able to get you out."

"The firebeast caught fire," Lusa added. "That's where all the yucky stuff on our fur came from."

Shila's eyes stretched wide with wonder. "Then you saved my life!" she exclaimed. "Thank you!"

Excitement had begun to rise inside Kallik as she heard Shila's story. "What was it like where you came to shore?" she demanded. "Were there other bears there? A bear named Taqqiq?"

Shila turned toward her, looking confused and scared. "My head hurts. . . . I'm sorry, but I don't remember anything."

Kallik let out a grunt of impatience. "I have to know!"

Yakone took a pace forward, giving Kallik a warning glance. "Shila, this is important," he began, his voice gentle. "Can you remember anything at all, even something that you heard before the no-claws came?"

Shila began to shake her head, then stopped. "I think . . . I think I remember walruses. . . . Yes, I was listening to the barking of walruses! There was a huge colony of them where I came ashore, and I had to go inland to avoid them."

Joy flashed inside Kallik, bright as flames. "I know where that is!" she exclaimed.

CHAPTER SIXTEEN

Toklo

Shila staggered to her paws. "Take me there!" she begged Kallik. "I have to get back!"

Toklo could see the gleam of excitement in Kallik's eyes as she replied, "Okay. Let's go! Tell me when you remember some more."

It seemed like Kallik hadn't noticed the note of desperation in Shila's voice, but it was clear to Toklo. He gave the white she-bear a wary glance.

Something isn't quite right about Shila. I'm sure she hasn't told us everything.

As his friends headed for the gap in the den wall, Toklo hung back. "Hang on a moment," he said. "Do we really want to travel with another bear when there are so many flat-faces around? It will be so much harder to hide."

"It's not far." Kallik sounded as if she was trying to suppress her annoyance. "We'll be at the shore in no time."

"Come on, Toklo." Lusa gave him a friendly shove. "At least we'll get away from all these flat-face dens."

Yakone nodded. "Right. And it's the same place Kallik wants to go."

Toklo realized that no bear was going to listen to him, and he wasn't ready to voice his doubts about Shila. "Okay," he said. "But we're *not* leaving now. Wandering around a flat-face place in daylight? Are you all bee-brained?"

Kallik let out a sigh. "You're right. And we all need to rest some more, especially Shila."

Scouting more carefully around the den, Toklo discovered some sheets of metal leaning against one wall; he hadn't noticed them in the dark the night before.

"It doesn't look as if flat-faces come here much, but they might. This would be a good place to hide," he announced, beckoning the others over.

Together the bears squashed into the cramped space behind the metal sheets. Toklo crouched with his head sticking out so that he could keep an eye on the gap in the wall.

"I wish my fur didn't sting so much," he grumbled as they settled down. "Kallik, are your ears still hurting?"

"A bit," Kallik replied.

Toklo guessed she was in more pain than she admitted. *She was really brave last night, leading us into the den.*

"I'll go out and fetch some snow," Lusa said, wriggling out of her hiding place again. "It'll be nice and cool on your burnt places."

"Lusa, no!" Kallik exclaimed, alarm in her voice. "It's not worth the risk."

"Don't worry." Lusa sounded cheerful as she padded off

toward the gap in the wall. "I'll be careful."

Toklo was pleased that the small black bear was managing to be patient with Kallik in her protective mood. *She really does treat Lusa like a cub sometimes.* He lay with his nose on his paws, wishing he could sleep, but knowing that some bear had to stay alert. It wasn't hard; the pain of his burns kept him awake, along with the rumble of firebeasts and the shouting of flat-faces.

"Maybe they're looking for me," Shila said nervously.

Fear tingled through Toklo as he realized the white bear might be right, but he pushed it down. "If they find us, we'll get you out," he promised, hoping that was true. "Just do as we tell you, and you'll be okay."

Shila sighed, as if she didn't quite believe him, but she said nothing else, and shortly her snores told him that she had gone back to sleep.

"Lusa's taking an awfully long time," Kallik muttered.

Almost as soon as she had spoken, the black bear staggered back into the den on three legs, carrying a huge scoop of snow with her fourth leg pressed against her chest.

"Here you are," she announced. "Spirits, it's cold! It's soaking right through my fur."

She gave some snow to Kallik, some to Toklo, and some to Yakone for a scorched place on his leg. As Toklo pressed the snow onto his burned skin, the pain ebbed, and he started to relax.

"That feels great," he said. "Thanks, Lusa."

"You're welcome."

Now that Lusa was safely back, and the stinging in his fur had eased, Toklo felt that he could have slept, but the disturbing sounds of flat-faces still came from outside. He could feel his friends' tension, too, and he was glad when the daylight began to fade and at last the noises started to die away.

"Time to go," Toklo announced, crawling out from underneath the metal sheets. "Kallik, wake Shila. Maybe she can tell us which way to go."

But when the bears ventured out of the den, the white she-bear seemed confused and frightened. "I can't remember anything about the journey on the firebeast!" she protested.

"It's okay." Kallik's voice was soothing. "I know you were asleep." She glanced up and down the path outside the den. "We'll go this way."

Toklo let Kallik take the lead as they moved off. He could pick up the tang of the sea beneath the stale reek of firebeasts, and he knew that Kallik would feel a powerful instinct pulling her onward.

I trust her . . . but I hope we don't meet any more flat-faces. We don't want to end up in that big white den!

The bears crept through the flat-face dens, keeping to the narrow paths and avoiding BlackPaths where firebeasts cast their shining eyes through the darkness.

Toklo jumped, startled, as loud barking came from the den they were passing, and Shila shrank away with a whimper of fear. Lusa was braced as if she was expecting to fight, while Kallik and Yakone gazed around, pinpointing the source of the threat.

"They must be shut inside," Lusa said with a sigh of relief, when the barking continued but no dogs appeared.

"Then let's get moving," Toklo responded, "before the flat-faces come out to see what's making them bark."

Kallik nodded, loping away at a faster pace, and the rest of the bears followed. At last they emerged from the narrow path and found themselves facing a vast expanse of darkness. Wind blew into their faces, bringing a stronger tang of the sea.

"The end of the denning place!" Lusa said, blowing out a gusty breath of relief.

As they stood beside the last flat-face den, staring into the night, Toklo felt a tremor of anxiety. Out there was the Melting Sea, Kallik's home, the place where they would have to say good-bye. Suddenly, even though he was desperate to get away from the flat-face dens, Toklo didn't want to take a single step farther.

But Kallik and Yakone were already striding away over the rough land, their pads leaving a trail in the thin, dirty layer of snow that covered the ground. Shila stumbled along in their pawsteps. Toklo exchanged a glance with Lusa, guessing that the black bear felt just as he did, and set out after them.

Away from the shelter of the dens, the biting wind buffeted his fur. Lusa stayed close to Toklo for shelter as they walked, trudging through the darkness until the lights of the flat-face place were no more than tiny twinkles in the distance.

"Let's rest," Lusa suggested as they paused to look back. "I think my paws will wear away if we go any farther tonight."

Her friends murmured agreement. Toklo looked around for a possible place to make a den, but there was nothing but the flat plain stretching away on every side. With no other choice, the bears huddled together in a heap. Warmed by Lusa on one side and Kallik on the other, Toklo finally managed to sink into sleep.

The grumbling roar of a firebeast woke Toklo. Dawn was long past; the sun had climbed high in a pale blue sky smudged with wisps of cloud. His friends were stirring sleepily, as if they, too, had been disturbed by the noise.

Toklo sprang to his paws, snarling in mingled fear and anger. Several bearlengths away he saw a huge white firebeast, crawling slowly toward him. It halted for a moment, as if his challenge had startled it, then crept forward again.

Lusa got up and peered curiously at the firebeast. "There's something wrong," she said, stiffening. "That firebeast isn't on a BlackPath!"

Toklo stared. "You're right. Come on, we have to get out of here!"

"I saw those firebeasts last time I was here." Kallik spoke around a huge yawn. "I don't think they're dangerous."

Toklo snorted. "Do you want to wait around to find out?"

Kallik thought for a heartbeat. "No. Come on, Shila. Let's get out of here."

With Kallik in the lead, the bears started to run. To Toklo's surprise, the firebeast kept pace with them, rumbling along without coming any nearer, but not falling back, either.

Spinning around, Toklo halted and bellowed at the fire-beast. "Maybe we should stand and fight," he suggested. "Yakone, are you ready?"

"Right here." The white male came to stand beside him.

"Don't be cloud-brained!" Kallik exclaimed. "We can't fight a whole firebeast. It's huge!"

Shila was shrinking away, mute and wide-eyed with terror. Toklo knew she wouldn't fight, and Lusa was too small to make much of a mark on a firebeast. It would be up to him, Kallik, and Yakone.

"Hey, look over here!" Lusa called out. She was peering ahead, and raised one paw to point. "There's a gully up ahead. We can scramble across it, and the firebeast won't be able to follow us."

"Good thinking, Lusa!" Toklo told her.

Glancing warily at the firebeast, the bears hurried across the tussocky grass and slid down the steep side of the gully. The far side was even steeper; Toklo and the white bears clambered up easily, but as Lusa drew close to the top, her hindpaws slipped and she began to slide back, her forepaws scrabbling helplessly. Toklo leaned over and grabbed the scruff of her neck to haul her upward.

"Thanks!" Lusa gasped as she flopped down on the flat ground at the other side.

Toklo gazed at the firebeast. It rumbled up to the edge of the gully, then stopped. "Great!" he said with satisfaction. "We've escaped."

The bears carried on. Lusa kept casting glances back at the

firebeast, and after a few moments she prodded Toklo with one paw. "Look!"

Toklo turned. To his horror the firebeast had traveled farther along the gully and had found a place to cross, bumping down on a shallower slope and bumping back up again with a deep roar.

"I'll say this for it," Yakone muttered. "It doesn't give up easily."

"What's going on?" Toklo demanded, slapping one paw against the ground in anger. "Is it hunting us?"

"I can't see any firesticks," Kallik said doubtfully.

"Look, there are flat-faces inside!" Lusa took a step or two toward the firebeast, clearly fascinated. "They're staring through those shiny gaps and pointing at us!"

"Oh, no! There's another one!" Shila was staring across the plain, back toward the distant flat-face dens.

Toklo followed her gaze. A second white firebeast had emerged from the denning place and was roaring across the plain toward them, moving much faster than the first one.

"Two of them stalking us!" Shila went on, quivering with fear. "We can't let them catch us again!"

Kallik watched the second firebeast for a moment, then gave a decisive nod. "There's nothing else to do," she said. "We'll have to go out onto the ice."

Toklo stared out at the sea, which was only a few bearlengths away. The ice looked a long way off, across the black, choppy water.

"Will we make it that far?" he asked. "Is the ice safe?"

"Safer than we are here," Kallik replied tensely.

Toklo could see that she was reluctant to leave the land, but with two firebeasts bearing down on them, it might be the only solution.

"I'm up for it!" Lusa said bravely.

Shila nodded. "We have no choice. We can't be captured by no-claws."

Together the bears crunched their way across the strip of pebbles at the edge of the sea and launched themselves into the waves. The cold almost took Toklo's breath away. The salt tang was in his nostrils as the water sucked at his legs and belly and fur.

I know we have to do this . . . but I wish we didn't have so far to swim.

The three white bears were forging slightly ahead. Toklo looked around for Lusa and spotted her close by, striking out boldly with paws that churned the water. He swam to her side, grabbing her by the scruff as a wave broke over her head.

"I'm fine!" she gasped.

As they drew away from the shore, Toklo glanced over his shoulder. Both firebeasts had halted at the edge of the water and crouched there, growling.

Ha! Toklo thought triumphantly, just before he took in a mouthful of water. His triumph faded as he spluttered and spat, and turned to face forward again.

Soon the water was very deep. Toklo remembered the orca that had killed Kallik's mother; Kallik was looking grim and worried, and Toklo guessed she was thinking the same thing.

This may be her home, but she has so many unhappy memories. . . .

Shila was swimming confidently, pulling herself along in the water. She seemed like a different bear here than the nervous creature she had been on land. Kallik and Yakone swam strongly, too, but Toklo began to feel himself tiring. Beside him, Lusa's strokes had weakened, and Toklo kept an even closer eye on her, ready to grab her if she sank.

But soon Toklo felt so exhausted that he was ready to sink himself. Every stroke took a vast effort. Lusa was even worse, looking barely able to force herself through the waves.

Just as Toklo felt as if he couldn't swim any farther, the ice shelf loomed up above his head. Yakone was already boosting Shila out of the water, and then he scrambled out himself and leaned over to grip Lusa by the scruff as her head went under. When he had hauled her out, the white male helped Toklo, then turned to Kallik, who was still swimming strongly at the edge of the ice.

Toklo stood next to his friends, catching his breath after the long swim. Behind him, the ice stretched away forever. Ahead, the land was a smudge across the sea. The firebeasts were too small to make out.

We're safe . . . but we're not on land anymore.

CHAPTER SEVENTEEN

Lusa

Lusa's legs felt wobbly after the long swim. She wanted to lie down and go to sleep, but she knew that she couldn't stop yet. *I have to find the strength to go on.*

Kallik padded over and looked down at her. "Are you okay, Lusa? I can carry you if you want."

Lusa was tempted to say yes, but she remembered how Kallik had started to fuss over her.

"I'm fine," she insisted, finding the trickle of energy she needed. "Where do we go next?"

Kallik raised her head and began sniffing the air. But before she could settle on a direction, Shila spoke decisively. "This way."

As the white she-bear strode purposefully across the ice, Lusa and Toklo exchanged a puzzled glance. *What made her so determined all of a sudden?* Lusa wondered.

There was nothing to do but follow.

Lusa could see Kallik's excitement rising as she traveled farther into the expanse of ice.

"It's so good to be home!" she exclaimed. "This is the ice where I was born." Padding past a seal hole, she added, "That seal hole could be where I caught my first prey!"

Lusa was impressed. "Really?"

Kallik let out a snort of amusement. "No. Even I couldn't recognize my first seal hole. But I know we are close to where Taqqiq and I grew up. I can feel it in the ice." Her amusement died, and for a moment she looked worried. "I just hope Taqqiq is here, too."

Yakone paused beside the seal hole. "Why don't we hunt here?" he suggested.

"No, no," Shila said; Lusa thought she sounded almost aggressive. "We can't stop here. We have to keep going."

Toklo turned to face Shila with a challenging expression. "What aren't you telling us?" he demanded.

Shila wouldn't meet his gaze. One of her forepaws scraped awkwardly at the ice. "Nothing, honestly," she responded. "It's just that . . . well, there are a lot of white bears around here, and there probably won't be any seals to catch at that hole."

Toklo let out a low growl, clearly not convinced.

I wish they would stop and hunt, Lusa thought longingly. *Then I could take a rest!*

Before Toklo could argue with Shila, Kallik touched his shoulder with one paw. "Come on," she said. "There'll be plenty more seal holes."

As the bears plodded on, with Shila still in the lead, Lusa noticed that it was getting harder to see into the distance. After a moment, she realized that mist was gathering

around them; soon it was so thick that they could barely
see a bearlength ahead. Daylight was fading, too, the sun's
warmth vanishing; Lusa shivered as the icy fog soaked into
her fur.

Shila's pace slowed, and she began glancing around nervously.

"What's the matter now?" Toklo grunted.

The white she-bear let out a snort of brittle laughter.
"Nothing. Just that we might fall into a seal hole if we don't
watch out."

Oh, yeah, sure, Lusa thought, her suspicions of Shila rising.
Like we can't see our own paws!

A few pawsteps farther on, Lusa jumped at the sound of
deep bellowing that echoed across the ice. Then she let out
her breath in a puff of relief. *It's only white bears.*

But to her surprise, Shila had halted, gazing around her
with wide, terrified eyes. *Why is she so scared?* Lusa wondered.
Doesn't she recognize her own kin?

Padding across to Toklo, she murmured into the brown
bear's ear. "What's gotten into Shila? Just what is going on?"

Toklo shook his head; he didn't reply, but his eyes were
wary as he looked at the white she-bear.

"I think we should stop and rest, now that we can't see,"
Kallik said. "There's no point in walking around in circles."

Staring through the foggy twilight, Lusa spotted a heap of
snow a few bearlengths away. Yakone had seen it, too, and led
the way over to it. He and Kallik began scraping out a rough
den.

"I wish we'd hunted earlier," Toklo muttered to Lusa. "It's too late now."

"Me too," Lusa responded. *I'm so hungry that I'd even be thankful for a few mouthfuls of seal!*

Her belly was rumbling as she snuggled into the den between Toklo and Kallik, but she was so exhausted that her hunger couldn't keep her awake. Even her growing anxiety about Shila faded as she lost consciousness.

Sunlight glittered on the ice as Lusa raced across it, beside Toklo and Kallik. Ahead of them, Ujurak was running: He kept changing shape from a brown bear to a white and then to a black bear. Then his fur dissolved into feathers and he lifted off the ground in goose shape, letting out a harsh, lonely cry. But just as Lusa began to despair of keeping pace with his wings, he glided down to the surface of the ice again. His form swelled and grew darker; antlers sprouted from his head, and he clicked off across the ice on the narrow hooves of a caribou. His strides lengthened and grew faster until he was only a dot on the horizon.

"Ujurak, don't leave us!" Lusa cried out.

The dot began to grow bigger again, but as Lusa drew closer, she saw that Ujurak had changed again. Now he waited for them in the shape of a flat-face cub, covered in bright pelts. The cub's mouth opened, but instead of the thin cry of a flat-face, the deep growl of a bear came from his jaws.

Lusa flinched. "What's wrong?" she asked.

Ujurak growled again, louder this time, and Lusa's eyes flicked open. At first she thought she was still staring into the chilly fog. Then as she became fully awake she saw that the sun was up; the whiteness in front of her took shape, and she realized that their den was surrounded by white bears.

Six of them! Spirits, they're big. . . .

Her friends were already awake, staring in dismay at the hostile glares of the newcomers. As Lusa tried to struggle to her paws, Toklo hissed at her, "Stay still!"

Obeying him, Lusa let her gaze travel from one white bear to the next. *Hang on,* she thought. *I recognize that one. . . . It's Salik, from Great Bear Lake! And that one . . . Manik.*

"Hey, Iqaluk!" It was Salik who spoke, nudging the white bear next to him. "A brown bear and a black bear. What are *they* doing on the ice?"

"They've no business here," Iqaluk growled.

Iqaluk . . . Lusa recognized that name, too. Her heart sinking, she realized that they had been found by the group of young males who'd been terrorizing the other bears who had gathered at the lake, and had even stolen a black bear cub from the forest.

But that means . . .

Lusa scanned the rest of the bears, her heart pounding. Beside her, Kallik was quivering like a leaf about to fall off its branch. Following her gaze, Lusa gulped.

At the same moment, Kallik gasped, "Taqqiq!" Leaping forward, her voice full of joy, she yelped, "I found you!"

Taqqiq looked stunned, his eyes bulging as he took a step back.

Before he could speak, Iqaluk shoved Kallik aside. "What are you doing, seal-brain?" he snarled.

"That's my brother," Kallik retorted, standing up to the huge male. "And this is our home! Don't you remember me, from Great Bear Lake?"

"I remember you," Salik sneered, pushing his way forward. "You tried to persuade Taqqiq to go on some fish-headed journey to a place that doesn't exist. Luckily, he came to his senses and came back."

"But we did find the Endless Ice!" Kallik protested. "It's true!"

"What are you doing back here, then?" Manik demanded.

As Kallik faced the male bears, Lusa heard a whimper of fear behind her and realized that Shila was still cowering inside the den. "Are you okay?" Lusa asked, ducking back to her side.

Shila shivered. "Don't make them angry!" she pleaded. "Let's just go."

Lusa heard Salik's voice outside the den. "Get out of here. This is *our* territory."

"Yeah." That was Taqqiq. "I never asked you to come find me. Like Salik says, this is our place."

"We have every right to be here," Toklo growled.

"I don't think so, *brown* bear," another of the newcomers snarled. "What's the matter, did you get lost?"

"Make it easy for yourselves," Manik said. "Leave before we make you."

"We mean it, Kallik," Taqqiq added. "I don't want you to get hurt."

Lusa backed out of the den again to see Kallik still facing the white bears, with Yakone at her shoulder. "White bears don't have territories," she argued. "You're just trying to push us around."

"We have territories now." Salik pushed his snout into Kallik's face. "Or haven't you noticed that there's not enough ice to go around? Challenge us if you want," he added smugly, "but the bears we found here before discovered that was a very bad idea."

For the first time Lusa noticed that the pile of snow where they had sheltered had once been a den. It had been crushed into destruction by gigantic paws with sharp claws. In the growing light of morning she made out blood spattered on the snow.

No . . .

Her heart thudding even harder, Lusa leaned in toward Toklo, feeling very small and vulnerable.

Without warning, Manik suddenly leaped forward, out of the group of his friends. "You want to fight?" he challenged Toklo.

"Just try me!" Toklo snapped, lunging at Manik and landing a hard blow on the side of his head.

The white bear paused for a heartbeat, shaking his head as if he couldn't believe that a brown bear could hit so hard.

While he hesitated, Toklo lowered his head and crashed into the white bear's side, knocking him off his paws. The two bears wrestled together, rolling over and over on the ice.

Lusa winced at the sight of Manik's powerful claws as they raked across Toklo's shoulder. Anger began to rise inside her as she saw the gleam of enjoyment in the other white bears' eyes—even Taqqiq's—as they watched.

"That's it, Manik!" Salik called out. "Show him what's what!"

"Flatten him!" Iqaluq snarled.

Lusa could hardly bear to watch. Toklo was smaller than the white male; Manik soon held him pinned down on the ice, though Toklo was pummeling at Manik's stomach with his hindpaws.

"Stop them!" Kallik shrieked at Taqqiq, shoving him in the shoulder. "You know Toklo is my friend! How can you be like this?"

Taqqiq pulled away from her. "Leave me alone," he growled. "You don't know anything about me now."

Kallik gasped in disbelief, her stricken gaze fixed on her brother. Lusa felt desperately sorry for her.

"That's enough." To Lusa's surprise, Salik stepped forward, thrusting himself between Toklo and Manik. "Save your strength," he added as the white bear struggled to his paws, shaking snow off his pelt with a thin rain of blood. "They'll leave now—won't you?" He swung around and fixed Toklo with a challenging gaze.

Before Toklo could reply, Lusa stepped forward, fury giving

her the courage to confront the huge white male. "Yes, we'll leave now," she said. "But you'll see us again, I promise."

She turned her back with dignity as the white males burst out into snorts and snuffles of laughter. Toklo got to his paws and joined her, and together they led the way across the ice, with Kallik, Yakone, and Shila following.

Kallik glanced back over her shoulder as she moved away, her gaze full of sorrow as she looked at Taqqiq, but she said nothing.

"Keep out of our way, if you know what's good for you!" Iqaluk bellowed after them.

Once the white males had been left well behind, Shila ran to catch up with Toklo. "I told you not to make them angry," she said.

Toklo halted and turned to face Shila; his gaze was stern. "You've met those bears before, haven't you?" he asked. "Now are you going to tell us what's going on?"

Shila couldn't meet Toklo's gaze. "You saw what they did to the den back there," she began. "They've been doing that kind of thing for a while. They smash up dens and steal food, and they try to make other bears hand over their catch, or risk being hurt in a fight."

Lusa could tell that as Shila spoke, Toklo was growing angrier and angrier, a low growl coming from deep within his throat. Kallik was staring at Shila in horror.

"They're even worse than they were at Great Bear Lake!" she exclaimed. "And there are more bears involved now."

Lowering her voice to a shamed whisper, she added, "Taqqiq is still one of them."

"Tell us *everything*," Toklo demanded, fixing Shila with a look harder than the ice.

Shila swallowed nervously. "Those bears attacked the den where my mother and brothers were sleeping," she began. "I tried to fight them off, but I couldn't. Then my mother, Sakari, made me go far away to hunt for food, and I got stuck on some broken ice. I ended up onshore, and that's when the flat-faces caught me."

"And then we found you," Lusa put in.

Shila nodded. "My mother and brothers could be dead by now," she went on, her voice rising in panic. "Tonraq and Pakak are too young to be out of the BirthDen all the time!"

"Calm down." Yakone stepped forward and touched Shila's shoulder with his muzzle. "Getting worked up won't help."

"Yakone's right." Lusa pressed up against Shila on her other side. "Calm down and we'll decide what to do."

"Yes," Toklo added. "We're here now. We can help."

Shila stared at him incredulously. "What can you do? You're not even a white bear!"

Toklo exchanged a glance with Lusa. "Maybe that's exactly what you need," he said.

CHAPTER EIGHTEEN

Kallik

Raising her head, Kallik let her gaze rest on the starry sky, the spirits thick as ice crystals strewn across the darkness. Her companions were all asleep in the shelter of another heap of snow. *Probably another destroyed den . . .*

Kallik had volunteered to keep first watch for Salik and his vicious group of bears, but instead she was looking up at the stars, seeking Ujurak. She felt as though her heart was breaking; she couldn't believe that everything had gone so wrong. White bears turning against one another. The Melting Sea turning into water before burn-sky had even begun. What else had changed?

Ujurak, did you know what I would find when I came home?

Kallik jumped as Yakone's white shape emerged from the pile of snow. "Do you mind having some company?" he asked.

Shaking her head, Kallik leaned against his warm pelt. It felt so good to have him there. "I was so excited to bring you back here," she told him, "back to where Taqqiq and I were born. But the ice is melting too fast, the bears are suffering more than ever, and Taqqiq and his friends are endangering lives with their greed and bullying. Nothing's right here," she finished with a sigh.

Yakone touched her ear sympathetically with the tip of his muzzle. "I know how you feel," he soothed her. "But we've traveled this far. We can do more than just watch what Taqqiq and the others are doing."

His strong, determined voice comforted Kallik, but she still felt overwhelmed by her terrible discovery about her brother. "Maybe I shouldn't have come back," she murmured.

"Of course you should have," Yakone responded. "You wanted to find Taqqiq, and you did! I'm so proud of you."

Kallik opened her eyes to see Toklo standing in front of her, muzzle raised to sniff the air. She had slept at last, tucked against Yakone's warm side; now he and the rest of her companions were waking, too. On the horizon a reddish glow showed her where the sun would rise.

"We need to plan what to do next," Toklo announced.

"No." Yakone heaved himself to his paws. "First we need to find food. We can't do anything to help Shila if we're weak from hunger. I'll go."

Toklo grunted agreement, and Yakone padded off into the distance; Kallik lost sight of him as the growing light dazzled off the ice.

Sooner than she expected, Yakone was back, dragging a seal behind him.

"Wow, that was quick!" Kallik exclaimed. "Great job."

Yakone nodded acknowledgment as he dropped the seal in front of her. "Too bad it's not bigger."

Looking more closely, Kallik could see that the seal was young and skinny. Trying to hide her disappointment, she realized how slim the pickings were, even out on the ice. *Times really are hard.*

But no bear complained as they gathered around the seal to eat, tearing off chunks of the oily flesh. Kallik noticed that Lusa was only picking at her share; worry stabbed into her belly as she realized again how hard the black bear found it to live on the ice.

We need to get Lusa back to land, but that means saying good-bye to her and Toklo, Kallik thought, deep sadness piercing her like thorns. *I can't bear the idea of losing my best friends. . . .*

"So," Toklo continued as the bears were finishing up the last of the seal, "the way I see it, the first thing to do is to find Sakari and the cubs."

Shila flashed him a grateful glance. Kallik thought that she looked calmer today, as if she was determined to keep fighting, whatever it took.

Rising to her paws, Shila studied the ice around her and lifted her muzzle to scent the air. A mist had risen while they ate, though to Kallik's relief it wasn't as thick a fog as the day before. She shifted her paws impatiently as she waited for Shila to make a decision.

Finally, Shila pointed ahead. "This way."

As they trudged across the ice, Kallik deliberately padded

alongside Lusa, half expecting the little black bear to need help.

"It's so amazing," Lusa began, "how you white bears can find your way across the ice when it's just . . . white nothingness. I mean, we black bears steer by landmarks like rocks and trees and bushes. But there's nothing like that here. Just ice and snow, and that's changing all the time."

"But there are loads of landmarks," Kallik protested. "There's the shape and color of the ice, and the feel of it. There are scents on the wind, and the sound the wind makes as it crosses the Melting Sea."

Lusa let out a little snort of laughter. "You mean like . . . that bit of ice," she began, pointing with one paw, "is different from that bit?" She paused for a moment and sniffed. "It all smells the same to me."

"Look," Kallik said, pointing in her turn. "The ice there has a greenish tinge, right? And over there it's white; that tells me that just there it's thicker. It's really easy when you know how. And as for scent . . . there's not only ice on the wind. There's . . ." She raised her snout and took in a long sniff, then froze with horror. "I smell bears!" she exclaimed. "It's Taqqiq!"

Spinning around, Kallik peered back the way they had come, to see several white bears in the distance, their shapes almost hidden in the mist. "Salik and his friends are following us," she reported tersely.

"Keep walking," Toklo said, with a glance back to confirm what Kallik said. "They know we know they're there, but we can't do anything about it while they're so far away."

"But we could be leading them straight to my family," Shila objected.

"That's a risk we have to take," Toklo replied.

As Toklo spoke, Kallik noticed that Yakone was bracing himself, ready for a fight. *I can't believe how lucky we are to have him on our side,* she thought. *He's never even met the bears from the Melting Sea before, but already he's willing to fight for them.*

Picking up the pace a little, they headed onward across the ice. Though they passed seal holes, no bear suggested stopping to hunt; they didn't want Salik and the others to catch up with them.

The hazy sun was rising toward midday when Kallik spotted more white shapes through the mist. As they drew closer, she made out two young females: One was crouching motionless beside a seal hole, while the other stood a little way off, alert as if she was on guard.

When she saw Kallik and her friends approaching, she strode over to meet them, her eyes glaring hostility. But then her gaze flickered into confusion as she spotted Toklo and Lusa.

"Get off the ice!" she snarled. "There's not even enough food for white bears here."

"It's okay, they're with me," Shila said, shouldering her way to the front of the group. "Have you seen Sakari and her cubs?"

"Yes, they were over there," the she-bear replied, jerking her muzzle in the direction the bears had been traveling.

"Oh, thank the spirits!" Shila exclaimed, her voice full of relief. "And thank you. I was afraid I'd never find them."

The she-bear let out a dismissive snort. "Now let us hunt in peace!"

"She's so angry!" Kallik murmured as she and her companions padded on.

"It's because the ice is melting too soon," Shila told her. "Burn-sky hasn't even started yet, and we're already hungry."

Poor Taqqiq, Kallik thought, though she said nothing out loud. *He made the long journey back from Great Bear Lake, but even the Melting Sea can't look after him.*

The journey continued until every bear was stumbling from tiredness. Kallik was wondering whether she should ask for a rest when Shila halted, her muzzle raised.

"I can smell something!" she announced.

Hesitating briefly to sniff the air again, she ran across the ice and dived into a pile of ravaged snow. For a moment she burrowed into it, throwing up a fountain of glittering crystals, then stood still and turned back toward Kallik and the others.

"My family was here," she said hoarsely. "But the den's destroyed . . . smashed up. And my family is gone!" She staggered as the full shock of her discovery hit her like a blow from a falling rock.

Kallik padded up to her, averting her eyes in horror as she spotted streaks of blood on the snow.

"My little brothers . . ." Shila whispered. "I can still scent them."

"We need to dig right down," Yakone said, coming to join them. "Just to be sure that they're not here."

"Good idea," Toklo grunted.

All the bears, even Lusa, began scraping at the mound of snow. As Kallik dug, she was aware that the scent of bears was growing stronger, and she uncovered a scrap or two of white fur. But there was no sign of Sakari, Pakak, or Tonraq.

Kallik's heart lurched. *Maybe we will find Sakari and the cubs here . . . dead and buried under the snow.* Panic and horror were building up inside her until she felt she was going to burst. *Why must bears keep dying?*

As Kallik went on digging, she heard pawsteps on the ice and looked up to see that Salik and his friends had appeared and were watching from a distance.

"Looking for something?" Iqaluk sneered.

Shila scrambled out of the heap of snow. Letting out a furious growl, she flung herself on Salik. "You killed my family!"

Instantly the white bears swarmed around Shila, pummeling her away from Salik. Kallik let out a cry of protest and heard Lusa gasp in horror. Toklo started forward, but Iqaluk and one of the others turned on him and forced him back, growling and raking at him with their claws.

Salik and the rest of the gang struck at Shila with heavy blows of their paws, sending her flying through the air. She landed on the ice with a yelp, and the bears loomed over her, snarling.

For a moment Kallik stared in disbelief. *What kind of bear has Taqqiq become?*

A red mist descended over Kallik's eyes, and her fury erupted. Racing across the ice, she flung herself on Taqqiq; her brother staggered backward, barely keeping his balance.

"Murderer!" Kallik snarled, her muzzle a paw's width from his eyes. "I wish I'd never found you again! I searched for so long, I never stopped thinking about you, but I'm ashamed that you're my brother. Cub-killer!"

Striking out with her forepaws, she raked her claws across Taqqiq's shoulders and tried to bury her teeth in his throat. Taken by surprise, Taqqiq struggled to fight back, snapping at the air.

Kallik was dimly aware that Taqqiq's friends were standing around, but they didn't interfere in the fight.

"Wow, what a dangerous bear!" Salik's tone was heavy with sarcasm. "You've got a hard job there, Taqqiq."

"Yeah, protect us from that crazy bear," Iqaluk added. "We're trembling in our fur."

"No wonder you left her and came back to us," Manik said.

Kallik hardly noticed Taqqiq's attempts to bite her. "What would our mother think?" she growled. "Nisa's spirit is stuck up there in the sky, watching you, and she must hate you just as much as I do!"

Taqqiq sank down onto the ice; blood from his shoulder where Kallik had scraped him trickled down and spread into the snow. Kallik was dimly aware that Yakone had thrust himself between her and her brother, while Toklo was nudging her away.

"You've made your point," Toklo said. "Now leave him."

Kallik turned away from Toklo. She didn't try to attack Taqqiq again but stood gazing at him, trying to put all her hatred and contempt into her gaze. "I wish you were dead!" she hissed.

CHAPTER NINETEEN

Toklo

Toklo was shocked by Kallik's strength and the force of her rage. Stepping up to her again, he nudged her away from Taqqiq, over to where Shila and Lusa were standing, watching with huge, horrified eyes. Shila was holding one paw off the ice, injured from where she had been thrown by the other bears.

"He deserves to die," Kallik muttered, though she didn't resist Toklo anymore as he moved her away from her brother.

Toklo and the others huddled together as the young males ambled away; apart from Taqqiq, who was still dripping blood as he went, they didn't look at all upset.

Once they had faded into the mist, Toklo turned back to his companions. Evaluating Shila's injuries, he guessed she had wrenched her shoulder and found it painful to put her paw to the ground. But worse than that was the stunned shock in her eyes.

"Sakari . . . Pakak . . . Tonraq . . ." she whispered. "Those bears killed them all."

When Toklo turned his attention to Kallik, he saw that she

wasn't badly hurt. Her white pelt was spattered with blood, but most of it was Taqqiq's. The only injury he could see was that one of her front claws had been ripped out, probably caught in Taqqiq's pelt.

Toklo's heart ached for his friend. *Her hopes were so high when she was looking for Taqqiq. Now she's found him, and all it's brought her is more pain.*

As he was gathering himself to lead his companions away, a quiet voice spoke behind him. "I didn't kill any bears. That's . . . that's not what we do."

Toklo spun around to find himself face-to-face with Taqqiq, who limped up to him and stood with his head bowed. Blood still oozed from his shoulder, and one eye was swollen shut.

Kallik was glaring at her brother. "I don't believe you!" she snapped. "Get away from us."

Taqqiq didn't move. "Please, don't think I'm a murderer," he begged. "Okay, we've caused trouble—destroying dens and chasing other bears away from their prey—but that's just because there's so little food, and not enough ice."

"Oh, sure!" Kallik growled sarcastically. "So that makes it all okay!"

"How would you like it if some bear stole *your* prey?" Toklo demanded.

Taqqiq hung his head. "We didn't kill any bears," he insisted, obviously taken aback that he hadn't been forgiven right away. "Please don't hate me. I can't stand it."

Kallik took a pace backward; her gaze was full of pain, but her voice still sounded as cold as the ice. "I don't know you," she said. "You are not my brother! I should have realized that at Great Bear Lake."

The silence dragged out. Toklo wanted to claw Taqqiq's ears off for hurting Kallik, and for all the trouble he had caused, but he kept his paws fixed to the ice.

At last Taqqiq turned to Shila. "I think I know where your family is," he told her. "They ran away when we attacked the den."

Shila drew in her breath in a rough gasp, gazing at Taqqiq as if she wanted to believe him but didn't dare.

"I know which way they went," Taqqiq added. "I'll help you find them."

"No, you won't," Toklo growled, taking a step forward. "Go away. We don't want anything from you."

"No—no, wait." Shila pushed her way past Toklo to stand facing Taqqiq. "Are you telling the truth?" she demanded.

Taqqiq nodded his battered head. "I am, I promise."

"Then prove it," Shila challenged him. "Take me to them."

Kallik gazed at Shila as if she could hardly believe what she had just heard. "You can't trust him!" she protested.

Shila turned her head and gave Kallik a sorrowful look. "What choice do I have?" she asked. "If he's lying, I'll just have to start searching again."

"Okay," Toklo said decisively. "We'll come with you," he told Taqqiq, "but put one paw wrong and I'll scatter your guts from here to the Endless Ice."

Shila turned and limped away beside Taqqiq.

Toklo gathered the others together with a jerk of his head

and trudged after them. He doubted they were ever going to find one little den in all that empty, snowy space. *I just hope Taqqiq really is ashamed of what he did and isn't leading us into a trap.*

As they plodded along, Toklo stayed alert, stretching all his senses to spot bears creeping up on them through the mist. He saw that Kallik was keeping well away from her brother, still looking very upset. Yakone padded close beside her, his concern clear in the gentle looks he gave her and the way he was talking quietly to her, his words inaudible to Toklo.

When they set off, Lusa had refused to ride on any bear's back, and was trudging sturdily along, but Toklo could tell she was exhausted. The injured Shila was just as bad, stumbling as she forced her paws across the ice.

Toklo halted. "This is ridiculous," he asserted. "We're all so tired we can hardly shift our paws. We have to stop and rest."

"I can't," Shila protested. "My family needs me."

"What help do you think you can be to them if you fall over from exhaustion?" Toklo asked.

Shila held his gaze for a moment more, then reluctantly nodded. "Okay."

"Hey, there's a seal hole over there!" Yakone pointed with his snout. "We can rest here, and Kallik and I will hunt."

"Good idea," Kallik agreed at once. "Come on, Yakone. You others, keep back."

She and Yakone padded over to the seal hole and crouched down beside it to wait for a seal to appear. Meanwhile, Toklo helped Shila to settle with her weight off her injured leg, and flopped down in the snow beside her. After a moment, Taqqiq limped across and sat beside them.

"So, Kallik's replaced me with a new brother," he growled with an unfriendly look at Yakone.

Toklo guessed that Taqqiq felt threatened by the presence of another male white bear in their group. "Er . . . no," he said. "I don't think Yakone wants to be Kallik's brother."

Taqqiq's eyes widened. He made no comment, but hostility was rising from him as clearly as mist from the surface of a lake. "So," he went on after a few heartbeats' silence, "what happened to the weird little brown bear that was with you—what's his name—Ujurak? Did you finally get tired of following him around?"

Fury started to swell up inside Toklo, and it took all his self-control to stop himself from giving Taqqiq a blow across the ear. "Ujurak's dead," he snapped.

"Oh . . . sorry." Taqqiq blinked in embarrassment, as if that was the last thing he had expected to hear. "I didn't know, or I'd never—"

A yelp of alarm from Kallik cut off his words. Whipping his head around, Toklo saw that Kallik had lunged for a rising seal. But as she moved, the ice around the seal hole crumbled away under her weight. Frozen with shock, Toklo watched as Kallik scrabbled vainly at the disintegrating edge of the hole. Yakone grabbed for her, but he was too late, and Kallik, still struggling, slipped down into the sea.

CHAPTER TWENTY

Kallik

As Kallik plunged down into the water, she tried to push with her paws and thrust herself back up again. But somehow her body wouldn't obey her. *I'm a strong swimmer,* she tried to tell herself. But panic was shrieking inside her head.

All she could think of was that Nisa had died in these waters. Now Kallik was certain that an orca was surging toward her from behind, its jaws gaping to tear her flesh.

Still she couldn't move. Black spots bloomed in front of her eyes, and the pale smudge of light that showed her where the seal hole was seemed to dwindle and fade with every heartbeat. She was sinking to the bottom; above her was only the ice, translucent and suffocating.

A shape swirled in the distance, heading toward her. *It is an orca!* Kallik felt a moment of pure despair.

Then she realized that another bear was in the water beside her. At first she thought it was Ujurak in white bear shape, and listened for his voice inside her head. But as her panic eased, she recognized who it really was.

Taqqiq! He dived in to save me!

Taqqiq's body pressed against Kallik's, urging her up toward the surface. Her fear ebbed as she realized she wasn't alone, and she began to swim, pushing herself upward through the water.

Kallik's head broke the surface, and she gasped in air. Behind her, Taqqiq gave her an enormous shove, boosting her over the edge of the ice, where she lay panting. When Taqqiq tried to pull himself out of the hole, the edge started to crumble away again; Yakone leaned over and grabbed him by the scruff of the neck, helping him to haul himself to safety.

"Are you okay?" Yakone asked Kallik anxiously.

Kallik nodded, but most of her attention was for Taqqiq. "I remembered how our mother died," she whispered. "It was like I couldn't move down there."

Taqqiq nodded jerkily. "I feel her here, too," he responded, his eyes sad as he leaned forward to touch his nose to Kallik's. "And when I saw you fall through the hole . . . it was like I was losing you all over again."

"And you saved me," Kallik murmured. "Thank you, Taqqiq."

"I couldn't stand it if you died, too," Taqqiq told her. "You're the only family I have."

A sea of emotions surged inside Kallik. *Taqqiq's my brother. He saved me—but he stays with Salik and those other fish-breaths.* "I know Nisa watches over me," she murmured. "She watches over you, too."

"I know she'd hate to see how I live," Taqqiq admitted. "But

I have no choice. You saw how the ice cracked beside that seal hole," he added defensively. "It's breaking up sooner than it ought to. That's why they—why we—felt we had to claim the territory. There's not going to be enough ice for every bear."

"But that's no excuse," Kallik growled, determined not to let Taqqiq get away with justifying what he had done. "There is *no* reason for terrifying these bears." She paused, pinning Taqqiq with her gaze until he looked away. "You're going to help us put things right," Kallik went on. "First by helping us to find Shila's family."

Taqqiq nodded. "I will, I promise," he said.

CHAPTER TWENTY-ONE

Lusa

Lusa padded across the forest floor. Sunshine angled through the branches of tall, leafy trees, and delicious fruit dangled from vines in front of her watering jaws. She enjoyed the feeling of good, warm dirt under her paws.

This is great, she thought. *So why are my paws and my nose freezing?*

Opening her eyes, Lusa let out a long sigh of resignation, wishing that the dream could continue. But the warmth and the scents of fruit vanished as she woke fully. Instead of wandering through the sunlit forest, she was still stuck on the ice, which was creaking alarmingly around her. Even the white bears were looking worried.

"Come on," Kallik said. "It's time to get moving."

The air was gray and misty; Lusa needed a moment before she realized that dawn was breaking. The night before, after Kallik's plunge into the seal hole, they had huddled together on the ice to sleep. But as Lusa rose to her paws, she still felt exhausted, her muscles aching, and she guessed that the others were suffering in the same way.

As they started off, Lusa noticed that Taqqiq looked especially tired, haunted, and sad. But she found it hard to feel sympathetic. *It's great that he saved Kallik yesterday, but I can't forgive him for what he did to the other white bears. It's no excuse that he and his friends didn't have enough food.*

Lusa turned away from Taqqiq, not wanting to encourage him to talk to her. Shila clearly didn't trust him, either: She kept well away from him, on the other side of Toklo. The whole atmosphere was tense and anxious, and Lusa plodded along unhappily.

Before they had been walking for long, Lusa noticed that Taqqiq was moving very slowly across the ice, often stopping to look around. Lusa still couldn't see any landmarks, and wondered what Taqqiq had seen that needed studying so intently.

"Taqqiq, can't you hurry?" Kallik asked after a while.

Taqqiq turned to gaze at her. "You want me to get it right, don't you?" he snapped.

Kallik let out a hiss of annoyance but said no more. Part of Lusa was glad that Kallik was distracted from fussing over her for the time being.

As they followed Taqqiq, Lusa spotted some other white bears, watching their progress from a distance. She nudged Toklo. "Look over there."

Toklo followed her gaze, then let out a growl, alerting the others. They bunched more tightly together, though the other bears didn't make any attempt to come closer.

"They look like a mother bear and two cubs," Yakone

pointed out. "Shila, are they . . . ?"

"No," Shila said with a sad shake of her head. "Those cubs are too old to be Pakak and Tonraq."

Even though they left the strange bears behind them, Lusa couldn't shake off the feeling of being watched. She stuck close to Toklo as she slipped and slid over the rutted ice.

We've been walking for ages, she thought, trying not to think about how sore her paws were. *Shila's limping even more from that shoulder injury, and my belly's aching.* Lusa thought longingly of the lush forest of her dream, with plenty of fruit and leaves for the picking. But all around her stretched the misty, inhospitable ice.

After another long time of trekking with no end in view, Taqqiq paused. Ahead, the ice had broken apart, leaving a broad stretch of open water. Lusa's heart sank at the prospect of having to swim again.

I've almost forgotten what it's like to be warm!

But instead of launching himself into the water, Taqqiq veered aside, heading along the edge of the ice.

"Are you sure we shouldn't go straight across?" Kallik challenged him.

Taqqiq turned to look at her. "I don't think so."

Kallik snorted. Lusa could tell she suspected that the ice was changing all the time, and Taqqiq wasn't certain anymore of where he was going.

"We're lost!" Shila exclaimed, her forepaws clawing against the ice. "I'll never see my family again!"

"Taqqiq, you promised!" Kallik hissed. "So get on with it."

"I'm doing my best!" Taqqiq snapped back at her.

While the others bickered about which way to go, Lusa flopped down on the ice, taking the chance for a brief rest. The ice creaked and gurgled beneath her, and she put her ear to it, listening.

Are those the spirits Kallik talks about? Weird! Lusa felt glad that her own ancestors were encased in warm, living trees.

The other bears were still arguing, so Lusa went on listening to the murmurs. Then she heard a faint scratching sound, like pawsteps. *Do spirits walk around inside the ice?* Lusa wondered. *There it is again.*

Lusa sat up and looked around. A little way off she spotted a pile of snow. For a moment she watched it thoughtfully. *I'm pretty sure spirits* don't *move around in the ice,* she decided. *Bear spirits don't move around in their trees, after all.*

Determinedly she rose to her paws and went to investigate the snow pile. Sniffing around, she found a hole; warm bear scents drifted out of it, and tiny scrapes of paws came from inside.

Lusa paused, gathering her courage, then poked her nose into the hole.

Instantly, a furious growl erupted from inside the snow pile. "Get away from my cubs!"

A she-bear leaped out, sending Lusa tumbling back onto the ice. Lusa braced herself for attack, only to see the she-bear halt as she loomed over her with one paw extended for a blow.

"What are *you?*" she asked, her eyes stretching wide in astonishment.

"I—I'm Lusa," Lusa stammered. "I'm a black bear."

The other bears were gathering around, Toklo in the lead. Then Lusa heard a gasp from behind her.

"You found them!" Shila exclaimed, her voice full of joy.

The she-bear backed away from Lusa, jaws gaping. "Shila! Is it really you?" Her voice was happy and astounded all at once, as if she could hardly let herself believe what she was seeing.

"It really is," Shila replied, limping up to her mother and pressing herself closely to her side.

The snow pile heaved again, and two small cubs pushed their way into the open.

"Shila! Shila!" they squeaked.

"Pakak! Tonraq!" Shila lowered her head to touch noses with her brothers, who bounced around her, letting out squeals of excitement. They butted their foreheads into her fur and tried to scramble all over her, as if they couldn't wait to play with her again.

Lusa scrambled to her paws and shook snow off her pelt. A wave of satisfaction swept through her as she watched Shila's reunion with her family.

"I'd given up hope of seeing you again," Sakari told her daughter. "It's been so long. . . ."

"The ice broke up, and I was cut off," Shila explained. "I had to go to land, and some no-claws caught me and put me in a firebeast. It crashed, and these bears rescued me."

Sakari's wondering gaze turned to Lusa and her friends. Toklo stepped forward. "You've met Lusa," he said. "I'm

Toklo, and the white bears are Kallik and Yakone."

Sakari dipped her head to them. "Thank you for saving my daughter and bringing her back to me." Then the joy faded from her face as she realized there was one bear Toklo had not introduced. "I know him," she growled, glaring at Taqqiq. "He's one of the bears who destroyed my den and stole the seal I caught." Bristling with hostility, she turned back to Toklo. "What's going on?" she demanded. "Is this a trap?"

It was Kallik who replied. "This is my brother, Taqqiq. He brought us here. He's sorry for what he did, and he wants to help."

"But it was Lusa who found you in the end," Toklo put in.

Sakari glanced from Kallik to Taqqiq and back again. Lusa could see she was still very suspicious. "Those bears caused so much trouble," she said.

Taqqiq did not respond, only stood a little way off, staring at Sakari sullenly.

Sakari pointedly turned her back on him. "Where is your family?" she asked Kallik.

"Taqqiq is the only family I have," Kallik explained. "My mother, Nisa, died saving me from orca."

Sakari drew in her breath sharply. "You're young to be out on your own," she said.

Kallik exchanged a wry glance with Lusa, who could read her friend's thoughts. *If only Sakari knew how far we've traveled!*

"I knew your mother, Nisa, when we were young," Sakari went on. "It grieves me to hear that she has gone to join the spirits."

Lusa felt a stab of sadness that she would never meet bears who had known her family. Ashia and King were so far away from the wild, in the Bear Bowl. *Kallik has come home, but I'll never be able to do the same.*

While her mother talked with Kallik and the others, Shila had been poking around the collapsed den. "There's hardly room enough for one bear in here, let alone three!" she exclaimed. "We need to build it up again."

Sakari shook her head, gently stopping her daughter with a paw on her shoulder. "There's no point," she said. "No she-bears build dens for their cubs anymore, because it gives away where they are. You know, to *his* friends," she added with a nod toward Taqqiq.

"That's terrible!" Shila's voice was full of dismay. "So you have to live in ruins?"

"I'll do anything to keep my cubs safe," Sakari told her.

Kallik stepped forward. "Well, that's going to change," she asserted. "Taqqiq, you have to tell those bears they can't keep doing this. They can't terrorize other bears!"

"I've already told you!" Taqqiq's anger flared up, though Lusa thought she could make out a trace of fear in his voice. "I can't change what they do. They think they have good reason for chasing bears away from their prey. How do you think I can stop them?"

"That's enough!" Toklo snarled at Taqqiq. "You're not even going to *try* to protect other bears from your friends, are you?"

"What can I do?" Taqqiq repeated, bristling as he faced the brown bear. "They think they're right to challenge other bears. Even if I was willing to fight them, they outnumber you and your friends."

"Hang on." Lusa felt a twinge of excitement as an idea struck her. "What if they didn't outnumber us?" Turning to Shila, she went on, "Didn't you say that Salik and his bears were bullying and harassing all the bears around here? What if they banded together to stand up for themselves and one another?"

Shila shook her head doubtfully. "It would never work. White bears are solitary. They don't meet up like that."

Yakone padded up to stand beside Lusa. "The white bears where I come from live and work together as a group," he told Shila. "I know the bears here don't, but it's possible."

"Yakone is right," Toklo agreed. "When they have to, any bear can find the will to fight in the best way to make sure they survive."

"But the ice is breaking up too fast," Taqqiq argued. "The hunting grounds are shrinking, and that forces the white bears to fight over the seals. There's no way around it. Every bear faces starvation once they have to go onto the land, so we have to eat while we're here on the ice!"

"No," Kallik said decisively. "That's not true. There's another way for white bears to survive when the ice melts. I've learned to use brown bear hunting skills to catch prey on land. When the ice melts, you can all do the same. Toklo can teach you."

"Yes," Lusa put in, her excitement growing. "And I'll show you how to find bark and leaves that you can eat. We did it for

Akna; we can help you, too!"

"And if you're going to band together to stand up to Salik," Kallik went on, "Toklo can teach you how to fight, too."

"We *know* how to fight, thanks," Taqqiq said brusquely.

Kallik turned to give her brother a hard stare. "It hasn't done you much good so far, has it?"

"And brown bears fight in a different way," Lusa added, gazing around at all the white bears. Optimism was flooding through her from her ears to the tips of her claws. "If Toklo teaches you that, you'll be able to beat Salik and his gang, because you'll have tricks they won't be expecting." She turned to where the brown bear was standing in silence. "What do you think, Toklo?"

CHAPTER TWENTY-TWO

Toklo

Toklo realized that every bear was staring at him. Kallik's and Lusa's eyes were shining trustingly, but the other bears looked more doubtful. He almost backed away from that intense regard.

Do I really hold all the answers for the white bears? It feels like a lot of responsibility—much more than just teaching Akna to stalk a snow hare.

Toklo's mind was whirling so much that he didn't want to make any promises. He remembered how Nanulak had tricked him into fighting on the Island of Shadows. *I could have killed Nanulak's father, and he'd never done anything wrong!* He knew that Salik and his friends' aggression had to be stopped, but he was still uncomfortable with the idea of teaching anything to the white bears—especially fighting.

"Let's just see what happens," he mumbled.

"I'm going to find a seal hole," Yakone announced. "Kallik, do you want to come and hunt with me?"

"Sure," Kallik replied, falling in beside the white male as he padded away.

"I'll look after the cubs if you and Shila want to hunt, too," Lusa offered to Sakari. Her eyes glimmered with amusement as she watched Pakak and Tonraq burrowing into the snow and leaping out at each other with mock growls.

Toklo saw that the mother bear was looking doubtful. "You can trust Lusa," he assured her. "She's good at taking care of cubs."

After another moment's hesitation, Sakari nodded. "Okay, thank you," she said to Lusa, and headed off with Shila.

"As for *you*—" Kallik halted as she passed Taqqiq, swinging around to face him threateningly. "Stay here at the den and start rebuilding it. And I'd better see some progress when I get back."

Toklo realized that even though Kallik had defended Taqqiq to Sakari, she was still furious with her brother.

Taqqiq was clearly fuming, but he just trudged resentfully over to the collapsed den and started to scrape at the snow. As Toklo watched him shove the heaps around, he felt a stab of sympathy for the white bear.

Hunger drives bears to do crazy things, he thought. *What Taqqiq and the others did was wrong, but I can't be sure I wouldn't have done something stupid, too, if I were starving.*

Turning away from Taqqiq, Toklo gazed around at the ice, hostile and white and creaking. He couldn't imagine wanting to live out here forever. *But then, I'm not a white bear.*

Tonraq and Pakak bounced up to Lusa, their eyes wide with curiosity as they stared up at her.

"You're a funny color," Pakak said.

"Yes, we've never seen a bear like you before," his brother added.

"Well, where I come from, there are lots of bears like me," Lusa told them, with an amused glance at Toklo.

The little cubs gave her an interested sniff, then seemed to accept what she said. "Are we going to fight the bad bears?" Tonraq asked.

"You're not," Lusa told them. "You're too little. But the rest of us—yes, we're ready to fight."

"We're not too little!" Tonraq protested.

"We want to fight now!" Pakak agreed. "We're *fierce*!"

Lusa exchanged another glance with Toklo. "Okay, I'll teach you a move or two," she said, adding in a lower voice to Toklo, "If things go badly, they might need to defend themselves."

Toklo didn't think there was much hope for the cubs if Salik and his bears won the fight, but he didn't say so. He settled down to watch as Lusa began to teach the cubs.

"The first thing you need to learn," Lusa began, "is how to dodge your enemy. You have to watch very carefully so you know which side the first blow is coming from." She pointed with her snout at Tonraq. "Run at me and try to hit me."

The little cub gave a bounce of excitement and then dashed straight at Lusa. Toklo could see that he was signaling quite clearly with the curve of his body and the direction of his gaze which paw he would strike with. Lusa sidestepped quickly so the blow never landed.

"You moved!" Tonraq protested.

"Yes, that's the point," Lusa said with a huff of laughter. "You'll soon get the idea. Pakak, now you try."

Pakak had learned from watching his brother, and Toklo could tell that he was trying to hide his intentions as he charged at Lusa, but she was still able to dodge.

"Now I'll show you," she went on.

As she ran at the cubs, feinting before striking out at them—though she checked herself before her blow could fall—Toklo realized that she was copying moves he always used. *Has she really learned how to fight from watching me?* She was using her weight in the same way that he did, and balancing in the same way to give herself the best use of her forepaws. *She almost looks like a brown bear!*

"You need to remember white bears are bigger than you," he called out to Lusa. "Try diving in *under* the blow and attacking that way."

"Thanks, Toklo!" Lusa responded.

"We can do that!" Tonraq squealed. "We're *really* small!"

Both of the cubs at once rushed at Lusa, who staggered backward, her paws slipping on the ice.

"You're a big white bear!" Pakak growled. "We're going to *get* you!"

Suppressing laughter, Toklo thought it was just as well that the hunters returned at that moment. Kallik and Yakone were dragging a seal, while Sakari had a huge fish clamped in her jaws. As soon as the cubs saw their mother, they bounded over to her, and Lusa was able to get up, shaking snow off her pelt.

"Save me from the fierce little bears!" she laughed.

That night, Toklo found it hard to sleep. However he lay down, there seemed to be a hard lump of snow or a spike of ice underneath him. He tossed and turned but couldn't get comfortable.

I guess I'd be okay teaching the white bears how to hunt on land. But there's so much they need to learn.

"Hey, you're squishing me!" Lusa complained.

"Sorry," Toklo grunted.

He rested his nose on his paws and forced himself to stay still, resigning himself to a sleepless night.

The next thing he knew, Toklo found himself in a sunlit forest clearing. Something about the way the trees grew seemed familiar, and so was the gurgling of the stream that ran along in front of his paws.

A rustling in the undergrowth made Toklo draw back into the shade of a clump of bushes. A moment later a brown bear cub emerged into the open, followed by a smaller cub. It took a couple of heartbeats for Toklo to recognize himself and Ujurak.

I look so young!

Ujurak was gazing happily around the clearing, following the flight of a butterfly and jumping up in a vain attempt to catch it.

"Concentrate!" Young Toklo growled. "I'm supposed to be teaching you stuff."

"Okay." Ujurak looked up expectantly.

"You have to keep your claws sharp," Young Toklo told him. "You do it by scratching a tree, like this." He stood on his hindpaws and scored his claws down the bark of the nearest tree. "Now you try."

Ujurak tottered a bit as he got up on his hindpaws, but he clawed vigorously at the bark, and Young Toklo gave him an approving nod. "When you're a full-grown bear," he went on, "you'll mark your territory like this, by making clawmarks on the trees."

I remember this, Toklo thought. *It was soon after I met Ujurak. We didn't have Lusa or Kallik with us then.*

"Okay," Young Toklo said. "Are you hungry?"

"Starving!"

"Then we'll catch a salmon. Do you remember what I told you last time?"

Ujurak nodded. "We stand in the water and wait."

"Right. Let's do it."

Toklo watched as both cubs waded into the stream and stood facing upstream, concentrating hard on the glittering water.

"Remember to pounce on the fish where it's going to be, not where it is," Young Toklo said.

"But how do I know that?" Ujurak asked.

"You watch the direction it's moving," Young Toklo explained patiently. "It takes practice, but you'll soon get the idea."

Suddenly Ujurak gave a bound, as if he had spotted a fish.

But as he leaped he changed, his body shrinking, his brown fur giving way to glittering scales, until he plunged back into the water as a salmon.

Young Toklo let out a groan. "Oh, no! Not again!" He waded over to a rock in the middle of the stream and clambered onto it. "Ujurak!" he bellowed.

Toklo stifled a snort of amusement, remembering how irritated he'd been. A few moments later the foliage overhanging the stream rustled wildly and Ujurak emerged, dripping wet, his fur plastered to his body. "Sorry," he said.

Young Toklo gave an exasperated sigh. "Honestly, Ujurak, you deserve to be caught and eaten, the way you go on." As the younger cub looked dejected, he added, "Never mind. Come over here, and we'll try again."

As his younger self slid back into the water, to meet Ujurak in the middle of the stream, Toklo heard a voice behind him. "You were an excellent teacher."

Toklo turned away from his dream vision. Though he still stood on the edge of the clearing, the older Ujurak had appeared among the bushes. Stars glimmered in his fur, and his eyes were warm and loving. For a moment the longing for the past, when Ujurak was alive and by his side, rose up and almost choked Toklo. He couldn't speak.

"You saved me," Ujurak said. "I didn't know who I was, and you taught me how to be a brown bear. You can help these white bears, too."

Toklo blinked in surprise. "But you were always a brown bear." When Ujurak didn't respond, he went on, "It's not the same, teaching brown bear skills to other bears," he confessed. "You said we had to learn to be truly wild," he reminded Ujurak. "Surely that means being true to our own nature?"

For a few moments Ujurak was quiet, his eyes deep and reflective. At last he said, "Let's walk."

At first the two bears padded side by side through the trees. But soon Ujurak picked up the pace until they were racing along. Then Toklo realized that his paws had left the ground. The trees dropped away beneath him. With a thrill of terror and excitement he mounted higher and higher into the sky; the sun had gone and stars glittered around him, blazing with an icy fire against the darkness of the night. Faster and faster, until he and Ujurak were pounding along, the wind rushing through their pelts.

At last Ujurak halted. Toklo found himself standing on the air, gazing down at a remote view of the world. The flat-face invasion was revealed in vast tracts of bright light, joined by hot BlackPaths where firebeasts crawled, their glaring eyes shining like beetles. The noise seemed to blast Toklo's fur and ears, even at such a great distance. The dark patches that indicated the unspoiled wild were pitifully small; Toklo imagined they were shrinking as he watched.

"Wildness is a rare and precious thing now," Ujurak said softly. "All bears must hold on to it, even if that means sharing the wildness of other bears. Or it will be lost like water running into sand." He touched Toklo's shoulder affectionately with his muzzle. "Sharing skills is a way to survive in spite of the flat-faces. Your spirits can be strong if you stand together."

Toklo gazed in astonishment as Ujurak's starry body swelled until it filled the sky. Then his bear shape faded, leaving Toklo standing alone beside the flaring stars of his friend's constellation. Air was rushing all around him.

I'm falling!

A jolt ran through Toklo's body; he opened his eyes and found himself in the rebuilt den. An icy wind was blowing through a gap in the wall, ruffling his fur. Toklo gathered together a pawful of snow and shoved it into the hole.

That fish-breath Taqqiq can't even build a decent den! he thought irritably.

Around him, the other bears were just beginning to stir. Toklo let his gaze travel over each one of them. *Yes, I can help you,* he decided.

"I'm going to find more bears who will help us against Salik," Sakari announced when all the bears had emerged from the den. She padded off in the pale dawn light, new energy in her pawsteps and the set of her shoulders.

"The rest of us had better hunt," Kallik said when she had gone. "Lusa, will you look after the cubs again?"

"I'll be glad to," Lusa replied, while Tonraq and Pakak let out squeaks of excitement. "Just come back quickly, before I end up as a few bits of black fur!"

Toklo joined the hunters, striding out confidently across the ice. He had spent so much time here, he had hunted seals so many times, that he knew he could do this.

Kallik taught me well, just as I taught her.

Spotting a seal hole in the distance, Toklo padded up to it

and crouched at the edge of the ice. As he waited, the ice rumbled and creaked in his ears, sending tingles of alarm through his fur.

Time isn't on our side, he thought. *How long before we're forced back onto land?*

At last a seal nose emerged from the water. Toklo flashed out a paw, sinking his claws into the seal and hauling it out onto the ice, where it flopped helplessly until he killed it with a blow to the head.

"Good catch," said a voice close behind him.

Toklo whipped around to see two white males standing a bearlength away, watching him closely. For a moment Toklo tensed, wondering if they were about to steal his catch, then relaxed as the bigger of the two dipped his head and spoke.

"Hi. I'm Tartok, and this is my brother, Olikpok. Sakari told us about the brown bear who's going to teach us how to fight and hunt on land. That's you, right?"

Toklo nodded. "Yes, that's me."

Tartok let out a snort. "I told Sakari I'd come, but I still think she's cloud-brained." His voice was defiant, and he raised his head proudly. "We don't need any help. Generations of white bears have survived without hunting on land. What's so different now?"

Olikpok shook his head. "The Melting Sea doesn't want us anymore," he said despairingly. "So what's the point of anything?"

Toklo was taken aback at the white bears' lack of energy. Then he realized that it must be so difficult for them to accept that things were changing.

"I can't argue with you," he said. "I don't belong here the way you do. But I'll teach you what I know, and it might help."

"Well . . . I guess we can give it a try," Tartok grunted.

Hauling his seal along, Toklo returned to the den, followed by Tartok and Olikpok. As he approached, he realized that several other bears had gathered there. He recognized the she-bear and her cubs who had watched them as they crossed the ice.

"I only came because you asked me to," the mother bear was telling Sakari as Toklo padded up. "But I really don't think we'll be able to fight off Salik and his bears. They're so strong!"

There was a murmur of agreement from some of the others.

"I think we should move on," a younger she-bear suggested. "I've heard there are other places where the ice doesn't melt so quickly, and there aren't as many bears competing for prey."

"Try it if you like, Nukka," Olikpok told her. "But how do you know Salik wouldn't follow us?"

Tartok gave his brother a shove. "You're always moaning, Olikpok! *I'm* all for fighting off Salik, but I don't see why we need a brown bear to tell us how to do it."

Toklo saw some of the other bears nodding, as if they agreed with Tartok. *If you can fight off Salik, why haven't you done it already?* he wondered. He narrowly avoided speaking the words aloud. Instead, he said, "I'm not trying to tell any bear what to do. But my friends and I have had experience—"

"You're not even a white bear," an older white male interrupted. "What do you know?"

"Yeah," Tartok growled. "Why do you get to boss us around?"

Toklo glared at Tartok. *A few heartbeats ago, you agreed to give it a try. Why are you changing your mind now?*

Before he could speak, Yakone stepped forward. "I know the bears I've traveled with are an odd group," he began, nodding at Toklo, Kallik, and Lusa, "but I've seen them fight off bears and other animals, and hunt together, and you wouldn't believe how successful they've been!"

"You're right: We wouldn't," Tartok muttered.

Toklo was surprised at Yakone's wholehearted support, and even more surprised when Shila squeezed through the crowd of bears to his side.

"I was inside a no-claw firebeast when it crashed and set the whole of a no-claw den on fire," she said. "Toklo and his friends worked together; they saved me and some other bears who were trapped inside the den. They've managed to do things no bear could manage on their own, and that's why we all need to listen to Toklo."

Toklo saw young Nukka nodding her head, and the mother of the cubs was looking interested, but some of the others were turning away.

"There's nothing for us here," Olikpok said.

"Wait!" To Toklo's astonishment, Taqqiq pushed his way into the center of the crowd and stood beside Toklo. "I was one of Salik's bears," he announced.

Growls of hostility rose from the group of bears. They hadn't recognized Taqqiq until now. The mother bear moved swiftly to place herself between Taqqiq and her cubs.

Taqqiq flinched, then seemed to brace himself. "You have to understand this," he said. "Salik and the others aren't anything special individually. It's only because they work together that they've been able to terrorize the rest of you. So it's only by working together that you'll be able to defeat them. And we need to do that before Toklo teaches you to hunt, so they don't come after that food, too."

He flashed a glance around the group, looking shamefaced and awkward, then sat down, his shoulders hunched as if he was trying to make himself inconspicuous.

Toklo wasn't sure that Taqqiq's words would change the mood of the gathering. But the bears who had been ready to leave were turning back, and even Tartok and the old male were looking less hostile.

"Okay," Tartok said at last. "So what do you want us to do?"

CHAPTER TWENTY-THREE

Kallik

Kallik watched, nervous and excited, while the white bears formed a ragged circle around Toklo. She gave Taqqiq a nod of gratitude as he shambled past her to take his place with the others. Lusa stayed on one side with Pakak and Tonraq, keeping them well away from the training session.

"What you need to remember," Toklo began, once the bears were in position, "is that Salik and the others think you're all scared of them. So the first thing in a fight is to show them that you're *not* scared. Growl. Bellow at them. Convince them that you're not going to back down."

Kallik could see a few of the bears exchanging doubtful glances, but Toklo went on before any of them could speak.

"Smaller bears can dart in, strike a blow, and dodge out of range again quickly." Toklo's gaze rested on the older cubs for a moment. "Salik and his group won't be nimble enough to follow you. But bigger bears can't do that. You have to rely on strength."

There were some murmurs of understanding at that. The

older cubs' eyes gleamed eagerly, as if they were imagining how they could strike back at Salik.

"When brown bears fight," Toklo went on, "we claw at each other's shoulders and try to sink our teeth into our enemy's throat. That means having a good grip on the ground with our hindpaws. It might not be so easy on the ice. On the other hand, it might be easier to knock your opponent off balance when it's slippery underpaw."

Kallik was surprised and proud at how confident Toklo sounded. She knew he sometimes doubted that he was strong enough or brave enough to take care of his friends. All the white bears were looking interested now, as if what Toklo was saying made sense to them.

"Another idea," Toklo continued, "is to try to push your opponent back to the edge of the ice, or into a seal hole. The edge might crumble away and pitch him into the water, and even if it doesn't, the thought that it might will make him nervous. And a nervous enemy is easily defeated."

"You're suggesting we kill them?" Sakari asked doubtfully. Kallik could tell that in spite of all the damage Salik and the others had done, she wasn't comfortable fighting her own kind to the death.

"No," Toklo explained. "But if your opponent falls into a hole, it will give you a break from fighting while they get out. And if one of their friends stops fighting to help them, that's *two* enemies you've dealt with."

"I think it's a great idea!" Nukka exclaimed. "Can we try it now?"

"In a moment," Toklo said. "There's one last thing I want to suggest. With all the bears we have here, we outnumber Salik and his gang. We need to practice with two bears joining together to fight one. Kallik and Yakone, will you help me show the others what I mean?"

Kallik stepped forward, her paws tingling with excitement. Yakone followed her.

"Okay," Toklo said. "Come at me."

He growled threateningly and raised himself up on his hindpaws. Kallik darted toward him, avoiding Toklo's sharp claws, which were groping for her shoulders, and slid underneath him. As Toklo staggered from her sudden onrush, she clawed at his belly, while Yakone jumped up onto Toklo's back, unbalancing him and sending him crashing to the ice.

"That'll do, thanks," Toklo said, his voice muffled by Yakone's fur.

As they broke apart and scrambled to their paws, a murmur of appreciation rose from the bears who surrounded them.

"That's cool!" one of the older cubs exclaimed.

"Okay, divide up and let's see you try," Toklo told them.

At once the bears split up into small groups, trying to copy what they had seen. Shila leaped up onto Nukka's back, digging her claws in and balancing as Nukka tried to throw her off.

"Come on, Olikpok!" Toklo roared. "Don't just stand there!"

Olikpok hesitated a moment longer, then jumped up, ramming his forepaws into Shila's side. Shila lost her balance and tumbled off Nukka to roll over on the ice. Together Nukka and Olikpok leaped on top of her, pinning her down.

"Get off!" she gasped. "You're squashing me!"

"That's great," Toklo praised them, as Olikpok and Nukka backed off, letting Shila scramble to her paws.

Kallik glanced over to where Taqqiq and Tartok were circling around Sakari, darting in to strike a blow at her and then leaping back before she could retaliate.

"Good," Toklo said, padding over to watch. "But when you're fighting for real, you'll have to hit harder than that."

"I *know*," Tartok growled. "But I don't want to hurt Sakari."

While Tartok's attention was distracted, Sakari leaped at him and dealt him a couple of hard blows around the head. Tartok paused, half-stunned, and Sakari swung around to face Taqqiq. The young male raised his paw to strike, only to lose his balance as Sakari ducked underneath the blow and swiped his paws out from under him.

"Good job, Sakari," Toklo told her. "Keep on like that, and Salik won't know what hit him."

Kallik could sense that instead of being doubtful, all the bears were becoming excited and more hopeful. Her own optimism brimmed over as she exchanged a glance with Toklo.

We might just be able to do this!

The sun was rising the following morning when Toklo roused the bears for another training session. Kallik looked on as he divided them into two opposing groups, with Tartok leading one and Shila the other.

"Tartok's one of our best fighters," Yakone commented, padding up to Kallik's side. "He's stubborn and defiant."

Kallik nodded. "I'm amazed by Shila," she said. "Her shoulder is still giving her trouble, but she's so cunning! She seems to know what her enemy will do before he knows it himself."

"Okay," Toklo called out when the bears had separated into their groups. "We're going to practice a battle. Tartok, you and your group can be Salik and his gang. Shila, you're defending your dens and your cubs."

"Got it," Shila said with an emphatic nod.

"Can we be in the battle?" Pakak rushed up to Toklo, with Tonraq hard on his paws. "We practiced all those moves with Lusa."

"No, you cannot." Lusa hurried up. "We'll watch from a safe distance." She herded both cubs away; they looked back over their shoulders with disappointed expressions.

While Toklo and Yakone were giving final instructions, Taqqiq broke away from his group and padded over to Kallik.

"I'm going to find Salik and the others," he announced. "I'll tell them that I've discovered Sakari's new den in their territory, and lead them over here, to where you're expecting them. If all goes well, we should be back tomorrow. I'll try to organize it so the attack comes at dawn."

"Have you discussed this with Toklo?" Kallik asked.

Taqqiq nodded. "He knows what I'm going to do."

I can't count the number of things that could go wrong, Kallik thought. She glanced around for Toklo, but he was busy watching the pretend battle.

"No, Olikpok!" he roared across the ice. "Stay on your paws! Use your claws!"

"What if something happens?" Kallik asked Taqqiq, anxiety welling up inside her. "It's been a few days now since you left Salik, and he must know that you're with us. What if he and his bears don't trust you anymore? Will you be safe?"

"I've left them before," Taqqiq reassured her. "Remember the time I came with you when you left Great Bear Lake? I've always gone back to them, and I've always been loyal. Why wouldn't they trust me now?"

"Very convincing." A voice spoke behind Kallik. "It makes me wonder if *we* should trust you. If you've always been loyal to Salik, Taqqiq . . . where do your loyalties lie now?"

Kallik turned to see that Shila had broken away from the battle and was gazing at Taqqiq with a challenging expression.

Taqqiq faced her. "I'll do what I say," he assured her. "I want peace on the Melting Sea."

Shila let out a faint snort. "You'd better come back," she warned him. "And you'd better be on our side."

As she watched them, Kallik was suddenly aware of some unspoken connection between Shila and Taqqiq, something that she couldn't understand. But this wasn't the time to ask them about it.

Taqqiq padded over to Shila and pressed the side of his face briefly against hers. Shila didn't respond, but Kallik could see uncertainty replacing the challenge in Shila's eyes.

"I will come back," Taqqiq promised, glancing from Shila to Kallik and back again. He backed away, then turned and began walking quickly in the direction they had first come from.

Kallik glanced at Shila, whose gaze was still fixed on Taqqiq, and wondered unhappily if they could really trust her brother.

I want to, but he's such a stranger to me now.

Standing beside Shila, she watched Taqqiq until he walked out of sight.

The mock battle was drawing to a close. "That was great!" Toklo called. "Remember everything you've learned when Salik turns up, and we'll show them!"

Kallik and Shila padded over to join the bears who were clustering around him; Lusa and the little cubs bounded over to their side.

"This is it," Toklo announced tersely. "We have to rest and eat well now, and prepare the den for the battle."

Kallik could sense the apprehension and excitement among the white bears as they exchanged glances, realizing that their great test was just ahead of them.

"I'll *gut* Salik," Tartok snarled. "And his bears. Or make them run so far and so fast their paws will wear away."

Toklo nodded. "I don't think any bear will need to worry about Salik after this."

"About the den," Sakari put in, gently nudging her excited cubs to one side so that she could approach Toklo. "Salik and his bears will be coming because they want to smash up our BirthDen. So maybe we should rebuild it properly. Otherwise they might guess that things have changed."

She has a point, Kallik thought, looking at the tumbledown den. Taqqiq had started to rebuild it, but he hadn't had time to finish. There were still gaps in the walls that let in the wind.

"We'll do that," Toklo agreed. "It's too bad we can't hide a few fierce bears in there, to jump out and drive Salik and his gang away."

Sakari shook her head doubtfully. "I can hide in there, but there's not enough room for another full-grown bear."

"Yes, there is!" Lusa exclaimed, her berry-bright eyes gleaming. "I can fit in there with Sakari."

Kallik drew in a gasp of dismay. "What are you thinking?" she asked Lusa. "It's far too dangerous! I won't allow it."

To her surprise, Lusa faced her determinedly. "Kallik, I'm not a cub, and you're not my mother. I've lasted this long. I helped hunt the bison, and I stood up to those two white bears when they attacked Akna's cubs. So why do you think I'll fail now?"

A gust of fear and regret shook Kallik like a storm wind. "I've let too many bad things happen to bears I care about," she whispered. "I abandoned Taqqiq, and my mother, and Nanuk. . . ."

"No, you didn't." Lusa's voice was sympathetic but firm. "What happened to them wasn't your fault. And you haven't abandoned me. You've kept me alive!" She hesitated, then went on, "But please, Kallik, don't try to stop me from helping. I can do this."

Kallik was still uncertain, but glancing at Toklo and

Yakone, she saw nothing but admiration for Lusa in their eyes. "All right," she sighed.

Once that was settled, Sakari and some of the others went to rebuild the den. The rest of the bears went back to training, while Yakone headed off to hunt, and Toklo padded around the area, finding places they could hide.

As night fell, they huddled on the ice. Kallik couldn't sleep and wondered how many of the others were awake, watching the stars as she was.

Ujurak, watch over us now, she begged silently.

Finally she drifted into sleep; no time at all seemed to have passed before she felt a paw prodding her in the shoulder. She opened her eyes to see Yakone.

"It's time," he murmured.

CHAPTER TWENTY-FOUR

Lusa

It was still dark when Sakari roused Lusa. The ice shimmered in starlight, and a soft breeze stirred loose snow on the surface.

"Come on," Sakari said. "We need to hide now."

As Lusa followed her toward the rebuilt BirthDen, the other bears were rousing around them. Toklo was in the center, directing them.

"Salik and the others should come from that direction," he began, pointing with one paw. "Olikpok, Nukka, head over there and keep a lookout for them. Warn us when you spot them, but make sure they don't see you."

The two bears nodded and padded off, side by side. Lusa thought they looked pleased to be chosen for an important job.

"The rest of you, hide," Toklo went on. "Tartok, I want you up close, ready to defend the BirthDen."

"Sure." Tartok headed for a pile of snow and crouched down behind it.

The rest of the bears looked for the deepest grooves in the

ice, or for other mounds of snow to hide behind. The mother bear lay flat on the ice while her cubs scraped snow over her.

"What about us?" Tonraq asked eagerly. "Where do we go?"

Lusa felt a stab of anxiety. In the BirthDen with Sakari, waiting for the attack, she wouldn't be able to look after the two little cubs.

"Over there," Toklo replied, pointing to a distant seal hole. "You're hunting for us today. We'll all be hungry after the battle."

"Great!" Pakak squealed as the two cubs scampered off across the ice.

Lusa was relieved. *They can't get into too much trouble watching beside a seal hole.*

She followed Sakari into the BirthDen and settled down beside her. Toklo appeared at the entrance, packing snow into the gap, leaving them in the dark warmth of the den. Lusa almost felt like a cub again, pressed against Sakari's side.

But I'm not a cub! I can fight!

The noises of the bears outside faded as they settled into their hiding places. Lusa heard a sharp bark from some bear, then silence. *That means they're all hiding and ready.*

Every moment dragged until Lusa was convinced that dawn must have come and gone and the sun would be climbing up the sky.

Maybe they're not coming, she thought worriedly. *Maybe they didn't believe Taqqiq. Or maybe he told them what's really happening, and they've gone to make trouble someplace else.*

Lusa was about to give up and wriggle out into the open

when she heard pawsteps outside the den. Some bear was sniffing around the entrance.

"They're in there." She recognized Salik's voice.

"Then let's get them out." That was Iqaluk. "Let's have some fun."

Lusa shivered as the rough, scornful voices surrounded her in the dark.

"Sakari needs to be taught a lesson." One of the other bears spoke, a voice Lusa couldn't put a name to. "We never said she could rebuild her den."

"Yeah," said Manik. "This time we should chase her and her cubs right off the Melting Sea."

"Salik, what are you doing here?" Lusa tensed as she heard Shila's voice, sounding young and vulnerable. "Why can't you leave us alone?"

"Oh, it's Shila!" Salik growled. "I thought we told you to get off our territory."

"It's *not* your territory." Though Shila's words were challenging, her voice was shaking. "We have as much right to be here as you do."

Manik let out a snort of contempt. "Strength and claws: That's what gives us the right. Where are yours?"

"And where are those weird bears you were going around with?" Iqaluk added. "I don't see them here."

If you only knew, Lusa thought, bracing her muscles, ready for the moment when the fight would begin.

"Yeah, did they leave you on your own?" Lusa's belly lurched as she heard Taqqiq's voice for the first time. It was sharp with hostility, nastier than any of the others. "You were stupid for trusting them!"

"Kallik's your sister, for the spirits' sake!" Shila went on. "Don't you have any idea what that should mean to you? Have you no loyalty?" She sounded nervous and full of dread; even though Lusa knew it was all pretense, she wanted to spring out and protect her.

Not yet. Wait . . .

"Just back off," Taqqiq hissed. "Or Salik will hurt you much worse than he did last time. I'm loyal to my friends. I can't believe you thought I would turn my back on them."

He sounds as if he means it, Lusa thought with an inward shiver. *Oh, Arcturus, which side will he fight on?*

"Enough talking!" Manik growled.

Pale dawn light spilled in on Lusa and Sakari as a massive paw swiped through the snow that blocked the entrance to the den. Lusa leaped up, her teeth bared and her claws extended, throwing herself upon Manik. He jumped back, howling with surprise.

Behind Lusa, Sakari hurtled out of the den. She barreled into Manik and sent him sprawling, then whirled to confront one of the other bears, roaring a challenge.

More roars answered her as the rest of the bears rose up out of the ice, galloping toward the knot of invading bears. Toklo and Tartok sprang out of hiding behind the snow mound and flung themselves on their enemies.

For a couple of heartbeats Salik and his bears stood frozen, as if they couldn't believe what they were seeing. Lusa briefly hoped they might flee without a fight. But then Salik let out a snarl of fury.

"Get them!"

Lusa found herself in the middle of a heaving mass of bears. After a moment of heart-stopping terror, she realized that she was so small the bigger bears ignored her. She was able to wriggle among their legs, clawing at her enemies and nipping at their paws. Now and then one of them would take a swipe at her, but she always managed to dodge.

The only danger is being trampled on!

Above her head Lusa could hear snarls and the heavy breathing of battling bears. Paws swished through the air. She caught a glimpse of Kallik facing an enemy bear, and the two older cubs darting in at Iqaluk, striking at him from both sides.

We're winning! she thought exultantly.

Then a heavy paw landed on her shoulder, throwing her to the ground. Claws sank into her flesh. "How dare you attack me?" Manik growled close to her ear.

Oh, spirits! Lusa thought. She struggled hard, her face pushed into the snow, but she couldn't dislodge Manik. The claws of his other forepaw raked down her side. She lashed out with her hindpaws and felt fierce satisfaction when Manik let out a sharp yelp of pain, but he still didn't let her go.

Then Lusa felt a jolt as another bear threw himself on Manik. She couldn't see, but she recognized Toklo's scent.

Thank you, Arcturus!

Manik's grip on her loosened, and Lusa could drag herself

free. She saw Toklo and Manik raised up on their hindpaws, gripping each other's shoulders as they swayed to and fro. Without hesitating, Lusa sprang up at Manik, fastening her claws into his back. He roared with rage and tried to throw her off, while Toklo got in a few hard blows to his head and shoulders. Manik dropped to all four paws and retreated, snarling.

"Great job, Lusa," Toklo panted.

"Thanks for helping," Lusa responded. "We make a good team."

Now Lusa found herself on the edge of the fighting. She spotted Nukka fighting together with Olikpok, driving one of Salik's bears back, pawstep by pawstep. Hearing a terrified yelping, she turned to see Iqaluk fleeing, pursued by Yakone. Tartok and the mother bear whose name she still didn't know had one of the others on the ground.

Where's Salik? she wondered. *And Taqqiq?*

As if in answer to her thought, Lusa heard a furious roaring. In the ruins of the BirthDen, Salik and Shila were grappling together. Though Shila fought bravely, Salik easily outmatched her in size and strength. His claws were fastened in her shoulders, and he was snapping his jaws perilously close to her throat. Shila battered at him with her forepaws, but the blows only seemed to enrage Salik more.

"I'll teach you to trap us!" he snarled.

"You're finished, Salik!" Shila gasped, but her struggles were growing weaker.

Toklo let out a growl and headed toward her, but before he

could reach the wrestling bears, a loud bellow sounded behind Lusa and Taqqiq hurtled past her, to throw himself on Salik. His claws scored down Salik's back; Lusa saw blood soaking into the enemy bear's white fur.

Salik let Shila go and tried to turn and strike out at Taqqiq. But his paws met empty air as Taqqiq clung close and kept on clawing him from behind. "Traitor!" Salik howled.

Shila took a pace back to recover herself, then sprang at Salik again and slammed her head into his belly.

Salik's attempts to fight back turned into struggles to escape, but Taqqiq and Shila bore him down to the ground and pinned him there until his efforts grew feebler and he was still at last, cringing in submission.

Taqqiq stepped back. "Now get out of here," he snarled.

Unsteadily Salik heaved himself to his paws. Looking around, Lusa saw the battle was almost over. Only two of Salik's bears were still fighting, being slowly driven back by Kallik and Tartok.

"Let them go!" Toklo roared over the sounds of growling and trampling paws. "They've had enough!"

Kallik and Tartok broke away from the combat and stood panting while Manik, Iqaluk, and the rest huddled together in a group and started backing away across the ice. Salik paused for a moment, his furious gaze resting on Taqqiq.

"Don't come crawling back to us," he threatened. "You know what you'll get if you do."

"I'm not coming back," Taqqiq retorted. "I've found better friends."

Salik still hesitated, until Sakari stepped forward. "I'm warning you, Salik," she said solemnly, "if you try to make any more trouble, we'll fight you again—and we'll win again. Now go away and don't come back."

Salik limped across the ice to join his friends, and all five bears turned and lumbered painfully away. Nukka, Tartok, and Olikpok pursued them for a few bearlengths, then stopped to watch them go.

Letting out a grunt of satisfaction, Toklo came to stand beside Lusa, with Kallik and Yakone close behind him. Shila padded over to Taqqiq, while the mother bear and her cubs joined Sakari. Every bear's gaze was fixed on Salik and his gang as they retreated.

Finally, they faded into the mist, and Lusa couldn't see them anymore.

CHAPTER TWENTY-FIVE

Kallik

Kallik stood gazing into the distance until she was sure that Salik and his bears had really gone. Then she turned back to her friends.

"Toklo, you're a hero!" she yelped, padding up to the brown bear and touching her nose to his shoulder. "The plan worked so well, with all of us fighting together and looking out for one another."

Toklo scrabbled his paws in the loose snow, looking embarrassed. "It's not my victory," he muttered. "It's every bear's."

"Who would have thought Iqaluk could run so fast!" Kallik went on, turning to Yakone. "And Lusa, you were great! I'll never forget the look on Manik's face when you came jumping out of the den."

"I'll never forget it, either," Lusa responded with a snort of amusement. "Or the feel of his claws in my shoulders," she added ruefully.

"Are you badly wounded?" Kallik asked.

Lusa shook her head. "I'll be fine."

Looking around, Kallik could see streaks of blood on the fur of most of the white bears, but none of them seemed seriously injured. They looked tired and battered, but joy in their success was fueling them with new energy.

Tartok was loudly describing to Olikpok how he'd wrestled with one of Salik's bears.

"I hit him like this!" he boasted with a swish of his paw. "And the stupid fish-breath turned and ran!"

Nukka and the mother bear were excitedly discussing the battle, while the two older cubs chased each other around them, rolling in the snow and throwing it around in glittering showers under the morning sun.

Taqqiq padded over to Shila, who was sitting in the ruins of the BirthDen, breathing hard. "Did Salik hurt you?" he asked. Kallik thought he sounded nervous.

"Not too much," Shila replied. "It's worth it, just to be rid of them for good." She looked up at Taqqiq and added, "I'm sorry I didn't trust you before."

Taqqiq stared at his paws. "I deserved it," he mumbled.

A warm feeling swept through Kallik, as if the sun had emerged from behind a cloud. In the end, her brother had made the right choice.

Tonraq and Pakak came scampering over from the seal hole, bouncing around their mother's paws.

"Did we win?" Tonraq demanded. "Have they really gone?"

"They've really gone," Sakari confirmed.

"Yes!" Pakak gave a huge leap off the ground. "And we *nearly* caught a seal," he added.

"That's great," their mother told them. "Now we'd all better think about hunting."

"Sakari's right." Yakone padded up to Kallik and spoke quietly into her ear. "We have to think about hunting." Kallik nodded, realizing that Yakone didn't mean quite the same thing as Sakari. "The battle's only half won," he added. "Now we have to teach these bears how to hunt on land."

Toklo and Lusa, who were standing close enough to overhear, murmured agreement.

Kallik felt energy flowing through her, as if all the power of the ice and the spirits was in her paws. "We'll help them," she vowed, looking around at her friends.

"You said you would teach us how to hunt on land," Shila reminded Toklo. "I think it's time we got moving."

"Moving?" Sakari looked up from watching her two cubs chasing each other around a heap of snow. "You mean, leave the ice? Now?"

Tartok snorted. "I'm not leaving yet. Why did we chase off Salik and his gang if we're just going to head for land?"

"It's okay," Kallik broke in hastily before an argument could start. "We can teach you the hunting skills right here, so when you have to go to land you'll know what to do."

Two days had passed since the victory over Salik. Sakari and Tartok had both caught seals, so the bears were all full-fed. They had decided to rest and recover before starting on the hunting instruction, but were eager to begin now. As they gathered around, Kallik could see how keen they were to learn how they could feed themselves when the ice melted and they had to go ashore.

"So what do we have to do?" Olikpok asked.

Kallik glanced at Toklo, but for a moment the brown bear didn't seem to know how to start. Suddenly Lusa jumped up and padded toward the edge of the ice floe.

"Look, there's a piece of driftwood in the water," she pointed out. "Now imagine that's a fish in a fresh-water river."

"Then the river would be flowing, and the fish would be swimming," Toklo objected. "You have to stand in the stream and jump where the fish is going to be. We can't practice that here."

Kallik could see the white bears were looking confused. Tartok leaned over and muttered something into Nukka's ear.

"I know," Lusa replied to Toklo. "But sometimes the fish rest in pools close to the riverbank, where the water is shallow. And then you can slip a paw in carefully and hook the fish out."

"That's right," Kallik added, hearing a murmur of renewed interest from the white bears. "Show them, Lusa."

"Okay." Lusa crouched down beside the bobbing piece of driftwood. "You need to make sure that your shadow doesn't fall on the fish," she explained. "If it knows you're there, it'll swim away."

Slowly, as if she was trying to catch a real fish, Lusa leaned out over the water, her paw poised. But she leaned out too far, letting out a yelp of alarm as she started to topple into the sea, paws flailing.

Kallik let out a horrified cry, imagining an orca lurking below, its jaws gaping. She was too far away to help her friend, but Yakone leaped forward and grabbed Lusa by the scruff, dragging her back onto the ice again.

"Thanks, Yakone," Lusa gasped. "Sorry," she added to the group of white bears. "I'll do it right this time."

Even more carefully, she slid her paw into the water. "You have to concentrate on not making ripples," she said. "The fish mustn't even know you're there. Then, once you have your paw underneath it—"

Swiftly she brought her paw up, hooking the driftwood so that it clattered onto the ice. Lusa slammed her paw down on it. "The fish will flap about," she explained. "Kill it right away, or you might lose it again."

"That looks hard . . ." Nukka murmured.

"If a black bear can do it, we can," Tartok declared. "Can I give it a try?"

Lusa nodded, dropping the wood back into the sea. Tartok took up a position on the edge of the ice and let his paw sink into the water. A moment later he brought the wood up again and let it fall onto the ice with a satisfied grunt.

"You forgot to kill it," Shila pointed out.

Tartok gave the wood a hard swipe with his paw. "Happy now?" he asked the she-bear.

"They'll soon pick it up," Kallik said, padding over to join Lusa and Toklo, while the other white bears gathered around to try catching the "fish" for themselves.

"I know," Lusa responded. "But it feels weird, teaching our skills to white bears."

"It's the right thing to do," Toklo told her. Kallik saw his eyes grow unfocused, filling with memories. "Remember how Ujurak taught us, in all his different shapes? So it must be okay to share our wildness with other bears. It's better than taking flat-face food, surely?"

Lusa nodded. "Ujurak told me not to do that again."

"Sharing our skills is the way to survive," Kallik said, grateful that she and her friends were able to help the white bears. "If it means that white bears have to behave like black or brown bears, then that's what we have to do."

"Hey, Toklo." Tartok's voice was muffled as he strode across the ice toward them, because he was carrying the driftwood fish in his jaws. "We've all done this fish thing. Can you show us how to hunt on land now?"

"Sure," Toklo said. "This time we'll make the driftwood a snow-hare."

Kallik watched as Toklo demonstrated how to stalk the driftwood, creeping up on it pawstep by pawstep, then landing on it with a huge leap.

"Anyone want to try?" he asked.

"Me!" Nukka exclaimed immediately. "I can do that."

She crouched a couple of bearlengths away from the driftwood, slowly edged her way toward it, and pounced. Her forepaws slammed down onto the wood; she scooped it up and tossed it into the air. As it landed, she brought one paw down on it with such a hard blow that it splintered into pieces.

"Yes! It's dead!" she cried.

Cheering rose from the group of bears standing around her. "Great leap," Tartok commented.

Toklo stepped forward, and Nukka looked at him anxiously. "Was that okay, Toklo?" she asked.

"Better than okay," Toklo told her. "That was great for a first try. But you'll need to remember that if that piece of wood really was a snow-hare, it could scent you. Keep downwind of it, and you'll be able to creep up and grab it before it knows you're there."

Nukka nodded. "I'll remember."

Kallik spotted Lusa picking up one of the scraps of splintered wood and carrying it over to Pakak and Tonraq. "This is something you can practice," she told the eager cubs, scoring her claws down the wood. "Now you try," she said.

Both the little cubs imitated her scratching. "Like this?" Pakak asked.

"Yes, that's very good," Lusa replied.

"But what's it for?" Tonraq asked.

"Well, when you get to land, there'll be a lot of trees—"

"What's a tree?" Pakak interrupted.

Lusa exchanged an amused glance with Kallik. "It's like this piece of wood," she explained, "only much, much bigger. Trees go right up into the sky, and they have lots of branches—other bits of wood—sticking out of them. They're covered over with this rough coating called bark."

"Bark? That's what seals do." Tonraq jumped to his paws

and demonstrated. "*Wah! Wah!* Like that."

"This is a different kind of bark." Lusa sounded as if she was hanging on hard to her patience. "If you claw it off, like I just showed you, the inside of it is good to eat. And sometimes you can find grubs inside. They're good, too."

"What are grubs?" Pakak asked.

Kallik left Lusa to it and padded across the ice, passing the white bears who were still practicing crouching and stalking. Close by, Toklo had taken Shila and Taqqiq to one side and was drawing something out on the ice with one claw.

"So if the bison herd is *here*," he pointed out to Shila, "you would need to skirt around them *there*, and Taqqiq could drive a young bison over to you."

"That should work," Shila agreed. "Then we can kill it together." Her tongue emerged and swiped around her jaws. "I had bison once last burn-sky. It was great."

"They're getting the idea," Yakone remarked, strolling up to Kallik. "I guess once they get to shore they'll figure out the details for themselves."

"I think they will," Kallik said, her gaze traveling over the group of happily occupied bears.

"Is it true that Toklo and Lusa are moving on tomorrow?" Yakone said quietly.

Kallik's jaws dropped open, and she stared at him. She'd been so caught up in the problems on the Melting Sea that she had forgotten their original plan.

Yakone and I can make our homes here, but Toklo and Lusa can't stay on the ice. They have to travel on to find homes of their own. . . .

* * *

That night, Kallik curled up with Yakone in a small den they had dug for themselves in the snow. But she couldn't sleep. All night she tossed and turned, unable to think of anything but the parting with Toklo and Lusa that was so close now.

Finally she felt Yakone heave himself to his paws. "Come outside with me," he said.

Kallik followed him into the open, feeling guilty as she realized that her fidgeting had kept him awake, too. "I'm sorry—" she began.

"Kallik," Yakone interrupted, "I think I know what's making you so unhappy. It's Toklo and Lusa, isn't it?"

Kallik nodded miserably. "We've been together for so long. We've been through so much together. . . ."

"And you don't want them to leave?"

"I know they have to leave," Kallik said. "This isn't the right place for them. But . . . oh, Yakone, I'll miss them so much!"

"Do you want to go with them?" Yakone asked.

Kallik blinked. Until Yakone had put it into words, she had never thought that traveling on with her friends was possible. Now she thought, *Could I really . . . ?*

Words spilled out of her. "This is where I've always wanted to be. I was afraid I would never see Taqqiq again, and now I've found him. This is my home. And yet . . ." Doubts crowded in on her. "So much has changed. The sea is melting so fast, the white bears must learn to survive on land as well as on the ice. And more than that, I feel like my journey is unfinished. How can I just let Toklo and Lusa leave, without knowing how their journeys end?"

"It's your choice to make, Kallik." The look Yakone gave her was warm. "I made *my* choice when I left my homeland," Yakone continued. "My home is with you now. Wherever we go."

He touched her shoulder gently with his muzzle, and retreated into the den again.

Kallik was left alone in the open. Starlight glimmered on the expanse of snow; in the distance she could hear the creaking of ice and the faint wash of waves. She gazed up at the sky until she found Ujurak's constellation.

Ujurak, please tell me where my path lies, she begged.

She waited for Ujurak to speak to her or to appear in some form or another, but all she could hear was a faint whisper on the wind. *Follow your heart. You know where it lies.*

Kallik suppressed a shiver. The voice wasn't Ujurak; it was her mother, Nisa.

I'm so proud of you, Nisa murmured.

Suddenly Kallik knew what she had to do.

When Kallik and Yakone emerged from their den the next morning, they found the other bears already up, standing in a ragged circle around Toklo and Lusa.

"We'll miss you all," Toklo was saying. He hesitated as if he couldn't find the right words. "It's been great knowing you," he ended at last.

"Mind you keep your claws sharp," Lusa told the little cubs, her voice quivering.

"There aren't enough words to thank you," Sakari said, dipping her head deeply. "We all owe you our lives, many times over."

Lusa caught sight of Kallik and Yakone, and nudged Toklo. Together they made their way out of the circle of bears and approached; Kallik could see the pain in their eyes.

"Kallik . . ." Lusa began, her voice choked.

"We're not saying good-bye," Kallik announced. "We're coming with you."

Lusa's eyes stretched wide, and she exchanged a joyful glance with Toklo.

"Just until you find your homes," Kallik added. "Then Yakone and I will come back here. But we want to finish the journey together. I couldn't stand not knowing where you end up." Catching sight of Taqqiq hovering a bearlength or so away, she added, "You can come with us, too, Taqqiq, if you want. I hope you will."

Taqqiq looked tempted, but Kallik could tell he was full of doubts.

Before he could speak, Sakari padded up with Shila at her shoulder. "I admire your courage and spirit—all of you," she began. "But this is the home of the white bears. I'd like you, Kallik, and Taqqiq and Yakone, to stay here with me and Shila and the cubs, just as you would have with your own mothers, until you're a year or two older and ready to live on your own."

"Thank you," Kallik responded. She was truly grateful for the offer, but she knew that Sakari had no idea of how experienced she and her friends already were. "But I've seen so much," she tried to explain, "and traveled so far, that I know I can survive on my own. Besides," she continued with a quiver in her voice, "I carry my mother in my heart, always."

Kallik already knew what Taqqiq's decision would be as she exchanged a sad look with him.

"I want to stay," he said, with a glance at Shila. "I want to be part of this family. And I'd like you to stay, too, Kallik. You're my only *real* family." Before Kallik could protest, he went on swiftly, "But I know you've made your decision, and you're traveling on with Lusa and Toklo."

Kallik nodded. "Yakone and I will be back," she promised him. "Just as soon as the others are safely settled."

She knew in her heart that she might not be able to keep her promise. The Melting Sea was so big that there was a good chance she and her brother would never see each other again. It was a miracle she had found him this time. She could see that Taqqiq knew it, too.

She thought that her heart would crack in two as she padded up to Taqqiq and thrust her muzzle into his fur, breathing his scent for the last time. She felt the touch of his snout on her shoulder and heard him murmur, "Good-bye."

"Good-bye, Taqqiq," she choked out.

But as she slowly walked away, Toklo's fur brushing hers, with Yakone and Lusa behind them, Kallik knew that she had made the right decision. Her long journey was not over yet.

LOOK FOR

RETURN TO THE WILD

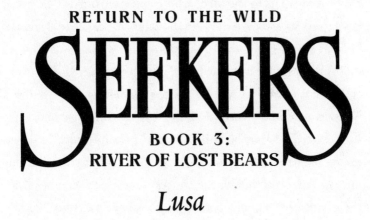

BOOK 3:
RIVER OF LOST BEARS

Lusa

Lusa lifted her muzzle and breathed in the scent of pine and water. Needles crunched, prickly beneath her paws, as she trotted through the forest. At the edge, she pushed through thick bushes, blinking against the brightness as she burst into the light. A river crashed past, wide as the sky and white with foam.

"Toklo!"

Her friend was standing at the edge, gazing into the water. It splashed his muzzle, but he didn't move.

"Toklo!" Lusa called again, but Toklo seemed lost in thought.

Lusa padded across the rocks and stopped beside him. "Are you sharing with the river spirits?" she whispered.

Toklo turned his head. "It's good to feel them near me again."

Lusa scanned the shore. "Where are Kallik and Yakone?"

Toklo nodded upstream. "They went hunting."

Lusa followed his gaze, still in awe of the churning river. They'd followed it since leaving the Melting Sea, sheltering

1

in the deep woods at night, fishing the shallows by day. "Will this river lead us to the place where you were born?" she asked.

"I think so. I know it must lead us to brown bears," Toklo replied. "I lived beside rivers that smelled like this when I was young."

"Why don't we just stay here?" Lusa ventured. "It has everything we need and we're still close to the Melting Sea. Kallik and Yakone would be near to their kin and we could live here." The forest stretched away on both sides of the river. It filled Lusa with excitement, to be back among trees. She hadn't tried climbing one yet but, even though the trunks were wider than her reach, their bark looked gnarly enough to hook her claws into. "Perhaps we don't need to travel any farther?" she suggested hopefully.

A splash sounded upstream and a moment later Kallik appeared, dripping, on top of a large boulder near the edge of the river. A fish glittered in her jaws. Yakone scrambled up onto the rock beside her, his wet pelt sticking out all over.

"Look!" Kallik tossed the fish down. It landed at Toklo's paws. "I finally caught one!" Kallik had been trying to catch river fish since they left the Melting Sea. But she'd missed every one until now. "I remembered your lessons, Toklo. Back from before we reached the Endless Ice."

Toklo sniffed the fish. "It's a fine catch, Kallik."

"It's a dumb way to hunt." Yakone shook the water from his fur. "How can anyone hook a fish out of the water when it's moving so fast?"

"I'll teach you," Toklo promised. "Once you've practiced, it'll be easy."

Lusa remembered Toklo's frustration when he'd first had to learn the patience a bear needed to catch seals on the ice. They were all bears, but each with such different ways of finding food. She flared her nostrils, drinking in the scent of soft brown earth. She didn't have to get her paws wet before she could eat here.

Wind ruffled the undergrowth at the edge of the trees. Yakone turned and bared his teeth. "What's that?"

"It's just the breeze," Lusa soothed. Yakone had been jumpy since they'd left the ice. He seemed unsettled in the strange world of trees and bushes and rushing water. He ducked out of the forest whenever he could and stared at the sky as though he was checking it was still above them.

Kallik skidded down the boulder and stopped beside the fish. Claws scraped behind her as Yakone followed, half-scrambling, half-falling.

"I can't dig my claws in here," he grumbled as he landed beside Kallik. "And they sink pawdeep in the soft forest muck."

Kallik touched his muzzle softly with hers. "I know you miss the ice."

Yakone snorted. "Who wouldn't?" He sniffed the fish. "Are we going to eat this, or what?"

Toklo tore the fish into four pieces.

Lusa pushed her portion away. "You can have mine."

Toklo glanced at her anxiously.

"I'm fine," she reassured him. "I can find food in the forest later." Her mouth watered as she imagined scratching up pawfuls of juicy grubs and beetles among the tree roots. She'd almost forgotten how rich the forest was, with ant-filled crevices in the tree bark and soft soil where she could dig for sweet roots. But it was still the season of cold-earth. Fruits and berries hadn't flowered yet and there were scant traces of soft green shoots in the undergrowth. Ants and grubs weren't always enough, so most days she was glad the river gave them fish. She'd eat anything rather than be hungry again. They seemed to have been hungry so many times before.

Toklo gulped down his share of fish. "Come on." He pointed his nose upstream. "The day is half over. We should move on."

As he ambled away, Lusa felt a stab of disappointment. He hadn't even considered staying here. She followed with a sigh. *I guess he misses brown bears.* Lusa glanced back at Kallik and Yakone, their white pelts pressed together as they jumped over the rocks after her. They had one another; Toklo was ready to cross half the world to find his own kind . . . was she supposed to miss her black bear kin more?

They followed the river until the rocks rose steeply, too jagged to climb easily.

"Let's go around," Lusa said, and without waiting for an answer she galloped into the forest. Pushing through a patch of thick bunchberry, she glanced back to see the others following. "I can't believe we lived on the ice for so long," she panted as Toklo caught up.

"Stupid ice!" he huffed. "It scraped our pads and clogged our claws. I remember icicles jangling from my fur." He shook his head. "Icicles! What bear is supposed to grow icicles?"

Lusa looked over her shoulder at Kallik and Yakone, trailing behind. Their white pelts stood out like snow in the shadows.

"I think Kallik and Yakone would choose icicles," she whispered.

"Then they should have stayed on the ice," Toklo grunted.

Lusa stopped and stared at him. "But they chose to come

with us!" How could he be so ungrateful?

"We came because our journey is not over until you've reached your home."

Toklo whirled around in surprise as Kallik's voice sounded behind him. The white bears had caught up to them.

Toklo dipped his head. "I know, and I'm glad."

Lusa heard honesty in his growl. She knew Toklo admired Kallik for leaving her homeland to travel with them. And Yakone too, for sacrificing the life he had known on Star Island to be with Kallik. *He really does appreciate it!* She willed the white bears to understand.

Yakone pushed past them and trudged away through the trees. "I thought we were trying to make the most of the daylight."

Lusa galloped after him, tearing through a bramble, relishing the prickles as they scraped her thick fur. As she raced past Yakone, the ground began to slope, plunging down into shadow. She could hear roaring ahead. "I think there's another river this way!" she called excitedly. She couldn't believe that she'd once thought the Bear Bowl was big. How had she ever been so bee-brained?

"Wait!" Kallik's terrified cry split the air.

Lusa tried to stop, but the ground fell away under her more steeply. Unbalanced, she tumbled down the slope, scrabbling to find a grip on the slippery needles.

"Lusa!" Yakone plunged after her.

Lusa flailed her paws. An acrid smell hit her nose. Lights flashed ahead. The roaring grew louder.

That roaring's not water! Terror thrummed in her ears as she fell. *It's a firebeast!*

DON'T MISS

OMEN OF THE STARS

WARRIORS

BOOK 6:
THE LAST HOPE

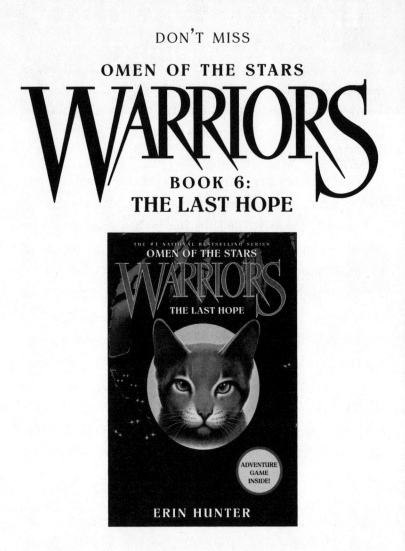

The battle between the Dark Forest and the warrior Clans
has come. As the cats seek out allies and enemies, Jayfeather,
Lionblaze, and Dovewing wait desperately for the fourth cat
who is prophesied to lead the Clans to victory—and who may
be their only hope for survival.

ENTER THE WORLD OF

WARRIORS

Warriors

Sinister perils threaten the four warrior Clans. Into the midst of this turmoil comes Rusty, an ordinary housecat, who may just be the bravest of them all.

Download the
free Warriors app at
www.warriorcats.com

Warriors: The New Prophecy

Follow the next generation of heroic cats as they set off on a quest to save the Clans from destruction.

All Warriors and Seekers books
are available as ebooks
from HarperCollins.

Also available unabridged from HarperChildren's *Audio*

HARPER
An Imprint of HarperCollins Publishers

Visit www.warriorcats.com for the free Warriors app, games, Clan lore, and much more!

Warriors: Power of Three

Firestar's grandchildren begin their training as warrior cats.
Prophecy foretells that they will hold more power than any cats before them.

Don't miss the stand-alone adventures!

Warriors: Omen of the Stars

Which ThunderClan apprentice will complete the prophecy that
foretells that three Clanmates hold the future of the Clans in their paws?

Also available unabridged from HarperChildren's*Audio*

HARPER
An Imprint of HarperCollins*Publishers*

Delve Deeper into the Clans

Warrior Cats Come to Life in Manga!

HARPER
An Imprint of HarperCollins*Publishers*

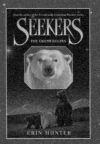
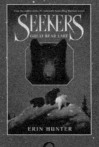